Praise for *Hippies*

"What Kerouac did for the Beats with *On the Road*, Gautier has done for the '60s generation with *Hippies* ... poetic and insightful."

Michael T. Tusa, Jr. author of *Advancing on Chaos*

"The quality of the prose is often immediate and compelling ... Gautier is at his best in the confrontation scenes between the idealistic protagonists and the authorities."

Steve Morris, author of *The Yoga Sutras* and *Strange Thoughts, Random Mutterings*

"An intriguing story with well-developed (and unique) characters ... not too sweet, not too sad."

Lorilin Meyer, bug bug book reviews

"Great job of incorporating fiction and nonfiction into an easily readable book that hooked you from the beginning ... made you feel like you were really living in the '60s."

Liz Gardner, Ski Lift Operator, Big Sky Montana

HIPPIES

Hippies

Gary Gautier

Shakemyheadhollow.com press
637 N Hennessey St
New Orleans, LA 70119
drggautier@gmail.com

Cover photo by Emily "Pink" Brown.

May 4, 1970

Spreading out to the west from the porch were tiers of landscape. Close in, the apple orchard, with a miniature dairy house just visible beyond and north. Then the rolling hills, every shade of green, tumbling down to the Hudson River. In the far distance, the Catskills.

"Do you want some mint tea?" the girl asked. Jazmine was coming out of a long sleep of exhaustion. Three days, it seemed, she had been hurtling through a black tunnel, unable to move, unable to speak. Now she was gaining her strength back.

"That would be nice," she said, and the girl went back inside. Jazmine sunk back down into the cushion on the wooden slat armchair. The bones in her arms ached. And the bones in her thighs. She rolled her head to the side. She could see into the room through the window, between dark green shutters, as the girl prepared her tea. But mostly she just wanted to think. Just three weeks ago, her life had been completely different.

A woman in her twenties, youthful but older than the first girl, brought out a mug of tea and set it on a small table by Jazmine.

"It's not just mint, you know," she said. "I added violet leaf and marshmallow root. We're going to bring you back stronger than ever."

Jazmine nodded, and the other woman continued.

"Are you still having those dreams?"

"I've always had dreams," Jazmine replied. "People, things, you don't even know."

7

"I don't need to know," said the woman. She rested her hand on Jazmine's for a couple of seconds and then went inside. Jazmine closed her eyes. Just three weeks ago. What had happened? She had been finishing her freshman year in college, in New Orleans, hanging out with a cool crowd of kids her own age, more or less, with all the breakthrough freedoms that came along as the 1960s turned into 1970. And then that fateful day. Would she ever go back? Would she ever see Ziggy again? Sometimes the whole thing seemed like a hallucination. She looked away from the orchard and the dairy house, toward the white picket fence brushed with knee-high weeds by the one-lane road. She ran her eye back and forth along the pickets until they blurred together. Just three weeks ago ...

Chapter 1

Jazmine lay flat on the massage table, tucked in from the hungry New Orleans night by panes of dimly lit glass. The powder blue sheet felt crisp and cool against the ivory skin of her back. It wasn't really a massage table. It was a solid table, though. Russian birch, the vendor had said when she and Ziggy bought it at a dusty flea market on the outskirts of town. Solid brown, now covered with a soft mat and the cool blue sheet. She felt her fingertips tingle. Then the skin on her lower back. The cells of her skin floating, blending into the liquid surface of the cool blue sheet. A flash of color darted in from the periphery of her visual field. Bright, bold color, but she couldn't say if it were blue or red or any other specific color. The elixir was taking hold.

Sure, they had all dropped acid before. But this was different. The idealist, genius, pointy-bearded kid they all called Ragman had his fingers in this one.

Now the room was undulating with digestive rhythm. The disembodied candle flames hovering around the massage table, the dark reddish-brown mahogany walls of this parlor relic of an 1830s house. Rippling and heaving in a visual ebb and flow. No, a tactile ebb and flow. Visual and tactile were only surface distinctions anyway, ludicrous human categories thrown over the primordial swell. She felt like a live animal swallowed by a snake. Bulging and undulating her way through the snake's body. Then she was the snake's body. Someone took her hand.

She had first met Ragman before Ziggy. She and two friends had gone to the nude swimming hole, a quiet cove in the lake where you could always find a few teenagers and twenty-somethings enjoying the full-body sun at the grassy edge of the cool water. But it was a little crazy that day. Something going on. Maybe twenty or thirty people. Balloons everywhere, and people in fantastic garb like Dr. Seuss figures mingling with the nudes. Jazmine stripped off her clothes and waded into the cool water, then plunged. When she came up, Ragman was next to her, smiling that child-rascal smile of his. He was a little shorter than average, with untamed brown hair, wide-set hazel eyes, that funny little pointy beard, and something irresistible. The folk menagerie was a bunch of kids he had met on the road, billing themselves as "The Red Queen's Naked Circus." Next thing you know, Jazmine and her friends were hanging out with the Circus in Ragman's back yard. That's how Ragman was. He didn't seem particularly spontaneous – actually he seemed rather methodical personally – but spontaneous things were always happening around him. And he made friends easily.

With her free hand, Jazmine moved her fingers around the edge of the sheet to feel the Russian birch. The painting on the wall, framed by a burgundy ceiling-to-floor curtain leading nowhere, a Madonna and child, was looking at her, talking. Not the Madonna but the painting itself was talking, the royal blue and shimmering gold, a visual language that she thought must be older and deeper than our normal language. An olfactory language, the cedar robe in its own obscure corner of the room. Then everything was shimmering. The candles, the creamy brown icing walls crystallizing, the window panes of deep black quartz, all a vibrating mosaic. She saw for the first time that all of this reality was just millions of tiny atomic bits of colored glass. How could she not have seen this before? Someone took her other hand. Yes, they were here with her. Ziggy and Ragman and Pepper. What love!

Then she went through the walls. Why not? Her body was 99% empty space. The walls were 99% empty space. She filtered through and was outside but in a wooded area, not a city. A village. Everyone in peasant garb. Like tunics, forest green and tawny brown, flowing in space. Goats and chickens on the dirt road. Earthy smells. Peat and straw and manure. She saw her own hand reach out into the space of the village.

"Rebecca," called a voice. She was facing a man with short-cropped curly black hair, beady eyes, and a prominent – almost a hook – nose. He was in the prime of life – thirtyish maybe – but had a stern ruggedness that made him seem older. "Rebecca, where were you at the matins? The Lord Bishop has come and gone. And you and me and Jeremiah with work to do."

At the mention of work, she felt a rush of anxiety. What work? Where was she? She saw the edge of her own face. Breathing heavily, reaching for something. Her stomach moving up and down.

"Jazmine, wake up," came a clear voice. She felt Pepper's voice wash over her and smooth her out on the cool crisp blue of the sheets. And she felt Pepper's hand squeeze hers firmly. She could always count on firmness from Pepper. Always ready to hug you or snap at you, never knew when to shut up, especially around the cops, but you could count on her as a friend. Ziggy held Jazmine's other hand, waiting for her to reach her own element.

She stirred and then rested again. Ziggy watched Jazmine's body relax into the mat. Raven black hair, straight but thick like woven black silk. Ivory skin with a slight undertone of pink, giving the impression of a radiant glow from some internal light source. Dark eyes with a hint of violet. Like a mesmerizing blend of Egyptian and Frankish. Her body shapely but soft, not taut. But it was not her beauty that defined Ziggy's connection so much as her purity. Even her sensuality had not initially triggered a sensual response in him.

Now, as she lay there, utterly relaxed and opening groggy eyes as if for the first time, Ziggy's thoughts carried him back to the night he had met her at Polo's Pizza. Ziggy had worked the kitchen there for six months and was already ranking pie maker. He was working that night with Beachbum, a skinny, goggle-eyed kid from California, always looking for a laugh. It was a boring night. When Jazmine walked in, her orange flower top swishing over jeans, "Watch this," Ziggy said to Beachbum. He dropped his oven mitts and went to the counter. He stood there, framed for a moment by the glass display of motley pizzas with ingredients covering all the color chakras a dharma bum could wish for. Then he moved to the side of the glass display where he could lean his tall, angular body over with his elbows resting on the red countertop between the display and the cash register. His hair was as black as hers, but wavier, cascading past his cheeks to shoulder length. Jazmine walked directly up to the counter, without looking right or left at the checker-topped tables. It put Ziggy off his game for a second. All he could think to say was: "Watch this," as if he were momentarily a parrot of himself.

He ran back to get a roll of pizza dough that had risen twice and was flattened about an inch thick. Beachbum honked a goofy little laugh out of his nose in anticipation. Ziggy stepped forth from kitchen to pizza, his two fists under the saggy disc of dough. And he began to twirl. Not just to twirl, but to twirl like only Ziggy could twirl. As the dough became more pliable he spun it in one hand, then the other, then spinning it from his left hand across his back to catch it in his right hand, still twirling.

"Can I help you?" he asked, twirling, smiling, knowing he was good.

"I'd like to fill out a job application," she said, point blank. He should have been insulted. But he was charmed. From anyone else's mouth, it would have sounded like disdain for his little show. But she had looked at him so earnestly, and said it so simply, so sweetly. She had a special kind of directness, a directness that comes from purity. That's what really got Ziggy. It wasn't love at first sight or even infatuation. It was the purity of heart.

One could see it still, the purity of heart, as Jazmine stirred herself awake on the powder blue sheet. Ziggy continued to hold Jazmine's hand but with his free hand fiddled with his shirt pocket. He did not want to think about the letter in that pocket. He wanted to think about Jazmine, what she was thinking, what she was feeling, what she would be doing a year from now. Was he in love with her? No, he didn't think so. More like a companion on the journey. But the letter in the pocket. Sometimes things change slowly and sometimes suddenly. Technically, the 60s were over. It was April 1970. But the war kept going on. And the anti-war movement kept going on. The Summer of Love had swept the Haight in '67. And all the naïve idealism of the Scene came together at Woodstock just eight months ago in that hot rainy summer of '69. No one knew at Woodstock that the Beatles were already breaking up then. They had their beautiful moment without the burden of that knowledge. And no one yet knew what the next big event would be. No one yet knew which way it would go. The forces pressing against Establishment thinking, or the Establishment's dark resilience pressing back. History seems all plotted out when you look back at the Roman Empire or the shift from Medieval to Renaissance times, but when you're in the middle of it, it's like spontaneous happenings everywhere, like soap bubbles in the park, blown and chased and popped. And Ziggy felt part of his generation, part of the Scene that had raised the hackles of the Establishment, and brought things to the point of no return. Something had to give. At least, Ziggy had said to himself, I know which side I'm on. "Peace, love, and flowers; not war, money, and machines," as Ragman always said.

And now the letter in his pocket: "Order to Report for Induction." You didn't really have to read the rest. For Ziggy, as for so many 18-year-olds during those years, Selective Service registration was pro forma and carelessly done. The Viet Nam war was to the teenage mind an occasion for bon mots of bravado between gulps of Boone's Farm apple wine or for vulgar gestures hurled at the Man from the windows of swirly painted VW buses. Every gulp, every hit on the joint, pushed the war further from the party at hand. But never completely away. Every kid had an older brother or cousin or friend on the block who had been there and come back changed.

And now – no one yet knew it – Ziggy's number had come up. He was drafted. He was suddenly not a kid guzzling Boone's Farm. His heart was with the draft dodgers but it was all a philosophical thing to him – the "peace, love, and flowers" thing – like something he had been watching on a screen. But now, with the induction letter, it was inside him. He'd always been what people call a "good boy." Protesting the war was one thing, but dodging the draft was another. A "good boy" could protest the war. But this was different. It was *his* induction. It was personal this time. The State was putting him on notice, removing everyone and everything else, and asking him to make a personal decision from which there would be no return. His Uncle Leo, the baby of the family on his mother's side, just a few years older than Ziggy and an unconventional lunatic before unconventional lunacy was hip, had made that decision and moved to Montreal. The older brother, Uncle Frank, on the other hand, was now a New Orleans cop. Funny how things work out. Now word was running through the underground, through every freak show and flower child gathering, wherever bell-bottomed waifs could find an open field to stick their toes in the grass and frolic, word was that six days from now – let's see, today is Monday, so that would be Sunday, April 19 – a gathering at Audubon Park would light another bonfire of draft cards. Fuck the Man.

Jazmine was fully awake now, but beat, so the others let her and Ziggy walk to the back steps and sit looking out over the spring garden in the yard. Though it was night, light cast from windows and soft street lights showed glistening cabbages and beans and leafy tomato plants in straight rows. Jazmine felt lucky to have Ziggy around to remind her that the world was a place to be at ease. Left on her own, she was never good at relaxing. She had inadvertently come to associate relaxing with victimhood. Her dad – a college professor – died when she was nine, and a few years later her mom took up with an abusive control freak. Jazmine left home at 17 and hitched to New Orleans, where her dad's old friend got her into the university Marketing program and she was damn sure going to stick with it. She would NOT let self-indulgent victimhood set in. Ziggy had taught her to relax again. But she could only relax so far. Maybe that's why she had insisted on trying out the tan acid, a spinoff hallucinogen Ragman had synthesized on an LSD base. She was more ready than anyone else to get beneath all this clutter of everyday life.

"What was it like?" Ziggy asked, not with excitement but with the soft-spoken manner that Jazmine loved. "Was it like acid? Mushrooms? Something else?"

15

"Something else," she said. "Well, a little like acid but, you know, it was quick in and quick out. And it seemed more like it was pointing you somewhere."

"How did Ragman know it would be quick in and quick out?"

"Genius," she said, smiled, looked at the square framed yard between the two houses and at the straight rows of growing vegetables and at the shadowy flowers and blueberry bushes at the perimeter, and took Ziggy's hand.

"You seem good," he said. "I think Ragman will be happy with this batch."

"Ragman's always happy," she said.

Chapter 2

The Magic Mushroom Head Shop and Dry Cleaners sprouted up like a beautiful extempore fungus in the Faubourg Marigny three years and some months back, one day in early 1967, after a heavy New Orleans rain. Things happened fast in those days, especially for a generation of rootless and unrestrained youth, so three years and some months was a long way back – before Woodstock and the Summer of Love, before Martin Luther King or Bobby Kennedy had been shot, before Sgt. Pepper's – and no one really knew from whence the head shop had sprung. The dry cleaners counter seemed to pre-date the shop, as the hippies swarming into the Marigny at that time had never seen anyone use those beneficial services and indeed were under the impression that the only people who used dry cleaners were over fifty, square, and enormously wealthy. In any event, the head shop that featured pipes, rolling papers, lighters, and other such bric-a-brac was certainly a product of recent cultural trends, and the folk wisdom of the neighborhood had settled on "one day in early 1967" as the definite nativity of the place in its current form.

The shop was on Frenchmen Street, down where the two-stories with wrought iron balconies yielded to one-story creole cottages. This particular cottage was brightly painted, with a banner on top of the door depicting an idyllic horizontal landscape and what appeared to be a brown-robed monk at one end happily smoking a long-stem pipe under the canopy of a fleshy mushroom. The smoke from his pipe curled up into the gills of the mushroom and around the cap and out across the horizontal blue space of blissful painted sky.

The owners were pair of drifting lovers, Claire and Cool Breeze, who had found their spot. They were no longer teenagers but had matured into their late twenties bodies as picture-perfect hippies from the heartland of Minnesota, the kind that editors of *Life* and *New York Magazine* loved to put on glossy covers to show the paradox of innocent beauty and hippie menace. Claire had long blonde hair and a model's body; Cool Breeze was medium-tall and well-made, with prominent features and a countenance both sweet and grizzly, like a Duane Allman lookalike, but with his own blonde hair knotted into a thick braid that hung to his waist. The pair had gone to the Upper Haight in the early days to escape the oppression of the Midwest. The Grateful Dead was already on the Scene, and Janis Joplin, but it was all new. You could still see Ginsberg and Ferlinghetti day tripping from North Beach to the Haight to see what was happening, and Richard Brautigan would show up looking half pioneer and half proto-hippie. Claire and Cool Breeze opined that the Scene in the Haight was already dead before that June of 1967, when Sgt. Pepper's was released and disaffected teens from everywhere would flow in a tidal wave to Haight-Ashbury for the "Summer of Love."

"You could tell by the tagline, man – 'The Summer of Love' – the Scene had already been co-opted by the Man and his mass media," Cool Breeze would opine. "Corporate branding and magazine stories for old ladies back east. That's what the 'Summer of Love' was."

Of course, there was no consensus on Cool Breeze's historical analysis. Indeed, the history of the Scene was – and still is – taking shape. Lots of people thought the Summer of Love was – and still is – an awakening moment for the counterculture. But Cool Breeze and Claire were real purists, happy to have found their niche in the old part of New Orleans after bailing from the Haight, but happy to reminisce about the authenticity of the early days. And they had the ears of their impressionable young hippie customers, who were, truth be told, often entirely innocent of history ancient, recent, or present.

When Claire and Cool Breeze first wandered into the Faubourg Marigny of New Orleans, it was a working-class neighborhood, just downriver from the French Quarter, rough and tumble. A few gay couples had come in, trailblazers as it were, restoring historical homes in a neighborhood they could call their own, but otherwise tourists and outside traffic barely made it as far as the creole cottages. So Claire and Cool Breeze got a place on the cheap and started sanding and scraping and hammering to make this one creole cottage into their head shop dream. They intended to top the building with a gigantic, brightly painted, sheet-metal psilocybin mushroom cap, modeled on the rotating root beer mugs that famously adorned Frostop restaurants. Perhaps thinking of the longboats of their Viking forebears, which were protected from ill favor by conspicuously sculpted figureheads, they may have thought

18

that their gigantic mushroom would protect their place of business from the Man. But, alas, it was not to be, for the Faubourg Marigny Historic Preservation Society still had enough squares on the council to torpedo the idea.

Inside the head shop were glass-blown pipes and ceramic pipes and rolling papers of every style and color, not to mention underground comics, used LPs, and incense sticks boasting various magical properties. There was even a corner shelf of handmade clothing – colorful ponchos, patch-laden jeans, polka-dot mini-skirts, tie-dye shirts and striped bell-bottoms. Adjacent to this shelf was a hat rack that would have appeared inexplicable to the traditional hat maker, in the unlikely event that a traditional hat maker ever wandered into the Magic Mushroom. There was a squarish hat adorned with rings of tiny plastic cavemen, a crooked stove-pipe Cat-in-the-Hat striped topper, a hat bursting with fabric long-stem flowers in an arrangement that had never occurred in nature, an oversized Mad Hatter chapeau, forest green with a blue-ribbon resting on the brim at the base of the crown, less spectacular but nonetheless cool leathery earth-tone patchwork hats, and a few other what-have-you hats.

At the counter stood Ragman chatting with Claire. After a year of settling in, Claire and Cool Breeze had taken in an abandoned preteen niece, Bitzy, and Rag tutored her in math in return for throwaway items from the head shop. Nearer the hat rack, Ziggy, Jazmine, and Tex Whittaker, another member of the tribe, were horsing around. The atmospheric sound of "The Court of the Crimson King" wafted through the air, creating a hazy etheric blanket over the things and people in the head shop.

"Just for you, Zig" said Tex, a big, bony crocodile of a man with a cowboy hat, boots and a handlebar mustache. And he plunked a knit, Rastafarian, rainbow beret on

19

Ziggy's dark locks. Ziggy turned to the small mirror on the rack and checked himself out a little too earnestly.

"Perfect," scoffed Jaz. "You look like a Cuban cigar dealer."

"More like Che," Ziggy said gravely. He eyed himself in the mirror again and swayed left and right. "Sexy, romantic, and ready for revolution."

"Wrong revolution, Zig," Ragman sang out as he bounced over from the counter. "Your revolution's here." And he put the extravagant floral hat on Ziggy's dark locks. "You're our flower child king," Rag continued.

Ziggy looked at Ragman a little funny. Wasn't Ragman the unspoken king? Ragman must have gleaned his thoughts because he turned his full visage to Ziggy – the hazel eyes and long light brown hair and high cheekbones. He cupped his chin and his small pointy beard between thumb and forefinger, eyed Ziggy dead on, and his bantering grin yielded to a more pensive smile. "No, Zig, you're the one who's going to get us there."

"Hey, Oat Willie stickers!" Tex's voice came from the FREE box over by the door. Sure enough, someone had brought in a box of stickers from the head shop of that name in Austin. "Onward through the fog" announced the Oat Willie stickers, the text running above Oat Willie's signature logo of an underwear-clad hippie, suspiciously happy, charging forward with a torch.

"And saints cards," added Jazmine, as she browsed stack of 2-by-4 inch cards, each with a medieval-style image of the saint on one side and a prayer associated with that saint on the other. And with this, Rag and Ziggy stepped back from their transcendent moment to join in the browsing of Oat Willie and the saints.

Walking down Frenchmen toward the French Quarter, Ziggy adjusted his new hat, the bizarre floral one.

20

Ragman donned the Mad Hatter's top and Jazmine had ended up with the rainbow beret. Tex wore his crumpled cowboy hat as always. Ragman was particularly jovial, and once they passed Esplanade and entered the more populous heart of the Quarter, he regaled passersby with good cheer, handing out Oat Willie stickers and saints cards. "Have a saints card, sister. This is your saint for the new age. Sticker for your briefcase, my man. Oat Willie, the madcap messiah. Love those dancing shoes, brother." And so on.

Tex tipped his cowboy hat at two sixtyish women from the Midwest, who covered their mouths with fat fingers and giggled on the sidewalk in front of their hotel as the group sauntered by. Jaz and Ziggy distributed cards and stickers as they walked. Some recipients smiled, some crumpled the tokens immediately, apparently unaware of their messianic value. But no one could really take offense, not faced with Ziggy's puppy-dog brown eyes and Jazmine's sweet sincerity.

The same could not be said for Tex, who could rub people the wrong way without trying. When the group hit Canal Street, passing from French Quarter to business district, Tex approached a man in a gray suit with black wingtip shoes and a solid bald head like a dented up bowling ball.

"Oat Willie sticker, my man," said Tex. Whether Tex simply lacked the charm of his compatriots or had chosen the wrong customer to deal with, his offer didn't fly.

"I don't want your sticker, freak."

"OK, then give it to your old lady," said Tex, a little testy.

The suited man held his jaw square, but seemed to yield a little. He took an Oat Willie sticker from Tex and a Saint Catherine card from Ziggy. He looked at them. Then he tore them up.

21

"We were just putting you on, man," said Tex, his black animal hairs bristling on his neck. "You need to ditch your hangups, man."

"Oh yeah, what hangups is that, freak?"

"Look at you man, white shirt, black tie, suit, the way you kiss up to the Man, that's your hangup." The two men glared, Tex tall and rangy, the other man smaller but carved of rock. Neither broke eye contact.

"At least I have a job," said the man, and he seemed ready to walk away when Tex spoke again.

"Maybe your job's why you're so fucking uptight, man."

The man glared back again. "What did you say, freak?"

Tex twisted the tip of his handlebar mustache as if he were thinking hard, and then adjusted the drawl and timbre of his voice for maximum impact.

"I said that's why you're so motherfucking uptight."

"Say your prayers, freak."

With impeccable timing, Rag stepped in and pushed Tex back with the surprising force of an old wrestling captain.

"I'm sorry, man," Rag said to the square. "We respect what you're doing. It's a big picture, man, and we're all in it together – you, me, Tex. Just cut Tex some slack. He's still figuring things out like we're all trying to figure things out." Here he smiled. "He just gets a little belligerent sometimes."

The square, who frankly heard little of Rag's salutary philosophy, looked Tex in the eye a little puzzled. "What part of Texas you from, freak?"

"The part that's called Meridian, Mississippi," said Tex, without skipping a beat. And it was true. Tex, despite the sobriquet, was indeed from Mississippi.

The square eyed him suspiciously. "You know about Weidmann's?"

"Cheese grits," Tex said laconically. "Every Sunday. After church." The square shook his bowling ball head, unsure in his own mind whether he were expressing disgust or camaraderie or some combination of the two.

"Creamiest cheese grits anywhere," Tex added, and he actually smiled.

"Cook'm in heavy cream to make'm extra rich," said the square. He caught himself starting to smile back, and quickly turned to walk away. Then he looked back over his shoulder.

"One more thing, freak. Get a haircut." The tone was ambiguous, but the smile on Tex's face reduced the ambiguity to insignificance.

"Hey," Jaz said, "the square had a good idea. Let's say a prayer."

Rag pulled out a card.

"Lord make me an instrument of thy peace."

They found a second Saint Francis card and went on together.

"Where there is hatred, let me sow love; where there is injury, pardon ..."

Jaz must have really been into it because she heard heavenly music coming in at the next line.

"Where there is doubt, faith; where there is despair, hope ..."

Was she hallucinating or tuning in all the way to heaven? A stringed instrument, the tinkling of small bells, a hand-played drum.

"Where there is darkness, light; where there is sadness, joy."

And then more voices in a polyphonic chorus. Two melodies, sweetly folded together and yet separate. A river of voices. What were the other voices singing? Now she recognized it.

"Hare Krishna, Hare Krishna, Krishna Krishna, Hare Hare …"

Coming from opposite directions on Canal Street, like heavenly armies the moment before engagement, were our heroes on one side and a coterie of Krishna disciples on the other.

"Hare Rama, Hare Rama, Rama Rama, Hare Hare …"

"Welcome, brothers and sisters," said Rag. "Have some Oat Willie stickers."

"Cool," said a chipped-tooth Hare Krishna girl who looked about 15. Three kids with her, robed in brown and green and light blue silk, seemed no older, and they gathered wide-eyed with their instruments as Ragman put the Oat Willie stickers into the girl's hand.

"Ah," Ziggy joked to himself silently, "finally, the chosen ones who see the mystical power of the Oat Willie stickers." But he knew it wasn't that. They were just kids, part of that generation of drifting misfits who gaped in wonder at every passing sight or sound or encounter, as if it too were a sign.

The girl whose hand held the stickers seemed the default leader of the little entourage.

"Y'all want a free book?" And she handed Rag a book with a cover image of colorful red and gold Eastern tapestry beneath bold text: KRSNA: THE SUPREME PERSONALITY OF GODHEAD.

Rag took the book, then took her small, dirt-mapped hand, and pressed it knuckle-side against his forehead.

"The sanctity of the saints upon you, my little Kali goddess," he said.

The girl looked a little confused, and Jaz gave her a saint card and a good hug. "Now play," Jaz said gently, and the little group began their song as they turned into the French Quarter, with our heroes dancing a free-form caper behind them.

"Couldn't give up that stupid cowboy hat, could you?" Pepper tossed the rhetorical question at Tex like a floating balloon, just to see which way he'd pop it. Our ragtag group of rambling hippies had stopped in her French Quarter shop, with their new hats and a group of Hare Krishna kids. Well, it wasn't really her shop. She worked in a room behind the shop, making voodoo dolls to sell to tourists. The priestess would come twice a week to bless a new batch to keep the gris gris off and stock them out front. Pepper was feisty, short but compact, like an animated bumper car, with a sharp mind and a good nature camouflaged by acerbic wit. She took her coloring more from the Gaelic than the Italian side of her stock, exhibiting fair and lightly freckled skin, reddish hair, and ice blue eyes, the kind that called every stranger for a double-take. Her lips seemed forever pursed into a fleshy, heart-shaped baby pout, but ready to smack down a tough-necked sailor should the need arise. She was a journalism major off and on, and her piece work as a voodoo doll maker was more for the monetary than the spiritual reward.

"Damn," she called out to the Hare Krishna kids, who had already hit the half-height refrigerator with a voracity unrivaled in the history of wandering mendicants. "Don't y'all get free vegetarian meals at the Krishna House on Esplanade?"

"Not like this," said the chipped tooth girl. She pulled a bit of green bean casserole from between her teeth with her thumbnail and rubbed it on the corner of the

25

tablecloth. The others had picked up their instruments and were tuning up.

"Namaste," said their diminutive leader, and she joined her palms, bowed to Pepper, and led the troupe out through the front of the shop.

"Why should I switch hats, man, just because these guys do?" Tex threw back at Pepper. "You want to see a stupid hat, look at flower child there," and he gestured at Ziggy.

Ziggy, always playful but never bellicose, stepped into the good-natured banter. "I think what Pepper's trying to say, Tex," and that broad Ziggy grin opened up, "is the same thing you were saying to the square. You're trapped in your old scene, man, the cowboy version of the Establishment. That hat is your hangup." He snatched Tex's hat and threw it to Pepper.

Tex was inching toward that vaguely marked frontier between good-natured banter and open irritation. "Look at you and Rag," he said. "Your whole hippie get-up is just another style, man. You talk about freedom, but you gotta dress the hippie scene just like the cowboys dress the cowboy scene and squares put on as squares." He couldn't help but smile at Rag.

"Like Rag, with his mismatched socks and gypsy pants and tie-dye shirt and now that hat. And Zig with his shirt hanging open. Y'all trapped like everybody else."

"You're right about me," Rag said, "but not Zig."

"What do you mean?" blurted Zig. "Tex doesn't even believe that, man. That's what the Scene is all about. Dress however you want, talk how you want, think how you want, create your own living spaces."

"The world isn't ready," said Rag. "Tex is right. I dress like this to disrupt the sensibility out there, shake it up, hippie shake scene. I'm trying to open the door. You're

26

already through the door, Zig. You really don't give a shit. You take whatever shirt's on top in that big empty Kleenex box you call your chest-of-drawers and put it on. You're free, man. You're effortless. You're where it's all headed."

Ziggy laughed. "Sure, man. Ziggy the Great. 'Sexy, romantic, and ready for revolution.' Except I don't know my ass from a hole in the ground." He thought for a flash of the induction letter. No, not now. He wasn't ready. He pushed it back below the surface of consciousness.

"You don't have to know," said Rag with the Ragman smile gleaming. "You just have to be. You're the flower child king."

"What about Jaz," Ziggy said. He stretched out his arms, took both of Jazmine's hands and spun in a circle. "She's cool, man. She's not trapped. She's through the door and into the heavens, man. You got it wrong, Rag. The floral scepter goes to her."

"If only you knew," said Jaz.

"She doesn't count," declared Tex. "She's a girl, man. She's gotta pay attention to how she dresses."

"Trapped by gender, you think?" said Pepper, her blue eyes burning ice and fire into Tex. "Don't you guys read shit? Betty Friedan. The Redstockings."

She fanned herself with Tex's cowboy hat. "I still got your hat, asshole. And this girl will burn your fucking hat to the ground."

Tex made a grab for the hat, and Pepper tossed it to Rag, who tossed it to Jaz, who put it on her head. Tex lunged here and there and froze in front of Jaz. "Can't fight that, man. You're beautiful, you're free. Whatever you touch, baby, it turns to gold."

"Now get your asses outa here," said Pepper. "It's Tuesday. Priestess be here in 30 minutes."

27

Chapter 3

The creative living space of which Ziggy spoke, habitation for our heroes, variously called "the co-op" or "the commune" or sometimes just "St. Roch" after the street on which it sat, consisted of two houses (known as the Duck and the Island) with a shared yard. It was easy to see how the Duck got its name – yellow paint with orange trim made it look like the rubber duck that was and still is ubiquitous in popular culture. The source of the Island's moniker was open to various legendary interpretations. The most current theory was that it got its name because of the water that pooled all around it after heavy rains, to the equal delight of neighborhood kids and transient hippies. An older and deeper story held that the name dated to the time of Biggles, a huge man with half a thumb missing from an offshore accident involving a hydraulic jack. Biggles was jolly and sneaky, and when everyone else had never heard of anything but Mexican dirt weed for $10 an ounce, he always had some kind of superpot. People joked that he had his own island where he grew this stuff. Then, around the time Ragman showed up, he disappeared. Drifters would occasionally pass through with sighting tales.

"I saw him in the summer of '68 at Mario's Trophy Case Lounge in the Upper Haight, couple of blocks from Golden Gate Park. He was entertaining the squares who still hung around the bar to reminisce the 50s and admire Mario's backbar of tennis trophies."

"Bullshit man, Biggles was down and out in Milwaukee in '68, had a bad acid trip and never got right again. I saw him myself mopping floors at the Oriental Lanes."

Still others said it was the strange design of the house. It was an odd-shaped little two-story, all vertical, on a very small lot, second house from the corner, and if it were not for the corner house, it would have looked like a miniature of one of those rock-column mountains you see in pictures from China, like an island rising out straight up out of nowhere. The corner house itself was the Duck House, a vast tunnel of a house, all horizontal, on a very long lot. So the Island's back yard was the Duck's side yard, a serendipitous, off-street communal space that fitted the still-forming cultural vision of the youthful residents.

The owner of the two houses, Mr. Anthony, had lied about his age to join the army in World War II and had subsequently been a prize fighter during the Friday Night Fights era at St. Mary's Italian Church on Chartres Street. He looked as square as square could get, but any neighbor who probed would find him an unlikely sympathizer with the 1960s youth movement.

"Nice polite kids," he would say. "I don't blame them if they want peace or to get out of the damned rat race. I'm sick of the rat race myself. I don't care how they want to wear their hair or clothes. They seem like nice kids, polite to me and always helping each other out."

In a way, you could say it was old-timers like Mr. Anthony who made the hippie vision possible, providing a kind of safe house while the building blocks of social organization were still being juggled. He kind of liked the whole idea, even if the rent was a little late sometimes.

In the kitchen of the Duck, Ziggy was cheerfully cooking mashed potatoes and steamed cabbage on the old white four-burner stove with a dish towel hanging from the waist of his pants. Rag was replacing the black knobs on the light blue cabinet doors under the sink. Well, not replacing really, but adding knobs where they had been missing for a forgotten number of months. Jaz sat at a square wooden table surrounded by mismatched chairs of metal, wicker, and wood. She was flipping through an early issue of *Rolling Stone* magazine, when Pepper walked in from the Island, wearing a green bandanna with a white paisley pattern wrapped tightly to her reddish hair.

"Hey, Pepper, that bandanna looks great on you."

"Thanks, sweetie."

"Did the priestess come in today?"

"Yeah, bitch was there," said Pepper. "Complaining about horse shit from the tourist carriages on Royal Street."

"I thought horse shit was her specialty," laughed Jazmine. She stood and stretched and tossed the magazine on the lower shelf of the open pantry.

Ziggy was plating up the cabbage and potatoes, all steaming with butter on top, and Rag opened a bottle of cheap chianti.

"Let's sit outside," said Pepper. "It's a nice, clear night."

"Go ahead. I'll bring your plates out. You want some, Pepper."

"No, I'll have a sip of wine, though."

They stepped out to the yard just as the spring sun set and sat on the benches at the small picnic table. The square yard was perhaps 40 feet long on each side, enough for the groomed vegetable plot 3 rows wide and 12 feet long, with thick grass otherwise. The night was clear but the air dense and humid, with a moist citrus scent coming from the small satsuma tree near the alley that ran from the yard to the street between the Duck and the Island. The opposite sides away from the Duck and the Island were open to the neighbors. Crickets raised their tiny voices in a rhythmic chorus.

Zig brought out the three plates and Rag filled four jelly jars with wine. Zig and Jaz and Rag dug in, and Pepper took a sip of chianti and looked up. She was engrossed with the sky, or something in it, but she said nothing.

"You make the simplest things taste so good," Jaz said to Ziggy.

"Sexy and ready," Zig countered, playing on his new punch line.

"How about you?" Pepper addressed Jazmine. "How you doing?"

"Good."

"I mean that trip the other day. The tan acid. What do you think? Was it good? Bad? Weird."

"Well, it was quick in and quick out, just like Rag predicted. That's good."

"That's really good," said Pepper, and she looked back up at the sky.

The others ate in silence, enjoying the crickets, the bird chatter of dusk, and the occasional sound of a VW bug torqueing around the potholes on St. Roch Street. Rag bussed the plates and refilled the wine.

"That's why I never did LSD after that first time with Gina and Tex," Pepper continued, as if there were no pause. "It was cool at first but then the long agony of coming down. I remember driving across the 24-mile bridge at night and seeing monsters coming out of the water with each turn of the waves, over and over in a hellish rhythm. And then I felt all the organs inside my body splitting open. I could see them and feel them tearing. Fuck that."

Rag had come back out and was lighting two tiki torches at the ends of the table.

"What the hell were you doing driving while tripping?" asked Ragman.

"I wasn't driving. Tex was."

31

"Oh, that makes it all better," joked Zig. "TEX was driving while tripping." They all chuckled at the reckless absurdity of it all, knowing that at least this time all turned out safe.

"But listen," Jazmine said. "You could even do this stuff, Pepper. There is no long, dark coming down part."

Rag fired up a joint. The match momentarily lit up his face. The hazel eyes gleamed, the cheekbones more prominent as they tapered down to the point of the light brown beard. He looked for a moment like one of the plastic devil heads that come from claw machines. He inhaled hard on the joint and then passed it to Zig, who sat on the bench next to him across from Pepper and Jaz. As Rag momentarily held the pot in his lungs, he ran his hand through his flowing brown hair, with one eye half-closed and his head tilted slightly. Jaz unconsciously recognized this as concentration on Rag's part and leaned in from across the table.

"What are you thinking, Rag?" she asked quietly. The flickering of the tiki torch pulled the violet highlights from her eyes.

Rag was equally quiet as he spoke: "This shit could change everything."

Zig took his hit and passed the joint to Pepper. The earthy sweet smell of marijuana mixed with the citronella fuel of the tiki torches, wrapping the four faces at the table into their own world. Jazmine, with her dark eyes and ivory glow, fiery Pepper with the ice blue eyes, Zig with his rectangular face framed by long curling black locks, and Ragman: faces close together, dimly lit against the darkening sky, all feeling the wrap and pull of pot-forged kinship, but the attention was on Ragman.

"Pepper's exactly right about LSD," he said, and he filled Pepper's jelly jar. As he set the bottle down, a red drop

32

of chianti ran down the side across the label and perched quivering the table.

"LSD breaks the traps. Once you do it, you see the world different and your connections to people different. You see that we can live together differently, not like the Man says we need to live, building machines and making war."

Ragman was animated now, flipping moods a madman. From Bodhisattva to dynamo in sixty seconds. He must have been a little self-conscious about it, because as if to calm himself he reached a finger gently to the drop of wine, which sat on the table like a drop of blood, and slowly spread in a circular motion into a dime-sized stain.

"But it's hard. Look at what happened to Pepper. People do flip out on that long, dark passage back. But what if it were easier? What if you could get that transcendence, that perspective, like people take a cigarette break? The new vision, the vision of the Haight and Woodstock, it would seep in everywhere." He was getting excited again.

"We could put it in Nixon's tea," joked Zig, pulling his earlobe evasively and trying to keep things light. Pepper, meanwhile, was fiddling with the lit end of the joint, apparently in her own world. Only Jaz was focused eye-to-eye with Rag, on the same page and intensity level.

Then Pepper blurted in a stifled voice, as she tried to speak and hold a hit from the joint in her lungs at the same time: "If it's so great, why don't you tell everybody."

"I thought about that," said Rag. "But we got to make sure we're ready, and we got to make sure *they're* ready, because it's going to be a lot to handle. I heard Abraham Lincoln once said, 'Give me six hours to cut down a tree and I'll spend the first four hours sharpening the axe.' I'm still sharpening the axe."

33

Zig caught Rag's gaze at this point and neither was keeping it light now. Ziggy didn't exactly like the axe-sharpening metaphor. But Rag was right – this was serious.

Jazmine pulled Rag's focus back, the magnetic draw between them too strong on this issue.

"And what about that weird part at the end?" Jaz continued. Her lush eyebrows knitted in concentration over the dark eyes, all beauty and intensity.

"I never had hallucinations like that. It was like the Middle Ages."

"Maybe reincarnation," said Zig, his fingers interlaced on the wooden surface of the picnic table. "Didn't you say when we started that you had some kind of ESP thing as a kid?"

Jaz turned to him, seeing a kind of elegance in his body the first time, the impeccable posture, the delicate wrists. She reached over and covered his hands with her own. She was glad he was here.

"The kid stuff was more like déjà vu. Not a clear vision with characters acting out their lives. Maybe you're right. Maybe it's reincarnation." She found herself admiring the feel of his knuckle. "That would be weird. Or maybe it's something from my own unconscious, something from my past, something personal and forgotten but with that drug relaxing the filters, it came up now, disguised and translated somehow."

Jaz noticed the tempo of her words increasing as she spoke. Was she rambling? There was certainly enough shit in her background to be dragged up. Good times with her dad. Bad times with the evil bastard, Ken, whom her mom had paired up with afterward. She was fucked up but she was forging ahead. "Onward through the fog," she thought, and smiled at the incongruous tone of the thought.

"Freudian bullshit," said Pepper.

34

"You don't believe in Freudian bullshit?" Rag asked Pepper, in earnest.

"Freud's a sexist and his time is over," Pepper retorted.

"Pepper, we're just trying to figure this out," Zig countered, halfway between a challenge and a plea. "If Jaz says maybe it's her own unconscious stuff, how is that sexist?"

"I don't know. You know I'm just a bitch," Pepper said, defensive, self-exonerating, but in her own peculiarly endearing manner. She got up and stood behind Jaz. She seemed to be positioning herself for another defensive maneuver. But then she sunk both hands into Jazmine's thick black hair and began a slow French braid, taking her time, doing it right.

"Maybe it's both," said Zig. "If removing the filters can open up stuff to your personal past, why not to past incarnations, too."

"Could be," said Rag. A bright green lizard crept up between the broken slats of the picnic table. Rag seized the little creature with superhuman quickness but then held it as gently as if he were holding a feather.

"Good catch," said Jaz.

Rag smiled and then seemed to catch himself. Compassion and pain flashed across his face so quickly that it could have been an illusion of the tiki lights. He set the lizard on the ground. It shot off through a patch of grass toward the blueberry bushes, where it crashed into Alfred, the cereal bowl sized box turtle that had established residency in the Co-op yard. The lizard took a ridiculous leap when it hit Alfred and disappeared into the high grass.

Ragman turned back to Jaz. "Or it could be the crazy power of imagination. Imagination unleashed."

"Sounds like William Blake," Jaz said. "You ever read Blake, Rag? Songs of Innocence, Songs of Experience, the visionary poems?"

"I like the concept," Rag said.

"I like the images," Jaz smiled.

"I like the conversation," Ziggy threw in roguishly.

"Well, kumbaya, motherfuckers, I'd like a hit off that joint" snapped Pepper. She'd been standing behind Jaz, knotting and knotting her black hair.

Ziggy passed the joint. He didn't actually get poetry or philosophy. He got the reincarnation thing – probably because the child in him found it interesting. When Jazmine and Ragman talked of Blake or of metaphysics, though, Zig was just a curious spectator, beating his own drum on the outside. He figured he didn't get politics either – at least not like Pepper. What did he get? He made friends as easily as Rag, and everybody seemed to think he was fun to hang around, but secretly he was nothing but a fucking blank slate. He just didn't know what to do about it. Anyway, he had enough on his mind these days. He had pulled the dish towel from the waist of his pants and was playing with it on the uneven boards of the table. Pepper knotted and knotted.

"Imagination alright," Pepper said. "The power of imagination is the power of bullshit. It's not the real world. Y'all as bad as the bitch priestess at work."

Rag gave a robust laugh. "In the end, Pepper, you might be the most right."

Pepper finished the braid, flipped it gently a couple of times to verify her work, sat back next to Jaz and spoke directly to her.

"You sure you want to keep testing this thing, sweetie."

"Absolutely," said Jaz without hesitation.

36

A screen door slammed, and the sounds of Grand Funk Railroad's Red Album came pouring through the open doors and windows of the Island. Tex had put side two on the turntable and came stumbling out toward the picnic table with his guitar case. He pulled a folding wooden chair from a nook where a small shed protruded from the main structure of the Duck and set it up near the edge of the table.

"Man, y'all should've seen these guys last summer at the Atlanta Pop Fest."

The introductory segment of "Winter and My Soul" was just yielding to the song proper.

"Even in the studio they sound like they're jamming to the crowd in an open field," Tex continued.

Stormy came out of the rear end of the Duck, brushed her skirt against Tex, and then pushed him on the shoulder. "Play that shit so loud," she said. A small crowd of Duck and Island denizens seemed to be gathering.

"I'll wash the dishes," Rag said. As he and Stormy walked back into the Duck, Gina and Hoss, with his guitar, came out of the Island. Gina was a tiny, quiet thing, and Hoss a big, garrulous walrus of a man – perhaps too garrulous. Like Pepper, he did not know when to shut up, but with completely opposite results. She was all waspish wit, ready for a smack-down, and he was all love and trust and geniality, with a ready bear-hug for any stranger. Indeed, it was his affability that led him to think that a tray of pot brownies would be enjoyable for all at a faculty/student social his sophomore year. That he was expelled for such a kindness seemed a cosmic injustice, but he was good enough with the guitar to make a few bucks at cafes and on the street, and he did contract work at bigger music venues like The Warehouse, so he took it all in lumbering stride. Gina's place in the Island was ambiguous, as the best anyone could tell was that she moved between the Island bedrooms of

Hoss and Pepper, occasionally shifting to the couch if she needed her own space and no bohemian transients were in town and on it. Tex held the remaining bedroom in the Island and he mostly kept his room to himself.

"Hey Gina, how'd it go with the baseboards?" asked Pepper.

Although it seemed vaguely inconsistent with her small frame, Gina was quite handy with a tool box, and she had been repairing a rotten baseboard.

"All done, sweetheart," she said, and squeezed between Pepper and Jaz affectionately.

Pepper cast an eye Tex's way. "You could have taken off that stupid hat and helped her." Pepper knew that Tex was a master carpenter, with an eye and hand for beautiful architectural detail. That he should possess such a virtue sometimes surprised people, but Tex was not really one to give a shit about what people thought. When the woodwork was in front of him, time disappeared and he became one with the object.

"You think way too hard about my hat, girl," he said. He plopped the crumpled cowboy hat on top of her green bandanna, stepped back, and shook his head. "I hate to say it, girl, but you and that bandanna make my hat look good. Anyway, Gina was digging the work. She was zenned out, man." His smile curved up into his handlebar mustache on both sides. "I didn't want to knock her out her zone."

Stormy came out of the Duck with another bottle of chianti.

"Hey, Stormy, where's the Rag?" bellowed Hoss.

"He's inside watching Rose Petal." Rose Petal was Stormy's two-year-old daughter. Together with Ragman, Ziggy, and Jazmine, this mother-daughter pair completed the permanent roster of Duck residents, at least for the time being. Of course, both the Duck and the Island had their parade of transients and hangers-on.

"Hahaha, that Rag," roared Hoss inexplicably, shaking his head like a giant potato all covered with coarse, bushy hair.

Tex pulled out his guitar and rumbled through a plucky version of Taj Mahal's "Fishin Blues." When he reached closure, Stormy began to tease him again.

"When you sing like that, I swear you just another damned white redneck from Mississippi." But Tex, despite his pedigree, was not what anyone would ordinarily call a redneck. In fact, he was the only one from the commune who had been at Martin Luther King's 1963 "I Have a Dream" speech in D.C. Maybe because he was the only one old enough. That was almost seven years ago. But still. He was there and it still brought tears to his eyes whenever the topic came up. Stormy knew that full well. Maybe that's why she walked over to Tex, leaned her taut, perfect brown body over and kissed him a slow, luscious kiss on the lips, and tweaked his nose with hers before standing back to full height. "Now keep playing, white boy." Tex smiled a Mississippi chicken thief smile, strummed an aimless chord, rattled his fingers on the box of the guitar for percussion, and started into "Crystal Blue Persuasion."

Meanwhile, Hoss had taken out his guitar, and as Tex strummed out the first chords of the song, Hoss laid on with the notes. Hoss would sing this one, mellowing his voice to the sweet timbre of a Jewish cantor on a High Holiday.

Look over yonder, what do you see?
The sun is arising most definitely

Stormy didn't sit back down but kicked off her peep-toe shoes with the short pointy heels, which she wore as

39

casually as the others did their tennis shoes and high-tops, and swayed barefoot in the tiki light.

> A new day is coming, people are changing
> Ain't it beautiful, crystal blue persuasion

Hoss and Tex continued the song in unison, but on the guitar Hoss was master.

"My god," Jazmine said after a pause. "Look at that crescent moon and Venus so bright. It's like something planetary is really happening. A sign of something coming."

"It's a sign that you're bogarting the reefer again," snapped Pepper. "Give us a toke every now and then."

Pepper's bon mot got chuckles, but everyone looked at the sky, a velvet blanket full of stars, no doubt, but with the moon and Venus most illustrious.

Stormy, still spinning as the song ended, chanted at the sky as she spun: "Gnomes of the earth, Nymphs of water, Sylphs of the air, and Salamanders of fire."

"Where do you come up with this shit, Stormy," asked Hoss cheerily, adjusting the guitar on his lap.

"Elemental spirits, baby, you can get 'em from a book if it ain't in your soul. Like Pepper says, don't y'all ever read anything?"

"Hoss never got past picture books," Tex quipped. Then he strummed another random chord while Hoss took a hit on the joint and sprawled back to look at the stars. But random as Tex's chord was, Stormy knew what he was thinking, and as soon as he hit the strings again, she was singing along:

> When the moon is in the seventh house
> And Jupiter aligns with Mars

She sang it from a soulful, timeless depth, like it was no joke, and kept swaying, the perfect blend of spiritual mystery and sensual presence.

> Then peace will guide the planets
> And love will steer the stars.
> This is the dawning of the Age of Aquarius

Under that Venus and that moon on that night in the spring of 1970, a half dozen hippies believed earnestly, joyfully, and perhaps a little naively, that indeed a planetary change was coming.

Chapter 4

As the night passed and the party broke, so passed Venus and the moon over the western horizon, and, in due time, the sun rose over the rooftop gables and camelbacks of the Faubourg Marigny, over the Magic Mushroom and Schiro's corner grocery, over the old ironworks on Piety Street near the Mississippi River, ushering in a beautiful Wednesday morning. Dew clung to the potted aloe veras on the cement doorsteps that tumbled out from the rows of brightly painted cottages on Royal Street and Burgundy, and to the broad-leafed banana trees on the easement closer to the street, and to the thick grass shrubbery and the 8' by 12' plot of vegetables at the Co-op. Birds squawked and crickets chirped as the sun heaved itself higher and higher, until the dew was gone and the next day had begun.

"Eat na appasauce, Alfwed," peeped a tiny voice. "Nu gotta eat." A ladybug, oblivious to the danger of giants, even baby ones, landed on the hand attached to the tiny voice. Alfred, a wiser beast, retracted his saggy neck and pulled his head into his yellow and brown splotched helmet shell. The ladybug was promptly pinched between a little fat finger and thumb.

"Eat da bug, Alfwed."

Stormy, adding leafy mulch by hand to the base of a freshly planted pepper bush, nodded her chin at Rose Petal. "Put that Ladybug down, baby. Quit teasing Alfred."

"Me not tease Alfwed. Alfwed hungry, mommy." She squished the ladybug tighter, perhaps thinking that the emphasis would highlight the deliciousness of the morsel in Alfred's eyes.

"Rose Petal! You gotta be gentle, baby. You're going to hurt it."

But perhaps gentleness was a learned trait in *homo sapiens*, as Rose Petal had in pure innocence already squished the life out of the unfortunate ladybug.

"No, mama, me NOT hurt waybug," she said fiercely.

"Watch," said Stormy. She stood and picked a ladybug from a tiny lavender wildflower that had sprung up at the edge of the garden. She sat with her face close to Rose Petal's and sang.

Three little ladybugs landed on a shoe
One flew away and then there were two
Two little ladybugs looking for some fun
One flew away and then there was ONE!

When she got to "one," she shouted it out, gently blew the ladybug into the air, grabbed Rose and spun her around. Rose shrieked in delight and the ladybug unfolded the orange and black machinery of its wings and floated away.

Stormy set Rose down in an unfinished corner of the garden with lots of nice mud and a small plastic beach bucket and shovel, easily distracting her into new activity and hoping the pill bugs and ground beetles in the new play area might fare better.

"Hey, Stormy, you want some coffee?"

Jaz was on the back steps.

"That's OK. Rose got me wide awake." Stormy sat on the cracked cement of the steps with Jaz while Rose played. Jaz moved one step higher and rubbed Stormy's neck and shoulders.

"I like your hair like that," she said. "I don't know what to call it, but I like it." Stormy had had a full Afro yesterday, but today her hair was bunched into little sprouts.

"Pepper did it this morning," Stormy laughed. "Once she gets something in her head, it's best to let it go."

Jaz reached up and patted the springy shoots of Stormy's hair.

"Don't know not to touch black people's hair, girl?"

"No," said Jaz, moving her fingers back down to the sinews of Stormy's neck. "Do you mind?"

"You are so innocent, girl." Stormy laughed out loud. "No, I don't mind. But don't try that on the street."

"I'm not that dumb, Stormy." Jaz worked her fingers out to Stormy's shoulders.

"But it's weird," Jaz mused. "People can't just be curious about each other without everything getting in the way."

"Ooh, that's good. Go down the right arm just an inch." She relaxed into it for a moment before going on.

"It's not that weird. What if you were walking down the street and someone pulled your lips up and down to see if you had strong teeth."

"Well, when you put it that way," Jaz said.

43

"When you bought and sold like cattle a few hundred years, you get sensitive about some things."

"Let me do your hands," Jaz said, and she scooted next to Stormy.

"It's getting better though, Stormy, don't you think? People are more liberal."

"I don't know. I'm not as hopeful as you. I know, the way we're living here. It's better than it was. But even the liberals. It's all politics. Who to blame and who to cuss. How to fight better. Politics – always us against them."

"But I heard you say yourself how good things were in '67."

Stormy's lips broadened into a distant smile. "Yeah, that's true. For about a minute everything was good." In her mid-teens, Stormy had been all fired up about the Civil Rights movement. She may not have been at the "I Have a Dream" speech like Tex, but she remembered it clear as day from TV. That's when she first noticed how different her father was around white people. Humble. Son of a bitch was not humble at home. And she started thinking about how white people sat downstairs and black people sat upstairs at the Pitt, the neighborhood movie theater on Elysian Fields. She saw a better world on the TV news and got a ride with a white kid from school out to San Francisco. It was the March before the Summer of Love. And it was true. She joined with a crew in one of the huge Victorian houses that run up and down the side streets of Haight-Ashbury, and she found a cultural window where racism really was uncool. Of course, they were all just kids. Which is probably why it worked. They didn't politicize it or overthink it. Hell, they didn't know the first thing about politics. They just lived it, armed with only the heart and imagination, as if the world were already the way they wanted it to be – open and all-inclusive and communal and everybody helping each other. And so it was for a little while. It couldn't last. For all sorts of reasons. But for Stormy, it couldn't last because she was pregnant before the Summer of Love hit, love child of a white hippie. Little Rose Petal, with her light brown skin and creole green eyes. So she had to come home for what shreds of family support she could find. Which wasn't much. But she had her place at the Co-op and that was a blessing.

"Still bits and pieces of good, I imagine. Like you." She put one arm around Jaz's shoulders, kissed her on the neck, and lay her head on Jaz's shoulder.

A record came screaming out of the Island's back window.

>Call out the instigators
>Because there's something in the air

"I guess Tex is awake," Stormy said.

>We got to get together sooner or later
>Because the Revolution's here

Stormy brushed her lips against Jaz's neck.

>And you know it's right,
>And you know that it's right

Ragman came down the alley between the two houses with a large plastic sack over his shoulder. He flipped it over at the edge of the garden.

"Thanks, sugar daddy," Stormy said.

"Sugar daddy, my ass," Rag replied. "We'd all be starving if you hadn't taken charge of this falling apart garden. Anyway, there's your sack of manure from Mr. Anthony." He flashed a smile, then sauntered back down the alley toward the street, doing his own thing.

45

Rose Petal had finally tired of the mud pile and had wandered back into the tall grass.

"Mommy. Alfwed hungry, mommy."

Jaz ran and scooped her up like a bag of potatoes.

"Hey Stormy, let's go get Bitzy from Cool Breeze and Claire and take her and Rose Petal to the puppet show in Washington Square park," Jaz suggested.

"You're late, girl," Stormy said. "Rag had the same idea. He's coming to get Rose after Bitzy's math lesson. But let's go with 'em."

* * *

It was hard to judge how many additions and subtractions had been made to the house in the century and a half of its existence before it took on its present life as the Duck. It had a cobbled-together appearance like the castle at Carcassonne, but without the grandeur. When you entered the small living room through the main door on St. Roch, you could turn left to pass through the kitchen and along the sprawling bulk of the house. To the right of the living room was just one room, which had become a kind of meditation space, a set-aside room for reading, reflection, and homemade yoga practices. This room, called "the shrine," perhaps because of the replica of Giotto's Madonna and child, which hung in a faux-gold frame on the wall, best preserved the character of the original construction. It felt old. This was the room of reddish-brown mahogany in which Jazmine chose to relax into the tan acid.

As Jazmine started her second trip on the tincture, which Rag had dropped in liquid form on a small square of blotter paper, she felt herself establishing a comfort zone in the room. There was the Madonna and child, and the burgundy curtains to nowhere. The familiar blue sheet and

46

Russian birch. Candles were lit at her request because she liked the mood they set. Stormy had added a pair of dark wooden akua ma dolls, about a foot in height, to the mantel. The akua ma was a female fertility icon from West Africa. According to the legend, an infertile young woman, Akua, was instructed to create a wooden doll and to carry, bathe it, and treat it in every manner like a living infant. She obeyed and was blessed nine months later with a healthy baby girl. Stormy, who could not frame a house like Tex but could rival him in woodcarving, made the dolls and sold them at the French Market. The point was not fertility in her case – she'd had enough of that – but the spiritual gravitas of Stormy's work was clear to the residents of the Co-op, and Pepper regularly referenced it as a foil to the "phony bitch priestess" who paid her salary. Jaz liked them in the room for the spiritual gravitas. And she liked Ziggy and Rag and Pepper in the room for the human love and grounding.

It was not really the akua ma dolls that caught Jazmine's eye; she was rather drawn again to the Madonna and child. The face of the Madonna, the gaze did not appear stylized and medieval but personal and modern. Jaz understood the gold leaf halo, but why the intricate knotted pattern on the halo. Then she heard rain. Torrential pouring rain. She didn't know if it was real or not. She was on the point of asking Zig, but decided not to. The Madonna's halo. The halo was just the topmost form on an endless series of haloes. You couldn't see them because they were stacked exactly behind the one in the painting. But they were innumerable, vanishing back through the walls into infinite space, like planets superimposed, vanishing back into time across centuries. And the rain washed back across centuries …

She was standing in a long hall with post-and-beam walls. The floor was covered with rushes, and on the timber

47

of the walls hung dyed linen cloths decorated with embroidery. There was little furniture – a couple of long wooden benches against the wall, a chest, a trestle table holding a small earthenware pot filled with sprigs of sage and basil and rosemary. The man who had spoken to her of Jeremiah sat on a stool at the table sopping a crust of dark rye bread back and forth in a mug of small beer. His sharp features and curly black hair and severe bearing had not changed. The narrow windows had no glass but were shuttered against the rain, which was coming down hard outside.

Another man opened the door and charged in, drenched. "God's Bones, William, we need to fix that gate."

"Is it done for the night, Jeremiah?" asked the sharp-featured man.

"Aye, for the night."

Jeremiah had softer features than William but more vitality in his demeanor.

William pushed back from the table and stood to move about, although there were not many places to move in the small house. The main room in which the three now stood was for cooking and eating, relaxing and performing other small domestic tasks. At one end, it had two wooden cots with straw-stuffed mattresses for William and Jeremiah. There was a hearth at the center with low-burning embers, and a lean-to addition protruding from the back, apparently to give a modicum of privacy to Rebecca and her decrepit bunkmate, the old woman who begat the sturdy William. Wait! How did she know she was Rebecca? Jazmine felt she was losing herself and being drawn into herself at the same time.

She noticed a separate chamber at the end of the main room opposite the men's cots. William strode over and into this chamber, which functioned as a workshop.

"What must it be like to be maidservant to such a man?" Jeremiah said, shaking his blond locks.

"What you to be apprentice to such?" said Rebecca.

"Ah, it's not so bad," said Jeremiah, stepping in closer to Rebecca. She could smell his scent – citrus and leather. He put his strong hands on her waist. Now she could feel his hot breath on her neck.

"Jeremiah, watch yourself! He's just in the workshop!"

"Aye but he'll be there for a while."

"But Jeremiah, William is my guardian. And he is thy master. His word to us is law."

"Aye, and what is his word?" muttered Jeremiah in exasperation. "That thou shalt never leave. That I remain another six year. It isn't tolerable, Rebecca. He shall keep thee forever bound. He'd a married thee yet if not for the ill-tempered hag that bore him. She thinks no caroling wench good enough for her William. But she shall be dead and buried one day. Aye, she hath a black lung now, the leech did say. One day soon she'll die and seal your fate. We must defy thy rough-hewn master before it's too late."

"His word is law," repeated Rebecca.

"Aye, for now," rejoined Jeremiah. "But we'll be free of him tomorrow, after the Lord Bishop arrives from the Michaelskloster with the Mohametman boy of which I told thee. Our time is ripe, Rebecca."

The hot breath closed against her neck. She turned her chin in to nudge against him, and he turned up and kissed her on the mouth. The diagonal scar on her lower lip tingled. The scar was a relic of a childhood disease. She had only been twelve, and when it hit, she raved in delirium. It was not part of a larger plague like the one that had taken her mother. She and only she had the illness, which elicited speculation of a divine cause. Sores had multiplied inside her

49

mouth and on her lips; it had felt like hot coals pressed and rubbing against tender skin.

At the time she had lived with her father, an already old man known as Meister Conrad to the local townspeople and peasantry, in a thatch cottage near the edge of the village. He had daubed what oils he could on Rebecca's lips against the pain, mainly at the little girl's own instruction since herbal lore had passed from her mother to her. He was, however, preparing for her death. Then fate intervened in the form of a traveler, a companion from Conrad's youth, who'd shared his wenching days at market towns and fairs, and with whom he'd ventured off on an abortive crusade, incoherently organized by a local lord to please a less local duke in the service of a quite distant king, who had hoped to gain the support of the pope in a family dispute with another royal dynasty. The Holy Land was never reached though many brave men were lost in battle against cholera and scarlet fever. Conrad had turned back at the Donau River and had never seen the friend again. But in Conrad's present time of sorrow, Berold, the companion of old, returned with his own mass of herbal lore to match little Rebecca's.

Berold immediately took a fixed interest in Rebecca's malady, and spent long hours gathering local herbs and fungi to combine with the tinctures and powders in his safekeeping. The townspeople, already on edge about the transcendental sources of affliction in Conrad's household, implored the local magistrate to suppress the witchcraft and heresy, which seemed to them more openly practiced since Berold's arrival, lest the pestilence spread to the faithful. The magistrate, a man of letters, did not share the superstitions of his constituents but was well aware of the material advantages – the casks of beer and oysters, fine English wool and fat capons – that come the way of a perceived deliverer.

Thus the wheels of destruction and death were set in motion for Conrad's house.

One morning Rebecca had recovered enough to work in the garden, which she tended with an old woman, the woman who would become her protectress of sorts, as this was the mother of William, who would take Rebecca into his household in her time of distress. On this morning, Berold, knowing his fate, came to Rebecca as she sat pruning a bush of black currants.

"Where's your father, lass?"

"Tending the poultry."

"Listen, lass." Berold's face came close to hers. She could see the red splotches on his bulbous nose and smell the beer on his breath.

"You're a young woman now," Berold said. His eyebrows furrowed with intensity as he gazed at her eye-to-eye, too close-up for comfort. "There's things you need to know. Aye, and perhaps best if your father does not know."

The girl's heart pounded. "Meister Berold, you're scaring me."

"Listen, lass. You see the sores upon your lips and mouth. You see the delirium that comes and goes. It makes you feel funny, doesn't it?" He showed rotten teeth in a terrible grin.

Rebecca couldn't answer. She couldn't breathe.

"Meister Berold," was all she could say before losing her breath. "Breathe, breathe," she said to herself. She sucked in air as if she were learning to breathe for the first time. She put her hand to her chest, hoping to keep her heart from hammering through.

"You're getting better now though. Aye. It's the herbs. You and I know the herbs, lass." There was that terrible grin again, creased between the sagging wallets of his cheeks. For a flash. Then he was all intensity.

51

"There's no time left, lass. They're coming to get your father and me. For witchcraft. Aye, witchcraft. And perhaps they're right. For what I know of herbs is more than natural."

The length of his speech brought the swell in Rebecca's chest down somewhat. But she had let go the currant bush and her hands were still shaking.

"Alchemists, lass, they look to transmute the dregs of earth to gold. But there's bigger things than gold. Secrets known only in the heavens. I have traveled far and wide, lass. The old Roman lands, the orient, Palestine, and a great continent below Palestine. And I have found a secret, lass."

His bulbous nose now almost touched her face. One more inch and she would die. Her breast heaved again.

"A secret bigger than gold."

Berold was becoming excited. He took Rebecca's tremulous hands in his own knobby paws.

"And you, Rebecca. YOU are the secret."

Rebecca felt tears welling up in her eyes. She could not speak. She could not think. Breathe, Rebecca. Breathe, breathe.

"This affliction that you and only you have, lass. It's not an affliction but the body's resistance. Something divine has chosen you."

Rebecca mustered all her strength and tried to pull her hands away, but Berold held on too tightly. She looked around for the old woman, William's mother, but the beldam had disappeared.

"No, child, don't pull away. There's no time, I say. This day your father and I will die."

As discomforting as Berold's presence was, this was the first time he had spoken harshly to her.

"Your delirium is not delirium but divinity. Divinity in chaos. Uncontrolled. But it can be controlled. Aye, it

CAN be controlled. Over the weeks, we've made a tonic, you and I, a tonic that's made you feel better, has it not?"

"Aye, Meister Berold."

"Can you remember the parts, lass, the formula?"

"Aye, Meister Berold."

"And make it again?"

"Aye."

"Good. There is a vast island many thousands of leagues below the Holy Land. You must find the sweet sap of a dwarf palm that grows thereon."

Rebecca was pulling away again, thinking she might faint from the beer smell on Berold's breath.

"Attend, lass!" he said with force. As he said it, Rebecca heard a scattering sound from the poultry pen. Chickens and geese screeched, but there was also the muffled sound of men's voices.

"Mix in this sap – one part to two parts – and your lips will heal. The divinity in you will break through and you will become the secret. Your delirium will break and you will see the underlying reality of which all these physical things are just signs. Attend, lass! It's said that this chance comes once in a thousand years."

A horseman rode up behind Berold, followed by two men and an oxcart. Cornflowers were in bloom and added shocking blue smears to the background and a peppery fragrance to the air. Something was in the oxcart, a large bundle of dirty rags.

"Say thy prayers, Berold. I arrest thee in the Lord Bishop's name for witchcraft and heresy. Art ready?"

"Aye." The men bound his hands and feet and stacked him into the back of the oxcart, lodged between the wall of the cart and the bundle. Rebecca could see now that the other bundle was not just old rags. It was a man. Motionless. Her dead father. A crack of a whip and the

53

oxcart slowly went into motion, carrying its bounty across a field of tall grass, known to the locals as St. Mary's Field, with a few long huts in the distance.

"You are the secret … you are the secret," Berold said in gasping breath as they took him away. And then he said nothing. But for a long time, his sad, bloodshot eyes held hers as he was carted across the wild flowers and dry stones and great clods of earth beneath the undulating surface of tall grass.

The rain had stopped at William's cottage, where Rebecca now found herself four years after that calamitous day at St. Mary's Field. Warier than Jeremiah of the man in the workshop, she took his hand and led him through the iron-hinged door to the front of the house, where the herb garden lay glistening and beaten down from the rain.

"Now what of the Mohametman boy, Jeremiah?"

"The Lord Bishop, my master before I was of age to apprentice, has since taken the boy by force from a family of Silk Road merchants in the Holy Land. Merchants with secret spices from far beyond Arabia for every malady, and some say for magic. The sweet sap you spoke of, the boy has it. I still have friends in the Lord Bishop's train and they confirm this."

It is true that Rebecca had confided in Jeremiah regarding Berold's proposed cure for her recurring affliction. She knew that Jeremiah had traveled as a servant boy in the Lord Bishop's train, and he was the first person she could trust in the four years since that evil day in St. Mary's Field. But even to him she did not tell the whole story. Even he did not know the elements and portions of the potions. He did not know how fully the cure was more than a remedy for the body. Yes, he was a good man and she trusted him, but she was clever enough to know that a young woman must not give away her secrets too freely in this world. She must keep what power she can to her own bosom.

Jeremiah put his hands on her shoulders and leaned his face toward hers with his bright-eyed smile twinkling. In his excitement, he almost forgot the seriousness of the subject.

"Rebecca, this boy's spices can harness the deliriums, ride them like an incubus."

"Jeremiah, come hold these cleats," came a firm voice from inside.

Jeremiah started to move. Rebecca seized both his hands in hers, stood tiptoe and pecked him a kiss on the lips.

Upon entering the house, Jeremiah strode directly to the workshop, and Rebecca followed at a gentler pace. When she looked into the room, Jeremiah was already at it with his master. William had carefully aligned three boards, about one foot by seven feet each, side by side to make a large, flat panel. Jeremiah now held a smaller board, about two feet long, crosswise against the larger boards. William popped three iron nails through the smaller board. William rapidly and gracefully tipped the final product on end, lifted it, and fitted it onto a great box. The great box, now covered, sat beside two identical fellow-boxes. Rebecca cringed, as she always did at the sight. Coffins. Gloomy apprenticeship, indeed.

Jazmine's head slowly rocked back and forth. She cringed as Rebecca cringed. Ziggy took one of her hands and Pepper took the other. A pattern was developing with which all three were comfortable. Ragman was studying one of the akua ma dolls, and then he started browsing the books on a built-in bookshelf that had come with the house. Rag could be intense, but at other times he masked concern with a feigned inattentiveness.

Jaz opened her eyes and smiled. Coming down really was easy, compared to LSD or mushrooms. The lightness of her look took Ziggy by surprise and was perhaps easily misread.

"You look happy," he said, and added jokingly: "Did you see the secrets of the universe?"

"Don't joke about it, Zig," she said. "Not right now."

Chapter 5

It was late Wednesday afternoon, and the sun slowly tracked its descent toward the far surface of the lake. The stretched-out bodies of Ziggy and Jazmine lay naked and soaking in the late afternoon rays.

"OK, so I get it that you think it's really a past life from the Middle Ages," Zig was saying. "Why Germany though? Were they speaking German? Were *you* speaking German?"

"I don't know. Something they said. No, not said. It's the way they were thinking. Or the way Rebecca was thinking. I didn't think about the language. It was just our – *her* – language. But now when I look back. Certain words. "Meister" kept coming up and "Michaelskloster." That's German, isn't it? Oh I don't know, Zig. I can't think about it anymore."

"Don't think about it," Zig repeated, reassuringly. He kissed her forehead, stood, stretched, and walked toward the beach. Jaz watched quietly, shifting gears in her mind to lighten herself up. She thought of the saints card in Ziggy's crumpled pants that lay beside her. Someone, probably Tex, had taken one of the Saint Francis cards they'd picked up at the Magic Mushroom, pasted Ziggy's picture over Saint Francis, and left in on Ziggy's pillow. "Maybe he is a saint," Jazmine thought as she sat there on the beach. "Or a god gone missing from the pantheon." As he ambled toward the water, she thought he did look just a little, maybe, like Apollo. "But a little skinny," she added in her mental narrative, smiling to herself, as she watched Ziggy plunge. Zig was a good guy, no doubt about it. It was the first time she had a guy best friend, with nothing sexual. Sure, she wasn't a virgin. There was the stupid car thing with Jason when they were supposed to be at the drive-in movie. Oh fuck, there was that night at Cassie's house, too. That was weird for all three of them. So she was experienced, although perhaps only comically so. And it was different here. It was easy to get close to people. Normal boundaries didn't seem to apply. When you met someone your age, the camaraderie was deep and implicit. Maybe it started with Viet Nam, with that feeling that wherever you went, you bonded instantly to people of your generation in a blood partnership against the ongoing horror of Viet Nam. So she met the kids at the beach, went to the party in the yard at St. Roch, and moved in the next week. Rag was great. He'd apparently had some reputation in the past – like his open relationship with Julia, sometimes quite open. Then Stormy and Rose Petal moved in, Rag toned it down a little, and Julia went to New York and never came back.

It was some months after she moved into St. Roch that Jazmine had applied for the job at Polo's Pizza and met Ziggy. In all that time at the Duck, Rag never tried to touch her, but she didn't have a best friend till Ziggy, someone she could love with all the doors and windows open. But not sexually. Maybe it was her problem. She had to separate sex and love, as if love were pure and sex were dirty. Like she was defending something inside but she didn't know what it was that was being defended.

"You look hot!"

Jazmine started out of her reverie to see a lanky teen boy with black frame glasses hanging over her.

"Thanks." The teen boy could see she was nervous.

"No, I mean sweating hot. I'm not hitting on you, I swear." He grinned. "We got some beers over by the Plymouth."

"No Thanks." Zig was walking up, squeezing water out of his long hair.

"Hey, man," said the kid, "I was telling your old lady we have some beers over by the Plymouth."

"Thanks. We're good."

"Y'all hear about the cops out here yesterday?"

"Never seen the cops out here before," said Zig. Jaz kept sunbathing in her own mental space, trying to put closure on her thoughts.

"Yeah, cops took my friend's weed and sent him packing."

Zig commiserated: "Shame, man. Cops getting into everything."

"Hey, I know you," said the kid. He scratched his big toe in the sand, as if he were trying to draw a secret symbol. Then he looked up and straight at Ziggy.

"I know where I seen y'all before. Y'all part of Ragman's army," he said, grinning a little more cautiously.

Ziggy laughed. "If we're the army, I feel sorry for whoever we're defending."

"Don't laugh, man," said the kid. Weird, Ziggy thought. That's the second time somebody told him that today.

"Be careful around Rag," continued the kid.

"Rag's cool," said Zig. The kid had touched on a point he felt strongly about. "Rag's the coolest guy I ever met." The kid fidgeted.

"Ever," Zig repeated, letting the kid know that this was not negotiable.

"I know, man," said the kid. "But be careful." Now he was nervous, whispery. He looked over at a small group standing across the beach by a palm tree.

"That's the problem," he hissed, under his breath. "Ragman's the one thing the cops can't stand. An idealist in the drug scene. You think they give a shit about speed and heroin dealers? Shit, the cops are dealing half the drugs in this town. And cocaine and downers? The Man loves that shit. Speed to keep people working; downers to keep'm tame. What the cops hate is a guy with the vision to change things. Fuck things up. And it ain't only the cops."

The more the kid hissed and whispered, the more Zig became intrigued.

"What do you mean, it ain't only the cops?" Zig asked, all ears, as if the kid were a street guru from a Jack Kerouac novel.

"Those fucking dealers coming in with the heroin and the coke. They just want money and zombies. They'd get rid of Ragman faster than the cops. Yeah, they got their fucking ways too." He rolled his foot along the sand, smoothing over forever whatever imaginary symbol he had started. "Their own fucking ways, man."

"Why are you telling us this?" asked Zig.

"I don't know. I like Ragman. I admire the guy. And your chick there looks cool." He thought for a second. Someone from the group by the palm tree gestured to the kid. Zig looked over and thought he saw Beachbum in the group. "And because I'm a fucking idiot," the kid said, and he walked briskly off.

* * *

Nestled between three-story sandstone buildings, a serious young man walked across a quad of thick but close-cropped green grass. Inside one of those sandstone buildings, Jazmine took a window seat near the stacks and stacks of books of the library. It was late Thursday morning and she was getting off from her work-study job at the circulation counter. It probably wasn't as much fun as Polo's Pizza would have been, but it was an easy job with time to read and catch up on homework. From the window, she could see the street that bordered the campus, and behind it a row of nicely kept two-story stone houses. But she was more interested in the books she had pulled from the shelves. She could not say why she was embarrassed. It made sense that she might try to find some history books to illuminate the weird experiences of the tan acid. But when she looked at herself from the outside – completely untutored at historical research, looking for books to prove something about reincarnation – it all seemed so ridiculous. Is this why she went to college? "No," she said to herself, "but this is in front of me now. This needs to be done."

She flipped through the narratives about barbarian invaders of Rome and the Islamic Caliphate moving up from the south, Charlemagne and Gregorian chants, the Black Death and the crusades. She even had a separate short stack of books on Medieval Germany. But it all started to blur together. She ran her finger back and forth on the page. She smiled and thought of Alice in Wonderland reading her book just before she spotted the white rabbit. What would Grace Slick say if she were here?

Jazmine closed her eyes and imagined the military beat to the opening bars of Jefferson Airplane's "White

Rabbit." Then she heard in her mind the psychedelic guitar bending in over that martial base.

"Hey you work here, don't you?"

Jazmine started and furtively closed the book as if she had really been Alice and up to something naughty. She looked up and saw the man who had been walking across the quad. His demeanor was not unfriendly but he retained his serious expression even as he engaged his interlocutor. Jaz was nervous but held his gaze. Stay the course, she always told herself. Don't let them see you flinch.

"Yeah, I just got off." Why did she say that? She sounded like she was apologizing.

"What's up with the German books?"

"I'm just trying to …" Jaz was stumbling. "… to find something."

"Maybe I can help. My people's from Germany."

"No, that's OK. It's nothing specific. I'm just browsing."

"OK, well, look, maybe you can help me then." The serious young man sat down at her table. He had a daub of pomade in his black hair, making it neat and slick, and he managed to combine the edgy intensity of James Dean with the handsome charm of Tony Curtis. Jazmine smiled as she thought of the comparisons, and it put her at ease.

"Maybe," she said bluntly, and pretended to look back at the book, leveraging the pressure to perform back toward him.

"Somebody keeps taking down my flyers," he said, unfazed by Jazmine's newfound sprezzatura. He pulled out a sample flyer for Jazmine to review. "S A W" read the banner across the top, with the subheading "Students Against the War." The central image featured President Nixon lying in a magician's box draped with an American flag. A student raged at the box with a hand-held saw, and a caption

61

underneath said, "No Justice, No Peace." The flyer promoted a meeting coming up in three days, on Sunday, April 19, at 6:00 p.m.

"Maybe if your student guy didn't look so pissed off, people wouldn't take it down," Jazmine said playfully.

"Ha, ha, ha, you're good," he said. "What about the slogan?" He held up his palms toward her and moved them in a circular motion as he spoke: "'No Justice, No Peace.' That was my idea. We're trying to decide whether to keep it."

"I don't know if it really fits the anti-war thing," she said.

The young man turned serious again and seemed to study the poster for the first time.

"You know what? You're right. Maybe we'll take that slogan off the next batch and save it for something else."

He stuck the flyer back into a folder. Jaz prickled with pride. Not that she had any reason to care about this guy's approval. But maybe her marketing studies were not totally useless.

"You should come to the meeting," he said. "I'm Saul." He held out his hand. There was, Jaz had to admit, something irresistible about him.

"Are you really a student, Saul?"

"Sort of. I'm taking one class. Poli Sci."

"I don't know if one class counts."

"What's your name?" he asked point blank.

"Jazmine." She laughed and shook his hand.

"I'll give you a tip," Jazmine continued. "Put your flyers in the Student Union, not in the library. And not in the hallway by the cafeteria, but in the side hallway by the club offices and the theater. If you put it by the cafeteria, Mr. Wilcox will take it down for sure."

"Great, Jazmine, you gotta come to the meeting. This is what it's all about."

"I don't know if my boyfriend will let me," she said. There was nothing remarkable about telling this particular white lie to deflect attention or feel out a guy's intentions. But why did she have to think of Ziggy when she said it?

"Tell your boyfriend to come," Saul said without hesitation. "I can tell you're cool, and he's probably cool, too. I'm sure he doesn't want to have his arms blown off just because somebody tells him he has to go kill yellow people halfway around the world. I'm sure he'll want to fight to keep all our brothers and sisters safe from the war and safe from the Man." When he smiled, it was like something special had happened. He was so concentrated, so serious – gaining a smile seemed like a bracing accomplishment.

"One other thing, though," he added. "Remember I'm not a 'real' student. You got ten minutes to show me where that spot is in the student union?"

"Sure," Jaz laughed. "Let me just tell Roxy at the desk that I'm done."

Ten minutes turned into twenty, and kept turning. Jazmine was intrigued. Saul had a kind of dangerous charisma. And he had ideas. How would Ziggy respond to Saul? And what would Ragman think of his ideas?

"This college is giving information about students' class ranking to the Selective Service. That puts their 2S deferment at risk. That's the topic for this meeting. If you can't fix the whole world, pick something you can do, and do it. We can make a big deal out of this and embarrass the administration. We can get this one thing."

Jazmine was impressed. Here's a guy who was out there doing something.

"Here it is," Saul said. A twenty-minute walk through the uptown university area had brought them to Saul's house – "The Den."

"When we go in, don't freak. There's some weird people cross paths here, but they're all working on something, they're all breaking templates. It's all cool."

Jazmine thought that a strange introduction, but she wasn't worried. Her self-consciousness didn't take that form. Maybe she worried too much about her focus or one-on-one dynamics, but she could handle nude beaches and far-out people in general. And she was good with breaking templates. At least she thought she was.

The house was a small wood-frame Victorian, built at the turn of the 20th century, purple with black trim. The front of the house was nearly covered with foliage, but a single brown oak door was half-visible through the verdant camouflage. As she walked up the three short brick steps, Jazmine felt, perhaps not unjustly, as if she were going into a funhouse.

The first room was dimly lit and almost empty, as if the space had been cleared for a transition of tenants that never took place. A man and a woman, who appeared to be in their early twenties, sat on the only two chairs at the only table. At the center of the table was a 1500-piece jigsaw puzzle. The box, tossed aside, featured a beautiful undersea image of a coral reef, populated by cheerful and brightly colored sea creatures. Presumably the completed puzzle would show the same, but the progress of the two players was hard to measure. The woman, small with close-cropped red hair, fitted in a piece.

"Got one," she said in a monotone.

The man had long sideburns, a corduroy shirt with suspenders, and a country bumpkin appearance. He looked up at Saul and Jazmine. He lifted a mirror with two lines of cocaine, a razor blade, and a straw. "Plenty for everybody," he said good-naturedly.

Saul spoke for both when he said, "No, Lonnie, y'all just keep doing your thing."

"Far out," Lonnie said, and he and his woman went back to the jigsaw puzzle and the two-liter bottle of Big Shot Crème Soda and the pack of Marlboros that seemed to fill the whole of their lives.

A curtain of blue and gold and silver beads divided the first from the second room, and Jazmine was torn between curiosity and trepidation at this point, as they brushed through the cascade of tiny glass orbs.

The second room was brightly lit by a bare bulb handing from the ceiling. Maybe it was the transition, but Jazmine thought it seemed like a 1000-watt bulb. The walls were a freshly painted pink, one with a window to the outside. At the center of the wall opposite the window, and of one of the remaining walls, stood elegant French hall tables, or knock-offs of elegant French hall tables, clustered with miniature ceramic animals, windmills, shepherdesses, and other such bric-a-brac. At the fourth wall was a baby grand piano, complete with middle-aged pianist. When Saul and Jazmine entered the room, the pianist rolled out a flamboyant flourish on the keys.

"Meet the Sheik," said Saul.

"Saul, baby," purred the Sheik. "You have company." He wore a velvet green smoking jacket over a white shirt with a purple kerchief knotted around the neck. When he smiled his teeth were way too white.

"Are you here for the show?" the Sheik asked Jazmine.

"No, Sheik," Saul answered. "She's going to help with the meetings."

One part of Jazmine bristled at Saul's need to answer for her, but another part, under the circumstances, took comfort in it.

"Ah, hahaha." An affected laugh rolled off the Sheik's tongue. He hit a few sparkly notes.

"You hippies," he said, shaking his head in good-natured dismissiveness. "You're so 'into' everything. Don't be so serious, Saul. It's a fad, baby. It'll pass. Relax and take in a little sensual pleasure."

"Thanks for the words of wisdom, Sheik," Saul said, without breaking his serious demeanor.

The threshold to the third and final room was a conventional door ("how quaint," Jazmine thought wittily to herself), and when they passed through it, all was busyness and bustle. This was the War Room. A city map extended across a large table at the center of the room. A young woman in straight clothes was leaning over the map writing dates and notes on sites with labels like "Army Recruitment Ctr," "University ROTC," "Administration Bldg," and the like. At a desk at some distance from the table, a pudgy guy with curly black hair and a dress shirt was going over what looked like record books of some kind. A broad-faced black man with a black beret and leather jacket stood between the pudgy fellow and the map woman. He looked squarely at Saul.

"They're burning draft cards in the park on Sunday, Saul. You sure you want the meeting on the same day?"

"Look, Clay, Jazmine and I – this is Jazmine y'all – Jazmine and I put out the flyers already. Anyway, the women's movement meets on Saturday and we *really* don't want to fuck up their gig."

"But Saul, people are going to be high, they're gonna burn out."

66

"We'll work the burning in the park and get them fired up to go straight to the meeting. What are we here for if we can't motivate people?" Clay eyed Saul and slowly – with a very deliberate slowness, Jaz thought – lit up a joint. He sucked in a full drag, languidly held it in his lungs for a few seconds, then blew out the earthy-smelling white cloud.

"My brothers are motivated, Saul. Panthers are gonna work with you guys. You work with us and we'll work with you."

"Now we're talking," Saul fired back. Little did either know that by the end of the year, Police Chief Clarence Giarrusso would send a force of 250 men, supported by a tank and helicopters, into the Desire Street projects to purge the Panthers.

"Hey, Saul," said the pudgy guy. "Listen to this: William Jerome Sherwood. Joined the SDS in Berkeley last summer, but the same name listed on our FBI feeder list."

The heavy earthy smell of the weed was making Jazmine ill. Everything about this room was smart, serious, suffocating. But especially the heavy earthy smell. With something perfumy in it. Maybe there was hash in it. She felt woozy.

Saul could see Jazmine was unwell. "Yeah, let's look into that, Martin," he said to the pudgy guy, and then he steered Jazmine through a door half-hidden behind an oversized calendar and out to a side alley. The lush vegetation of saw palmetto and elephant ears made Jazmine feel better immediately.

"I'm fine now," she told Saul. "I just don't know what happened in there."

"It's a weird space," Saul granted. "But you take the hand you're dealt and you get things done. This is the hand I was dealt."

"I know that feeling," Jaz said.

Later, back at the Duck, Jaz was stirring bits of herbs and vegetables into rice while Rag was refinishing some end tables Hoss had brought home to sell at the French market.

"Why me, Rag?" she asked over the sizzle of the rice.

"Why me what?" he said, still concentrating on his work.

"Why did you pick me for the tan acid? Not because I'm pliable. Zig is more pliable. Not because I'm a bitch you want to get rid of, that would be Pepper."

"I don't want to get rid of Pepper," said Rag honestly.

"So why?" asked Jaz.

"I didn't pick you. You volunteered. Remember?"

"Oh yeah," Jaz laughed. It was true. Jaz had practically implored that she be the guinea pig. For one thing, she'd always felt that vaguely psychic thing as a kid. But she felt a stronger pull toward this task, something personal, like she was searching for something lost, some part of her identity, that the tan acid might give her. Ziggy talked about her so-called purity of heart, but if that were true, she had become closed off from it somehow. She couldn't see it like he could. She needed something to open her back up. Maybe the tan acid.

"But you still could have gotten anybody," she pondered out loud, whimsically adding sunflowers seeds and lemon and mint to her rice pilaf.

"Not really," Rag said. "Pepper wouldn't feel safe. Zig ... well, Zig's *too* pliable. Believe me, we need Zig, but his time is not here yet. Right now I need somebody who can take the reins a little. You won't fold, you won't freak, and you'll ride the beast with direction."

"Why not yourself?"

68

Rag looked puzzled for a minute. "I don't trust myself," he said bluntly. Then he put down his stain brush. "You don't need to do this, Jaz."

"No, you misunderstand me, Rag. I'm going into this with both eyes open and both feet moving forward."

She smiled and added: "I just like to know what everybody's thinking."

Chapter 6

Friday, April 17. It had been only one week since the letter had come, but Ziggy's secret, like anything forcibly pushed into the unconscious and kept from light of day, was starting to grow tendrils and roots in his psyche. Letter to Report for Induction. Why had he not mentioned it to Jazmine or Ragman? For one thing, Jazmine was a worrier. She was smart, fun, everything else. And she had drive. She could get things done – a "warrior" too, thought Zig, and he smiled inwardly at the homonym – but he recognized another layer to her. Something to do with perfectionism maybe. If she thought something were to knock her – or him – off track, she'd worry about it. Definitely. With Ragman, he had a different reason for keeping mum. In Rag's case, Ziggy was shrewd enough to recognize his own insecurity. He knew Rag would tell him what to do. And it would be the right thing. But Ziggy felt that he had to own this one himself. It wasn't a philosophical issue about war and peace, or love or creative freedom. It was personal.

"Damn, boy, grab that branch," shouted Uncle Frank.

Zig steadied the broad oak branch that Uncle Frank was chain sawing off a streetside tree in front of his Irish Channel house. Uncle Frank completed the cut and Zig steered the branch artfully to a heavy thud on the grass, safely away from parked vehicles, the fire hydrant, and Aunt Louise's roses. Uncle Frank leaped off the ladder with athletic assurance. From the way he behaved, one would think that the Irish Channel was his own sole proprietorship. It was a working-class neighborhood, settled by the Irish in the 19th century, then the Germans, then Italians, and now an occasional African-American or Latino leading into the mix. Regardless of ethnic changes, cops, firemen and riverfront workers were always the core residents. Uncle Frank was right at home. He and Ziggy seemed a graceful team as they loaded sawed wood into the bed of an old Ford pickup.

"How you kids live like that, I'll never know," Uncle Frank said.

"We just want to find our own way, Uncle Frank." Ever since he was a kid, he and Uncle Frank always got on well.

"See that bar over there." Uncle Frank nodded toward the corner where a wood frame bar and grill sat with air conditioning window units hanging precariously from two windows and a dilapidated sign touting the masculine virtues of Falstaff Beer.

"That man was a second district cop for 35 years, then he retired and took over that bar. Never lived anywhere but the Irish Channel. His wife and kids serve up food at the bar every Sunday to anybody comes – black, white, Mexican, they don't care. See them young fellas at the picnic table?"

Zig had not noticed, but two men sipped beers at a weather-beaten picnic table on the side of the building: a suave, mustachioed fellow and a shorter guy with thin lips and a weightlifter's body.

"Them boys next generation cops. It's the thread that keeps things going. How you think this city's been here near 300 years? People pass the torch. That's life, boy. Not floating around in pipedreams like you kids. You'll see. Everybody settle down someday."

"I know, Uncle Frank. It's a nice little bar. But look at the bigger picture. We don't want this world full of wars and scrambling for money."

"Nobody wants wars, Ziggy." In casual fulfillment of the bar sign's prophecy, Uncle Frank popped open two cans of Falstaff and gave one to Ziggy. They sat on the easement by the tailgate of the truck. "But the world's full of imperfect people." He took a swig. "And long as it is, some people gonna act out. You can't always talk'm down. Sometimes only fighting can keep things right."

Ziggy had to admit that beneath the blue-collar exterior, Uncle Frank, cop and all, could see into the world quite well in his own way.

"Like these kids burning draft cards," Uncle Frank continued. Zig silently tensed up. "That ain't no way to fix things. You can't just say I'll quit fighting and defending myself, so all y'all other people can stop now too. Somebody's gonna take advantage." He drained his beer and opened another.

"I hope your crazy kid friends ain't mixed up in that. Burning draft cards is a crime, no joke."

Ziggy shuffled his feet. "I don't know, Uncle Frank. I guess some are and some aren't."

Uncle Frank eyed him for a few seconds and spoke lower, in what seemed a beer-induced confidence. "I'm telling you, Zig, get a regular job, something stable. This hippie shit can't win in the long run. Feds canvassing the districts right now to crack down on draft dodgers. They been going easy. But there's new blood down here now. Hungry blood. Next time your hippie friends make a big show of burning draft cards, these feds gonna mark every name and face. I wouldn't give them poor kids a week after that." He shook his head. "Federal crime."

"Thanks for the warning, Uncle Frank," was all Ziggy could think to say.

Uncle Frank took a particularly long draught of Falstaff.

"I'm not giving any warnings. Just stating a general fact."

Ziggy didn't know how to take this. Did this mean that Uncle Frank *was* giving warning but was layering himself with plausible deniability to avoid incrimination? Uncle Frank's next comment made it clear that plausible deniability was intended and that Uncle Frank was not very good at covering himself.

"I don't give warnings, Zig, but I like you. You kids are careless. You think you're indestructible. But you gotta be careful in this world. There's always people watching and being watched. Fifth district detectives watching right now." He stared at Zig intensely, his bushy salt and pepper eyebrows pressing in and down toward the bridge of his nose.

"Watching kids for drugs." Now Uncle Frank was chewing on the tip of an unlit cigar. He pulled the cigar out and looked at it nonchalantly. Then he looked back at Ziggy.

"Skinny kid for example." Ziggy found Uncle Frank's oscillation between nonchalance and intensity a source of enormous anxiety. Uncle Frank shifted back to nonchalance and let the "skinny kid" comment sink in. Ziggy felt the blood rushing to his neck and face. Was he a "skinny kid"? He wasn't *that* skinny. He felt a smothering

72

apprehension and a self-deprecating humor at once, as if her were playing the lead in a Kafka novel.

"Short skinny kid works at a pizza place. A body's not careful a body could be on a list. Name could come up – oh, I don't know – a week from today, say."

A *short*, skinny kid, thought Ziggy. Beachbum. Beachbum's in trouble. Could he believe what he was hearing? Was Uncle Frank telling him that Beachbum was on a drug bust list for a week from today?

Uncle Frank continued. "Hate to see good kids get into drug trouble. No telling what kids might do when they in trouble."

Ziggy braced himself up. "So Uncle Frank ..."

"Nah," Uncle Frank blurted sharply, cutting Ziggy off. "I don't give no warnings. You just stay to yourself and don't get into no trouble."

"Ok, Uncle Frank," resigned Ziggy, his metabolism downshifting but his brain still troubled.

Uncle Frank stuffed his unlit cigar into his top shirt pocket and leaped up, apparently sober as a cop should be, alert and ready to go.

"You want I should buy you a poboy for lunch, Zig."

Zig looked at his wristwatch. Quarter to two. Shit.

"No Uncle Frank, I gotta meet Jazmine in the park after her 1:00 class. I'm late already."

"Thanks for helping me crop that tree, son. And best keep to yourself and stay out of trouble."

A pleasant breeze picked up through the open windows of the streetcar between every stop, but Zig paid attention only to his own thoughts: "Fucking Beachbum. Careless little bastard." They were scheduled to work together tonight at Polo's.

As Zig walked from the streetcar line into the oaks and lagoons of the park, past indignant cackling geese and egrets standing motionless in the shallows, he saw Jazmine at a particular oak, whose splendor had earned it the nickname, "the Tree of Life," and which functioned as an informal meeting place for hippies, squares, and in-the-know tourists. Its massive arms sprawled out low and bountiful, and made it easy to climb. Jaz had climbed to a broad, shady branch about eight feet off the ground. Ragman was with her.

"Remember that girl who hitchhiked in and stayed with us for three weeks," Ragman was saying. "What was her name?"

"Nancy Green," said Jaz.

"Yeah, Nancy Green. Whatever happened to her?"

Ziggy reached up and hoisted himself through the branches to their level. "Primate behavior," he thought to himself. "Easy." But his dark thoughts were not yet cleared.

Rag pulled out a small packet with tiny purple pills. "You want a hit of purple microdot?" he asked Ziggy. "They're mild. You'll still be able to work tonight." Zig put one of the diminutive hits of acid under his tongue.

"Last I heard Nancy was working at a strip club on Bourbon Street," Jaz said.

"Too bad," said Ziggy. "She seemed nice. Maybe a little lost, but nice."

"Why too bad?" queried Jazmine.

"To each his own, but it seems a little rough, a little degrading, like out of the frying pan and into the fire."

"You sound like a square," Jaz rejoined good-naturedly. "It's her body. She's liberated to do what she wants. There's nothing dirty about it."

"So now she's just a sex object," Zig mimicked the language he'd heard on TV. But he felt it, too. "I know what

74

you're saying, Jaz, and I can't explain it, but I picture her in those clubs, and it just doesn't seem liberating to me. What do you think, Rag?"

Jazmine and Ziggy both knew that Ragman had probably saved more lost kids than the NOPD and the evangelical missions combined. He'd feed them, clothe them, and put them up around town. It was like he had his own underground railroad. Sometimes he'd send them to his contacts in San Francisco – the Diggers, Stephen Gaskin's Monday Night Class, the Skyline communes – but he wouldn't proselytize. He wouldn't box them in. Maybe that was his flaw. Maybe that's why he lost some of them. Maybe he could have saved more.

"Why am I always the arbiter?" asked Rag, with far too little humor.

"Come on, Rag, you know you're the genius of St. Roch," Jaz shot back.

"Genius or not, I don't know," was Rag's reply.

"Either you're for open sexuality or you're against it," Jaz continued. She was on a roll. "And if you're against it, then you're just like the squares, same old Establishment control of sexuality."

"You really think that's where I'm at," asked Zig.

"No, Zig, I know that's not your thing. But I'm just saying. Think about it." And with that imperative, a glumness fell on the threesome.

"There's nothing dirty about it," Jaz insisted absently, almost to herself, as the three of them pondered separately.

Then Rag broke the silence.

"I know what Pepper would say. She'd say, 'Fuck people who don't like the open expression of sexuality.'" Jaz smiled at the apparent corroboration. But then Rag went on.

"And she'd say, 'Fuck people who want to stick women on a stage in a strip club.'" Jaz found this a little confusing. But she sensed that Rag was right. Any expression that began with "Fuck people who ..." seemed likely attributable to Pepper.

"But what about you and Julia, Rag? You're an open sexuality guy."

Ragman gazed out across the lagoon. "Sexual openness means different things, I guess." And he just sat gazing.

"Pepper, explain thyself," prodded Jaz, teasing Rag for his Pepper imitation.

Rag squinted one eye. "Well," he said, and paused. "Open sexuality can be beautiful, man, can break down all the old bullshit inhibitions, it can wipe away all the bullshit values of capitalism and bring out beautiful human values." Here, he pulled out a small tobacco can and some rolling papers and began rolling a joint to facilitate the juices of the brain.

"Or it can be pornographic, erasing the beautiful whole human being from sex and making it just another commodity for sale. It can turn the whole gig back into abject capitalism. In that case, you don't feel liberated, you just feel like shit."

"I take it you don't like pornography."

Rag fired up the joint, inhaled, ruminated, then exhaled, and passed the joint to Ziggy.

"No," he said. "Not my bag."

"I hope she's doing alright," Ziggy reflected after taking his hit.

"Who?" asked Jaz, who had lost the train of thought.

"Nancy Green." And he offered the joint to Jazmine.

"No, the tan acid's heavy enough for me right now." Her barefoot leg hung from her cutoffs and rocked against

76

the alligator bark of the oak. "I'm going to back off the weed till I see where that goes."

"How was the trip yesterday?" asked Ziggy. "Easy in, easy out?"

"Yeah, easy in, easy out," she said, kicking her legs and casting her eyes groundward so only the long dark lashes showed. She seemed reticent.

"Hey, dig this," exclaimed Ragman. Jaz looked back up into his clear, wide, sand-and-sea eyes. But he wasn't looking at her. He gestured across the green to the narrow road that ran along the side of the park. A man in a suit emerged from a black Buick parked at the edge and walked toward the tree. A convertible parked behind him, followed by several more cars. A dozen well-dressed people were gathering under the opposite side of the tree. They could see the three pot-smoking hippies through the broad trunk and jumble of branches, but they didn't care. They didn't even look, really. It was as if the hippies were a natural part of the tree, like leaves or branch buds or butterflies.

Zig addressed the tan acid trip again: "Did you get any clues about whether it's your own unconscious dreams or something real from a thousand years ago?"

"Yeah, Jaz," Ragman mused. "Are we going backward in time or downward into your unconscious?"

"I don't know," Jaz said. "It seemed so real. Rebecca – that's me …" This clarification of Rebecca's identity made Jazmine feel weird, to say the least. "Rebecca has this lover, Jeremiah, but it's still secret right now. And William – that's the coffin-maker …"

"There's a coffin-maker?" enquired Ziggy in wonder.

Jazmine filled Ziggy and Ragman in on whatever details she could remember – Meister Conrad and Berold, her affliction as a child and the soothing herbs applied and the tragic end of Conrad and Berold. Meanwhile, the well-dressed assemblage beneath the tree began to take shape as a wedding. A photographer stepped back and forth, lining up shots in his mind's eye. A celebrant stood with his back to the tree. And then the bride and groom, casual, stylish, strode through the company and up to the celebrant to hear and speak their vows. A little girl with a wreath in her hair threw flowers from a rectangular box about the grounds randomly.

"Wow," murmured Ziggy. "Am I tripping or is that a wedding?"

"What wedding?" teased Jazmine.

Ziggy thought she was joking but wasn't completely sure. "Hey Rag, what's in this pot? You sure this isn't some of that super shit Biggles left in the Island?"

"Ha, ha, ha, no," laughed Rag robustly. "I got this from that Honduran waiter at Café du Monde. It must be the purple microdot."

"Oh yeah," was Ziggy's droll response. "I forgot about the microdot."

"I'm gonna have to watch what I give you, man," Rag joked.

"That's right, man," Zig tossed back. "I might freak out." He grabbed both of Rag's shoulders and pretended to throw him out of the tree. It was just play, but both men's bodies tensed as they became one in mock-struggle, each powerful in his own way: Ragman compact, smooth, solid; Ziggy lanky but with knots of muscle. Then they laughed, sat back, and became two again.

Zig sat back against his branch. "But there is a wedding, right?"

"There was a wedding," chuckled Jazmine. And it's true the wedding party had spoken, laughed, cried, kissed all

78

around, and left the scene for a reception apparently to be held somewhere else.

"So wait, Rag," Ziggy said. "You still think that whole Middle Ages scene is all imagination?"

"I didn't say it was all imagination," Rag stuttered from out of his own reverie.

"Yeah, last time, in the yard at St. Roch," Zig insisted.

"I don't know," Rag said. "I'm trying to think it through like Pepper, in some kind of feet-on-the-ground, no nonsense way. What if it's DNA?"

"What's DNA?" asked Zig. "Is it something like LSD? Something in the tan acid?"

"No, no, no," corrected Jaz. Ziggy thought at that instant what a beautiful schoolmarm she would have made 100 years ago.

"It's the big thing now in the Biology Department," Jaz resumed. "It's the biological info stored in your body. Passed from one generation to the next over and over. Tells you how to grow two arms and two legs and all that."

"Wow," was Zig's running response at this point, delivered with childlike sincerity if not with burning insight.

"It's like cellular memory," Rag added. "You dig? Memory. In the cells. So Jaz is remembering shit that was passed down in this cellular DNA for a thousand years. Even Pepper could dig that, man. It's science."

"So why aren't we all remembering shit all the time?" asked Zig.

"Not everybody's on acid all the time, man."

"Thank God," Jaz injected.

"Something about this tan acid." Rag was excited. "Or something about Jazmine."

"Yeah, add one hit of tan acid and one mental case and cook them in the oven," Jaz quipped.

79

"No Jaz, you know you got that deep intuitive thing, man. Maybe it's that. Maybe the tan acid. Maybe it takes both."

Jaz looked out over the lagoon. Some kids were feeding the ducks on the other side.

Zig picked up: "So, Rag, you really think LSD – or this tan acid – can awaken cellular memories in the DNA."

"That's how LSD works generally, right? It opens up what's been closed off."

"Yeah, man, but it doesn't peel back time. It brings you into the super present. It's like all those webs you build from the time you're born, breaking the flow of reality into chunks you can fix and name. You throw these webs over reality and then you name all the little squares in each web, and just when you got it all figured out, LSD comes along and pulls the nets away, and you're face-to-face with reality again, predigested reality, before it's been all chopped up to feed to the brain."

Ragman smiled. "I think that purple microdot is making you smarter, Zig."

"Sexy, romantic, and ready for revolution," grinned Zig.

"But, Zig, maybe time is one of those webs that we put on reality. If LSD pulls that web away, too ..." Rag squinted his eye in thought.

"But you can't go backwards," Zig insisted.

"No, you're not going backwards. The past isn't somewhere back there like some invisible string disappearing into the past. It's somewhere in here, inside the present but at a depth. It's like the rings of this tree. This tree's probably 200 years old. Two hundred rings. They're all right here, man." Rag pounded his open hand against the tree. "You can't see them because they're inside the tree but

80

they're all here right now, making the tree solid. If they weren't here right now, the tree would collapse."

Ziggy had to think about that one. If all of time were here right now but at a depth …

"So Jazmine's cells are like this tree," Rag continued. "The DNA is the rings. Maybe she's digging down into the rings. She doesn't have to magically go back in time. She just has to drill down."

As Ragman weighed the philosophical implications of his epiphany, Ziggy weighed the personal side of it.

"So," Ziggy started out slowly, "if you're right, this Rebecca would be a direct ancestor of Jazmine, part of her DNA."

"Yeah, I guess so," said Rag. He wasn't thrilled with the idea. It sounded limiting. But it was logical.

Jazmine had been quiet throughout this little crescendo of drug-induced epiphanies, thinking her own thoughts. She had told them enough, that's for sure. But she hadn't mentioned Berold's prophecy about the undelivered potion and the transcendental secret of Rebecca's body. She was too embarrassed to do so. It would be as if she were claiming some cosmic divinity for herself. Rebecca had kept the full secret from Jeremiah and now she was keeping the same secret from Ragman and Ziggy. Perhaps for her own reasons. Perhaps for the same reasons as Rebecca.

Ragman and Ziggy, meanwhile, finally lapsed into a post-epiphany silence.

"Hey! Dig this!" Ragman said. It reminded Ziggy of something. It could have been a year ago or it could have been ten minutes ago. He followed Rag's gaze back across the green where the wedding party had come and gone. Some discarded geraniums from the service lay around a forest-green steel trash barrel. A group of cars pulled off the road and parked, one by one. It was happening all over again. But this time, the cars seemed more downscale – VW bugs and beat-up Ramblers and beat-down station wagons. One young woman held what looked like a large ceramic cookie jar, blue and silver and gold. Two young men walked beside her, as if she might fall. Zig suddenly thought, at that moment, that all of life and all of human history seemed scripted. "This better fucking be real," he said. "Shhh," Jazmine shushed him and they all marveled at the new scene forming.

The young woman set the urn down in the grass. An older couple, though probably no more than late 30s, set a circle of tea candles around the urn and lit them one by one. Where first group was all white, this was a mixed race group, although Ziggy had not noticed this fact until a black boy of 10 or 12 stood up, like some archetypal figure, with a large box in one hand and a small American flag in the other. He stepped outside the circle of tea candles, threw the cover of his box on the ground, and put the small flag into the box. The box was filled with what looked like wildflowers – pink and blue and yellow – and the boy walked around the tea candles, dropping the flowers on the ground and making a larger concentric circle. Then one of the young women began to speak, but Ragman and Ziggy and Jazmine could not hear the words.

"Weird, all these life and death rituals," mused Ragman.

"I know, right here," Zig said. "Like life and death decisions being made right under our noses, under our tree."

"Not decisions, really," added Jazmine.

One of the young men in the group picked up the urn, opened it and stepped to the ring of tea candles. Then, as if on second thought, he stepped past the tea candles, past the ring of flowers, and sprinkled the ashes in still larger concentric circle.

"I swear it's all like a magic show script," Zig said.

"A very serious one," Jaz reflected.

As the funeral group gathered up their things, a dog – it must have been a yellow lab – ran into the group wagging its tail, looking to be petted. Gaining only a few mechanical pats, she ran to the Tree of Life and looked up at the hippies, still wagging her tail. Ziggy could hear her panting in expectation. It must have been the microdot, because when she ran off, Ziggy continued to hear the panting. There was nothing eerie or disturbing about the continued sound; it was just part of the landscape. Traces left behind. "Maybe that's how the past gets tangled into the present," Zig thought to himself, and the thought seemed comfortable and incoherent at the same time. Panting, breathing. Zig noticed the grass waving in the wind near the lagoon. And as the grass waved and blew in the wind, the movement rippled out from the grass to the trees and the geese and the sky. It was all waving and rippling with the wind. Trees, grass, sky, all the people in the park, the city bus rumbling down the main road in the far distance. All caught in the same wave, like so many two-dimensional, technicolor planes stacked and swaying against one another. And the serious young man walking through the blowing grass with fatigue-green pants and white button shirt half open.

"Oh, shit!" Jazmine exclaimed, breaking Ziggy's trance. "I forgot, y'all. I told my friend, Saul, to meet us here."

Saul stopped beneath the tree, perplexed. Jazmine thought it hilarious that everyone else – wedding revelers, funeral mourners, the dog – had seen the tree-bound hippies, but Saul just stood there, ground level, looking around.

"Just what we need," Jaz called down. "A blind revolutionary to lead us to the Promised Land."

Saul looked up with that peculiar smile of his, a smile that presented itself as a minor act of condescension from an otherwise serious person.

"Hi, Jazmine. Hi y'all."

He swung into the tree with breathtaking speed and dexterity.

Jazmine introduced all to all.

"I thought y'all might want to meet Saul. He's organizing something against the war."

Saul pulled out a tight, skinny reefer and rolled it between his fingers to make sure the pot was evenly distributed. "Jazmine told me about your scene, Rag." He fired up and took a hit. "It sounds cool." He passed the joint to Rag, who took a hit before he spoke.

"Just trying to spread the love, man."

"I'm hip, man. That's cool. I wish it were only about the love. But it's about the fight, too." He pulled a sheet of paper folded in quarters from his back pocket and handed it to Rag. Rag took it and offered the joint to Ziggy.

"Naw, man, I'm too far gone already." Zig's comment elicited confederate smiles from Saul and Ragman. But Jazmine was in her own world, and so was Ziggy. Zig leaped from the tree. The yellow lab had wandered back to the high grass by the lagoon and Zig went and sat next to it. The other three followed Ziggy down from the tree instinctively and sat at a distance from him and the dog with their backs against the broad trunk. Rag unfolded the paper. It was the "S A W: Students Against the War" flyer Saul had posted at the Student Union.

"Cool, man. I'm glad you guys are out there fighting the fight."

"Don't just be glad, man. Come join us."

Jaz was surprised to see Rag put off a little by Saul's tone. Normally, nothing put Rag off.

84

"No Justice, No Peace," Rag recited from the flyer. "That's pretty heavy."

"That's what I thought," added Jazmine. "It doesn't fit the anti-war theme, does it?"

"Y'all got something better?" asked Saul, although it wasn't clear if the question were genuine or rhetorical.

"How about 'All You Need Is Love'?" offered Rag. And as he said it, Jaz noticed that he had acclimated to Saul's tone, and she could not tell if his suggestion were sincere or sardonic. In any event, Saul was slightly flustered by it.

"I dig the whole Beatles thing, man. And I dig what you're doing, Ragman. But the gentle scene won't make it, man. Love is NOT all you need. That's what's wrong with Beatle politics."

"I hear you," was all Rag said.

But now Saul was channeling Abby Hoffman and the Chicago Seven, and he couldn't stop. "You need JUSTICE. Fight fire with fire."

"But once you choose to fight violence with violence, how do you unchoose it?" Jazmine was surprised to hear – or was she imagining it? – an uncharacteristically pleading edge to Ragman's voice.

"We're not choosing it," Saul shot back. "They're choosing it." Now it was Saul's turn to plead. "Look, Rag, I want peace and love just like you do. I don't want violence. But the enemy sets the terms. If they use violence, we have to fight them on their terms or we cave in."

"Were you at Woodstock?" Rag asked inexplicably.

"No," Saul replied tentatively.

"Well this guy at the mic there –Shurtleff I think was his name – he said that this revolution is different from all other revolutions in that we have no enemies. I keep trying to wrap my head around that, but it's taking me a long time.

85

When you talk about the enemy, I have to try to put all this together, man, but I just can't do it."

"Oh, don't worry, there's an enemy," Saul assured Ragman. "And the one thing he wants more than anything else is for you to not see him as the enemy."

"I dig what you're saying," Rag admitted. "But I can't figure in the violence when I look down the road. Once you've accepted it as cool in some scenarios, then it's always an option waiting to be dug out again. Then the peaceful way can never be an absolute."

"But look at World War II. They tried talking to Hitler but he just kept taking more shit till they hit back."

"Yeah, but," Rag started. Now he was enjoying the point-counterpoint. "Look at Gandhi. He liberated more people in India than all the people in Western Europe combined. And he did it with non-violence against an armed occupier, with beautiful principles intact. And Martin Luther King. That's where he got all his power. From the beauty of the non-violent way. You think he could have *beaten* the Birmingham cops into submission?"

"I know this," Saul said. "Where did Gandhi and MLK end up? How did they both die? Both shot dead. They were cool, no doubt, but they underestimated the violence of the oppressor."

Perhaps the two had reached an impasse or perhaps the dialectic would have spun on ad infinitum, but Jaz put an abrupt stop to it with a simple question.

"Where's Zig?"

The three looked toward the lagoon. Geese, yes. Kids in strollers, small birds pecking for bugs in the grass, yes. But no yellow lab and no Zig.

"I hope he's OK," Jaz mulled.

"Of course, he's OK," reassured Rag. "He's just digging the scene." But there was uncertainty in his voice.

86

"Let's go find him," said Saul. "Might as well be sure. Let's spread out a little. I'll take the lagoon and keep an eye out on both sides." Rag instinctively went across the green to walk along the narrow road, and Jazmine took the middle. As they walked south, away from the streetcar line and toward the river, Jaz heard the neighing of a horse and then the heavy thud of hooves. For a second she thought Rebecca's thoughts, as the thudding seemed to come up behind her. She turned. Indeed, there was a man on a beautiful chestnut mare. The mare had huge soft brown eyes but seemed confused and the man comforted her. Then Jazmine remembered. Yes, there were stables in the park, for horseback riding and for the animals that populated the petting zoo. But horseback riding was not allowed in this area. Something was wrong.

She looked over to Rag but he merely continued his pace along the side of the road. Saul had stopped and was talking to someone. It was Martin, the pudgy guy from Saul's war room. She could only catch a few muffled words here and there, but it did not sound like the sort of conversation you'd find among the kids at St. Roch. "Firebombed," she heard, and "recruitment" and "SDS" and "burn it to the fucking ground." The man had turned the horse and gone his way, and Jazmine mechanically drifted toward Saul.

"Always on Sunday," Martin was saying. "Nobody's there on Sunday." Saul's back was to Jazmine and his reply was inaudible, but she heard Martin's next words: "Not this Sunday, but next Sunday, that's April 26, Ken Kesey and the Pranksters will be in the park. I guarantee they'll suck up all the oxygen. Everyplace else will be deserted." Whether Martin saw her coming or not, he abruptly parted before she reached Saul.

"Hey, here's your prodigal hippie," called Ragman. Rag and Zig walked nonchalantly toward Saul and Jaz and the lagoon.

"Where the fuck were you?" was Jazmine's lead-in.

"Just grooving on the park, Jaz. It was weird. The dog looked at me with so much love, like the Buddha or something, and it was like he wanted me to follow him. And we took this curve behind the stables and I met this goat girl from Cuzco."

"Far out," said Rag, but Jaz was skeptical. "You sure you're not just tripping?"

"No, man, it blew my mind. Y'all want to hear the whole story?"

Rag and Jazmine were all ears, but it was Saul's turn to be distracted, as perhaps he was thinking about his conversation with Martin.

"So the dog charged right around the curve where the road goes behind the stables, and there were these goats – like three of four goats – and then there was a Shetland pony. They were just standing around in the grass but one of the goats starting walking into the road. The dog charged off on some other mission, like he was tired of me. But I had to nudge the goat back off the road. And then the goat girl was there, with a staff thing like out of a fairy tale. But not your blonde-haired princess fairy tale. She was plain and pure native Indian – reddish brown face and long, straight, burnt-brown hair.

"'They got out of the stables' she said. 'Can you help me get them back in? The stable master's looking for Big Boy – that's the horse – but it will be better for me if I have these little ones in the stable when he finds Big Boy and brings him back.'"

At the mention of Big Boy, Jazmine thought of the horse she had seen. For a moment, her life blurred with Rebecca's. Goats and chickens on the dirt road.

"The goats for Walpurgisnacht," she said in a whisper.

Zig stopped and looked at her. "What?"

But Jaz had collected herself. "The goats. I was wondering about the goats? What were they like?"

"I don't know. A baby white one kept bouncing up and down like a jumping bean. But they were all stupid friendly. Even the big brown one with devil horns."

"'Where you from?' I said as we corralled the goats.

"'Cuzco,' she said. And she told me about the Andes Mountains and the ancient Incan city of Cuzco. She actually lived on a farm near there, but merchants would come to her mother for cloaks and scarves of alpaca wool. Her favorite thing was to wander the Urubamba Valley and sing ancient Incan songs that came into her head. She didn't realize that it was weird for songs to just come into your head, but she had a beautiful voice. A voice that got her into trouble."

Rag and Jaz and even Saul were now glued to the story.

"Her mother had fallen on hard times and there wasn't enough to eat. Nothing but edible roots and tubers. So this merchant who had always been kind offered her mother 100 soles to take the girl into his own family, to put her in school with the merchant class. She cried and hung on her mother, but she knew it was no use. She would go on with her life and the money would see her mother through.

"At first all went well. She would run up and down the narrow maze of streets in Cuzco, singing as she had sung in the valley. But then the merchant's wife died and the merchant changed. He would look at the girl and then turn away and chew on his own inner cheek as if he were fighting with himself, loathing himself. He was becoming mean. She didn't know what to do, or if she were making him miserable. The next time she saw him behave this way, she would sing her heart out, sing to him, and he would feel better.

"Not many days went by until the merchant called her to him, looked at her with meanness but with watery eyes. 'Dear God,' he said and turned away. And she began to sing. With all her heart she sang, sang to save the merchant. But his self-loathing was too strong.

"'Curse you for that song,' he shouted. 'Curse you for that damned singing that tortures me like this.' She froze up, horrified. She felt guilty of the blackest ingratitude. Never would she sing again. Never. She was soon sold again to a man who brought her to the United States. He was neither kind nor mean, and she had no idea why he had bought her, but she escaped the very first night while he slept. And she managed in time to find her way here and to find work at the stables."

"That would blow anybody's mind," marveled Ragman.

"She told you all that?" asked Saul. Jazmine could tell that Ziggy didn't like his tone. In fact, Ziggy just looked at him.

"Did she ever sing again," asked Jaz.

"I asked her that," Zig said. "She said she'd never sung again. I told her the ingratitude thing was all wrong. She was guilty of nothing. But she already knew that. She said all she could figure was sometimes you get a little knot twisted up in your brain and you can't untwist it. Maybe she would sing again when she was ready. And at the end, I asked her if she was ready. Dumb question, I know. If she was ready, she wouldn't have put me on like that. But looking back, I'm surprised that she paused before she

90

answered. She had scooted the last of the goats into the corral with the Shetland pony, and the gate was still open. She froze up for a second, maybe just like she froze up when the merchant cursed her. Then she unfroze. 'Not yet,' she said, and she walked in and snapped the gate behind her."

This led to a moment of reflection, which gradually became an awkward silence. Jazmine was perhaps most awkward in the silence, as she was thinking how everything was starting to echo of Rebecca. This whole Cuzco girl trip. Fuck this, she thought.

"So Saul," she said, "What was that about the SDS? Who's the SDS anyway?"

"You don't know the SDS?"

"No," Jazmine said innocently. Saul seemed stumped for a second, and then he spoke.

"Students for a Democratic Society. They're national. They're talking about burning down ROTC buildings and recruitment centers. California, Ohio, different places." He paused and looked furtively at Ragman: "That's how you secure your 'All You Need is Love' scene."

It all sounded so far away and impersonal to Jaz. "You gonna burn down an ROTC building?" she laughed.

Saul looked at Ragman, then at Ziggy. "What if I did? Y'all in it with me?"

Rag scratched the ground with a stick. Saul became more animated.

"Man, the university's handing those cats student data about 2S deferments. The whole draft card scene's about to get a lot worse."

Rag kept scratching, concentrating on his own hieroglyphic.

Zig came in self-consciously. "Isn't it enough to burn the draft cards? I mean, buildings, too?" He seemed almost snide and received no answer.

91

"I'm still with Gandhi," Rag finally said. "It's like the goat girl thing from Cuzco. Once you give up your own thing, you give up your vision, or let somebody take it away, you twist a knot in your brain, you can't get it back."

"You're right about one thing," responded Saul. "She LET somebody take it away. She didn't fight fire with fire. Maybe she couldn't. I'm not blaming her. But WE can fight fire with fire. And when we shut those bastards down, then we can sing. Otherwise, they'll be singing over our body bags."

"So that frantic guy in your flyer, sawing at the other guy in the box ..."

"Nixon," Saul corrected.

"Sawing at Nixon in the box," Rag continued. "He's going to fix this?"

"That's right. I know deep down you're with me, Ragman. Just come out of the clouds and put your feet on the ground and think about it. Either you saw that son of a bitch in half or he will take control."

The more worked up Saul became, the more distant seemed Ragman.

"The man in the box," Ragman said absently.

Jazmine felt a vague shudder at the image. Then Ragman went on.

"The man in the box. He always walks away unharmed at the end of the magic show. It's like what Ziggy said about the script. Your guy with the saw doesn't see he's just part of the script."

"Clever," Saul conceded, the smallest of grins curling one corner of his lips. "But I'm guessing Ziggy doesn't want to be the part of the script that dies in Nam because we didn't take it to the Man with real force. What do you think, Zig?"

92

Saul could not have known how close to home his scenario had hit for Ziggy. Zig replied curtly: "I think the Cuzco girl didn't mean all the shit y'all are reading into it."

Jazmine interpreted this exchange as confirmation of Ziggy's antipathy for Saul. She felt a deep urge to support Zig, to rescue him, to envelop him with a comforting balm.

"Zig's right," she said in a matter-of-fact tone. "She's not trying to save the world. She just wants to figure out how to sing again." She looked at Zig's face. For once, she had put him at ease instead of the other way around.

"So maybe that's it," said Zig, in a rare moment of lit crit clarity. "It's not about saving the world. Maybe if each of us learns to sing again, the world will save itself."

Jaz brightened up. "I think Rag's right, Zig. That purple microdot is making you smarter."

Chapter 7

Saturday morning. Jazmine shivered this time as she looked at the Madonna and child, the liquid blue and glittering gold. The burgundy curtains were not curtains but waves, cosmic billowing waves. Of course they led nowhere. Where would there be to get to? All the other curtains in the world – those that seemed to lead to windows or doors – it was all a charade, a game, a magic trick. A million ways of hiding that there is no place to get to. Nothing but cosmic billowing waves. She closed her eyes. Her hips ached. And the joints in her fingers. An arthritic ache. Bagpipes and bone flutes, tumblers in procession past the front arches of the church – a small, rectangular church, but attractive, with long vertical windows and carved figures of saints and goblins, the latter clandestinely modeled on local figures resented by this or that craftsman. The church faced east over a dirt-and-grass town square disputed by goats and chickens. The remaining perimeter of the square consisted of smithies and workshops, timber-framed houses of the more prosperous merchants and tradesmen, and taverns, linen and wool shops, each with a colorful sign indicating its trade. A few towers and spires could be seen rising from the background jumble of the town.

The circus people, truth be told, were making as much noise as possible to attract an audience, and annoyed geese scattered at the pipes and timbrels, flapping themselves in half-flight to the patchwork warren of rutted alleys and streets spreading out on either side of the church. Jazmine was tempted to smirk at these itinerant performers. "Damned be all these gypsy tramps," she was thinking. She felt an arthritic pain shoot through her left hip. "So this is what it feels like to be an old woman," she thought, as she faded into the avatar of a hobbling crone. She eased her aching bulk onto a small, rough-hewed stone wall. "Damn their money-grubbing ways." A few townspeople gathered about the square as the gypsies circled: artisans in bright tunics and hose, monks in plain brown robes, housewives with gowns and shawls and white caps tied in the back. The traveling circus had caught wind of the Lord Bishop's visit and smelled a chance to get what copper coins and bartered goods they could from visiting curiosity-seekers and from proud locals, whose native severity was known to yield to a more festive and generous spirit on such occasions. Whether they deserved the old woman's damnation for thus seeking a ration of daily bread we will leave for the philosophers to decide.

"Ach! Christ's blood!" said the crone, and she cackled out in laughter. "We's all the same, aye. Gypsies,

94

Christian, heathens. We draw people in to visit our pretty church so we can take their money in our shops; the gypsy ragamuffins come to take our geld."

As she rubbed her crusty feet, one at a time, a box turtle wandered through a breach in the stone from the dry grass behind. It plodded along but stopped to look at her skeptically. She kicked it with surprising force for an arthritic, and it landed upside down on its shell, spinning for a moment like a coin. "And damn all the devil's vermin too."

This wholesome exercise with the turtle seemed to give her strength. She stood, pulled a twig of oregano, pinched and put it into her pocket, and began hauling herself, hip by hip, past the timber-framed houses thatched with straw and heather. "Aye, hell is for saints and sinner alike. All be damned is justice served. Aye, but what's this?"

She stopped suddenly and looked diagonally across the square. Jeremiah – Rebecca's Jeremiah, William's apprentice – loitered by the irregular limestone blocks of the church's wall, near the rounded arch of a heavy wooden side door. The crone peered closely and kept up her muttering.

"Aye, I know thy craft. But my boy, my only son, William, is too good for thee. Thou'st so smart with that Rebecca, so cheery, but I know the game. You two's can be quiet and sneak and talk. Aye, but others can sneak too. And listen. I can hear the demons, Jeremiah and Rebecca. I heard thy devil words, thy will to get rid of William – she the orphan wench that William took in when her curséd father was beat to death. Aye, beat to death fairly for a witch. Aye, I know the whole tale. 'A secret bigger than gold,' says the devil Berold. 'Something divine has chosen you.' And now the wench to plot with Herr Brighteyes against my William."

She crinkled up her voice in mockery. "'We'll be free of him tomorrow,' says he. 'But what of the Mohametman boy,' says she. 'Tomorrow,' says he again.

95

Aye, but there's some got more wits than thee. By's blood, my boy shan't be put upon by the likes'a thee! Nor she neither! But wait!"

A brown-skinned boy, barely a teenager, had joined Jeremiah at the side of the church. Draped over his small frame was an absurdly rich gown of black and purple, finely trimmed in gold with geometric patterns and clasped at the waist by a thin, decorative leather belt. The costume was completed by a simple winding cloth for a headdress and sandals filled with smooth, beautiful brown feet. That he was engaged in some secret discourse with Jeremiah was beyond question.

"So that's the Mohametman to do the trick. A lamb, he appears. Aye, but my William shall not be anyone's lamb."

The old woman hitched in closer. She pulled the oregano from her pocket, along with seven scalded black beans she had placed there earlier, and rubbed them vigorously together between her hands to make herself invisible, as local lore would have it. She crept still closer. Jeremiah looked flustered. "In a few hours," she heard the Mohametman boy say. "After the Lord Bishop's audience with the Burgermeister." She was all ears, but her bean-scalding technique must have fallen short, because she was startled by a princely horseman on her heels who apparently found her quite visible.

"Hold thy course, woman," commanded the horseman. It was Darian, the son of the Lord Bishop, in his own noble dress on a chestnut mare. His wavy, shoulder-length blonde locks and pointy nose and chin framed a haughtiness of visage than none could miss. As soon as he arrived, Jeremiah and the Mohametman boy went their ways.

"What is thy name, woman?"

"Gammer."

"Don't fool with me. Thy proper name."

"Guda is my given name m'lord, but all call me Gammer these twenty years past 'a child-rearing. The other old ladies is Gammer Elsa and Gammer Kate and such, but Gammer Guda is too much for the tongue, your honor. My old man used to say, 'Christ's blood, Guda, if ever in thy …'"

Darian cut her off. "Dare you taunt the Lord Bishop's son with such a blasphemous oath! I should whip thee here and now for thy insolence." He cracked his whip to emphasize the point.

"Oh, Jesus, m'lord, I mean no insolence. The Lord Bishop is a gentleman, to be sure. As fine a gentleman as that rascal before him, in faith …"

"Hold thy tongue! That man hard by at the church wall just now. Thou wert watching him. Is he of thy household?"

"No kin of mine, m'lord. I wouldn't claim such a bright-eyed demon for all …"

"What business has he with my father's boy?"

"None, m'lord."

"How call you him a bright-eyed demon? What knowst thou of him?"

Guda could see that she had revealed too much already. But there was nothing to do but go on.

"Know him!! God's wounds, m'lord, how should I know him? One can tell by his looks he's a clever one, m'lord. Lord Jesus bless me if I know such a creature. My old man …" At this second reference to her long late husband – for husband he was in all things but the law – she made the sign of the cross to impress her inquisitor. "My old man used to say when Old Nick gets in a body …"

"God damn thy old man! May he rot in hell!" exclaimed Darian, perturbed by the crone's loquacity and perhaps exercising with his own oath a right reserved for his rank.

The chestnut mare gave a quick, sudden snort, startling Guda a second time. She staggered but continued.

"Oh, Jesus, m'lord, she's a pretty one, she ..."

Darian wheeled away, unable to withstand the chatter, and in his wake, Guda saw that where the Mohametman boy had parted, Jeremiah had made it just a few steps before Rebecca had joined him. She heard Jeremiah's sonorous voice, and a chill ran up her spine.

"Be strong this one last night, Rebecca, then you and I shall have our day with none to block us evermore."

Jazmine shivered again and opened her eyes. She was back in the shrine at St. Roch.

"How was it?" asked Zig.

"Weird," she said.

Jazmine seemed more reticent after each trip. Ziggy didn't like it. But he'd let it rest until later.

"Sweetie, you up for the Big Lake Fest in the park? All the bands are free and pot will be burning."

Jazmine closed her eyes and didn't answer Pepper's solicitation.

"I'll get you some tea," Pepper said more quietly and went to the kitchen.

Ragman had gone to the Magic Mushroom to get some Arabian dates, which Claire had ordered in bulk for intestinal cleansing as well as for the delicious taste, so Ziggy and Jazmine were left alone in the room. Ziggy thought she was sleeping but she spoke.

"What happened with Beachbum last night?"

Ziggy wondered if she were deflecting attention from the tan acid trip.

"There was no Beachbum."

She opened her eyes and looked at Zig.

"What do you mean?"

"He quit. Walked out before I ever got there."

"Fuck!" was all Jaz said.

Zig rubbed her arm. "I'll find him. I'll let him know what's happening."

Pepper returned with the tea and Jazmine sat up. She was ready to come back to this world. For a time, at least.

* * *

A skinny blonde girl wearing a red headband and little else spun a whirling dervish across the grass holding a blank flag of purple fabric in her outstretched arms. Spinning and spinning through the loose crowd, knotted here and there into groups of three or four hippies of mixed race and gender, until she careened into a group of four – namely, Ragman, Pepper, Ziggy, and Jazmine – and collapsed into the arms of the unsuspecting, bare-chested Ragman. She and he crashed in slow motion into a sitting position and began to talk quietly as if nothing had happened. Pepper sat with them, leaving Ziggy and Jazmine, although only a few feet away, in their own space.

"Whatever she's high on, I hope there's more of it," Ziggy grinned.

"No you don't," said Jazmine seriously. "She's losing it."

Zig looked back at the seated group of three.

"They just look like they're talking."

But he saw the concern on Jazmine's face.

"You OK, Jaz?"

"I don't know. I'm just tuned into things lately. Sensitive. I can tell she's full of joy but freaking out at the same time. Like euphoria and psychosis are two parallel lines that just crossed in her mind."

99

"Heavy," said Zig.

And then she was crying. The girl in the headband. Her friends came to collect her and Ragman passed her gently over.

"You think the tan acid's getting to you?" Zig queried.

"I'm not always Rebecca," Jazmine said abruptly.

"What?" asked a startled Zig. Pepper and Rag joined them.

"Is something wrong?" asked Pepper. "Y'all look like you just seen a ghost – oh wait!" she quipped. But then she could see Jazmine wasn't in a festive mood.

"I'm sorry, sweetie. I didn't mean to make fun." Jaz smiled at Pepper and touched her flowing red hair. "Like a Druid princess," Jazmine thought to herself. "It's OK, Pepper," she said out loud. And all four sat in a circle.

"She's not always Rebecca," Ziggy repeated, still grappling with the meaning of the words.

A concert dignitary had taken the stage and was making announcements, but the grassy field was large, the stage perhaps 100 yards away, and the sound production team still learning on the job. Thus, our heroes could continue their conversation untroubled by whatever idealistic declarations or promises of spectacle were being broadcast. All eyes were on Jazmine.

"It's true. I felt like I was an old woman this time. I saw everything – the same village – the same characters, but from her eyes. Gammer – or Guda is her proper name – she's the mom of William the coffin-maker and I think she means trouble for Rebecca and Jeremiah. She's definitely not happy. Bitter, really. Why would she pick me? Or why would I pick her?"

Jaz seemed to be lost in the troubled waters of which she spoke. Pepper stood behind her and massaged upward

100

from her shoulders to her neck, finally sinking her fingers into Jazmine's lush black tresses and massaging her scalp.

Slowly, Jazmine smiled again. "I'm gonna fall in love with you one day Pepper, you keep this shit up."

"Anytime, sweetie."

"Well, Jaz," Rag said. "I guess that takes down the DNA theory. I don't see how you can trace DNA memories back to two unrelated people at the same time."

"If there *are* DNA memories," Jaz teased, moving into a wry distance from her own predicament as a case study.

"And there goes my reincarnation theory," said Zig.

"Oh, was that *your* theory?" Jazmine continued to tease.

Zig went on, mindless of her tone.

"Same thing. How can you reincarnate into two different people at the same time?"

He shook his head, "Then again, who knows how all this shit works?"

"No, Zig, maybe you're onto something," said Ragman. "Y'all ever hear of the akashic record?" Jaz and Zig had not, and Pepper, despite her encyclopedic appetite for cultural and current affairs, could only respond with a question: "What the fuck is that?"

"Don't you ever read shit, Pepper?" Rag teased. Pepper smirked and nodded, more eager to hear than to banter.

"Well, dig. I don't even know if this shit's written anywhere. I heard it from Tim Leary's friend, Richard Alpert."

"You and Timothy Leary have mutual friends!" Pepper scoffed.

Rag brushed off the jab and went on. "In Eastern religions or ancient Sanskrit, I don't really know the source, this akashic record is the record of everything normally considered past, present, and future. Our linear sense of time is just clumsy bullshit, anyway, right Zig?"

"Why you asking me?"

"The Tree of Life, man. Remember the Tree of Life. You said something about LSD bringing you into the super present."

"I was higher than a fucking zeppelin, too."

"No, dig. The akashic record is sort of like the super present. Every thought, every movement of every leaf, is contained in this vast catalog, as it were. But the akashic record is more than a catalog. It's the ultimate reality. All our daily actions are reflections of this akashic record. We are right now living the akashic record, experiencing it from one orientation point. What we're seeing is just the shadows being cast."

"So why didn't you say this at the Tree of Life?"

"Pacing my train of thought, man. Like the Lincoln story, I'm still sharpening the axe."

"I never liked that axe analogy, Rag," continued Ziggy. "It makes you sound like Saul." Rag gazed thoughtfully out at the growing crowd of bell-bottomed waifs in the background. Ziggy went on: "But what about the tan acid? What about Jazmine?"

"What it means," continued Ragman, becoming excited. "It means maybe you were just thinking about reincarnation the wrong way. Reincarnation's not linear, man, not one life, then the next, then the next. If you can use prayer, fasting, meditation, yoga – or even tan acid – and go all the way down to the akashic record, then you're at the bottom, man, the deepest level of our existence. You're viewing reality not from the orientation point of your individual consciousness but from the orientation point of the akashic record. Then you see that you're living all lives past, present, and future simultaneously."

Zig and Jaz shared Rag's excitement at the thought. Pepper limited herself to a skeptical "pff."

But Zig caught himself. "So what about Jazmine?" he insisted.

"See, with the tan acid, Jazmine's dipping down into the roots of consciousness in the akashic record, and bringing fragments of these other lives back up to the conscious level. At least that could explain tapping into two separate lives from the same time."

"Damn, Rag, that's elegant," said Jazmine, admiring the theory at a distance, not quite remembering how it applied to her personally.

"Hmm," pondered Ziggy. "But why *these* lives?"

"Ay, there's the rub," said Ragman cryptically.

Pepper, who had been sitting there folding and unfolding the flower of her skepticism, spoke out.

"Is that your only problem? Why *these* lives?" she asked rhetorically before answering her own question.

"I'll tell you this. It's not all that crazy shit y'all made up. It's got to be inside Jazmine. That's the only way she could be both Rebecca and the old lady. It's Jazmine's own shit after all. Rebecca's the part of Jaz that lost her dad and is looking for stable love. The old lady's the skeptical part, the part that's watching her ass, the part that doesn't want to get burned again. I mean, think about it. Rebecca loved her dad, he died, and this old guy creeped her out. Jazmine loved her dad, he died and her mom married an asshole. Jaz is working her shit out in a dream – sorry, sweetie," she said to Jaz, thinking she'd vaguely been disrespectful.

Now Rag shifted back toward teasing Pepper. "Pepper," he poked. "Last week you said Freud was all bullshit; now you're Freud's coy mistress." He gave a hearty laugh.

"At least it's more scientific than your akashic record bullshit," Pepper said.

Jaz offered her opinion in a quiet monotone, not quite part of the present conversation. "It shows you what people are really like – not scientific, not spiritual, just practical. 'Oriented,' as Rag says, but oriented only to the problem at hand. Instinctive, reactive, survival of the fittest. People – and that includes all three of y'all – will flip-flop through every contradiction, rewrite every theory to suit the shit in front of them. Every one of us, a walking contradiction. One thing today, another thing tomorrow. Whatever's in front of us."

"Is there a little bitterness, there, Jaz?" asked Rag, not entirely playing.

Jaz smiled, but it seemed rather a dark than a festive smile. "Must be Guda. I'm becoming a hybrid you know."

"Becoming a bitch like me," jibed Pepper. "Welcome home."

"Angel in the flesh, that's your hybrid," said Zig, trying to rib Jaz back down.

"Look, sweetie," Pepper said to Jaz, "I know you're drawn to this whole tan acid thing. It's interesting, it's eye-opening, and it's a little creepy, too." Here she looked at Rag with a trace of that Pepper fire in her eye. "But it doesn't take magic to see her owning her own shit in a dream."

Rag fired back with measured focus: "OK, Pepper, you study journalism, how do you get a printable story past the editors here?"

Pepper looked at Jaz. "Think about the details, Jaz. Rebecca's house, the town. Is there anything there about Medieval Germany that you could not have known from movies or books or your own imagination?" Jaz thought but

104

said nothing. Pepper nudged gently: "Anything we can corroborate to prove these people are historically real?"

"Not really," Jaz said.

Pepper leaned back and resumed character. "So fuck you, Rag. No magic here."

"Maybe not," Rag said, chewing the inside of his cheek.

"But look," Zig said. "Who cares if it's magic? Y'all are missing the point." Rag lifted an eyebrow and Pepper scoured Zig's face as if to read it. He went on: "This is not about philosophy. This is about Jazmine. What's it like for her? Is it making her feel better or worse?" Jazmine wasn't really sure if this were a question, and if so, whether it was addressed to her or Ragman, but she felt best keeping mum.

Zig continued: "Is it raising consciousness for her? Is it making her happier? I mean, Rag, that's the whole point, right?"

"Yeah," Rag said. "You're right, Zig. That's the point." But his enthusiasm was drained and he was thinking hard.

Zig wasn't quite finished, though. "And, yeah, 'easy in and easy out' is great, but it seems like it's not just an acid vision of what a new world can be like without the Establishment. It seems like this whole past life thing is taking over."

At that point, another reveler came barreling into the circle, pretending to crush Ragman and mashing a cowboy hat onto Pepper's head.

"Brothers and sisters," announced Tex Whittaker. "Making the scene." He had been drinking and had a plastic milk jug half full of the red beverage that had given him his present joyful swagger. "I bring peace, poppies, and pink lemonade for the army of love."

105

He offered the jug, but only Ziggy took a swig. Tex looked at him in expectance of high praise.

"It tastes like the shit they give poison victims to make them throw up," said Zig.

Tex looked puzzled. "It's sloe gin fizz," he said, as if the words themselves were ample explanation to correct Zig's faulty assessment.

"Sit your cowboy ass down before you fall," said Pepper.

"Watch these guys," Tex said, gesturing at the stage. "I saw them in Lewisville, Texas, a few weeks after Woodstock."

"Why the fuck were you in Lewisville, Texas?" interrogated Pepper.

"The festival there was no bullshit. Led Zeppelin, Janis, Grand Funk, Santana. These guys got lucky to be on the scene. How you think they got Uncle John Turner to sit in on drums today? They probably met him with Johnny Winter in Lewisville. Let's move in closer."

Drunk or not, Tex could be trusted when it came to music. They stood and ambled toward the stage. Engrossed in their little circle, they had not fully registered the festive environment around them. Frisbees of varying colors floated across the field in multiple directions. These little slow-motion UFOs, barely heard of a few years ago, marvelously suited the psychedelic age of which we were in the midst. A few hula-hoopers and jugglers worked on their skills, but the Frisbees randomly flying between strangers seemed the symbolic paste, the atomic chords that held a generation of people together in internal exile from the Establishment. People spun and danced with arms outstretched, huddled in groups smoking pot, or just walked around greeting each other as fraternal partners in crime against the Man. The St. Roch group had just shared a toke with two clean-cut kids on baseball scholarships at North Carolina, down from Chapel Hill for couple of days of weed and whiskey in the French Quarter, when a female mime, naked and painted all white with black outlines, caught their attention and held a flat, white palm toward them, directing them to stop. As if trapped in an invisible box, she moved her flat palms step-by-step, up and down, then repeated the movement to her left, rear and right, completing the box. She looked at our group pleading, gesturing for Jaz to come up, and signaling her to pick up an invisible key and unlock the box, at which point she leaped out and with true cat-like agility, climbed up to Ziggy's shoulders and led him on a charge to the front of the stage. Then she kissed his check and walked away.

"I guess I was the tallest in our group," Ziggy said.

"That doesn't even make sense," said Pepper.

"You're just saying that 'cause you're the shortest," Jaz chuckled.

"None of this makes any sense," said Tex.

"That's life untethered to the Establishment," opined Rag. "No rules, no sense, a celebration of the non sequitur."

"So wait," said Jaz. "Why is the Big Lake Festival at the park and not at the lake anyway?"

Tex was on this one. "You see that mime that was just fucking with you?"

"She wasn't fucking with me."

"Ok, well, see that mime. Now look at those cats." Tex nodded.

Jaz and the others followed Tex's gesture to a group, some with painted faces, but in particular two young women completely painted wearing only panties and swaying trance-like.

"The festival producers aren't stupid. Why give the cops an excuse to shut down our nude beach? They're not

107

going to shut down the park. Uptown society people still do shit at the park."

"Funny," Jaz said, "how we're saved by integrating with the Establishment minions."

"And one day we'll return the favor," Rag said.

"What's that mean?" asked Zig. "You speaking in riddles like the great oracle?" He pushed Rag's shoulder in mock attack.

"Our vision, man," Rag said. "Those uptown people will come around one day. They'll acclimate. When the Age of Aquarius comes, we'll return the favor and welcome them in."

"Fuck'm," said Tex. "I say wipe'm out."

"You sound like Saul," said Zig. "Let's just wipe everybody out."

"We can't wipe them out, Roy Rogers," chimed in Pepper. "We need them."

"For what?" asked Tex.

"Remember the Altamont Free Concert in California," said Pepper. "We said we'd provide our own security, right? The Hell's Angels. No cops. And they beat that guy to death while the Rolling Stones played 'Sympathy for the Devil.'"

"Not that simple," mumbled Tex.

"Why not?"

"Guy had a fucking gun," barked Tex. Apparently his mumbling was not an admission of defeat but a trick of the sloe gin fizz.

"Guy was climbing up the stage with a fucking gun. What do you want them to do? If it had been the cops on top of that guy, the crowd would have descended on them in a riot. It would have been bloody chaos."

Pepper replied with sarcasm: "Ok, ok, peace, love, and flowers for the army of love. And Thank God for the Hell's Angels."

"I wouldn't be too sure about the Hell's Angels," came a voice from behind.

"Saul, hey man, you spying on us?" said Jaz coyly.

"Just checking out the scene."

"From what I heard, I thought you'd be all for the Hell's Angels," Pepper said. "Militant resistance, all that."

"Controlled, baby," said Saul. "The Hell's Angels is chaos. I got the same goal in mind as you guys. I don't want some endless fighting scene. I'm for peace and love like Ragman there's for peace and love. I just think, in the short term, we might need some controlled, limited force-against-force to get us through this period where the other guys have all the weapons."

No one was quick to respond, so Rag spoke up.

"Makes sense," he said. And then the band started with a Hendrix-like version of Bob Dylan's "All Along the Watchtower."

Chapter 8

It could have been a Greek temple in a far-flung Mediterranean outpost, an open-air structure of heavy masonry supported by a colonnade of Ionic columns and featuring a scene of fauns and naiads on the pediment under the roof. Two stone lions guarded the front steps. But a temple to whom? Sunday, April 19, 1970, had arrived, and the gathering crowd showed more barbarian energy than classical restraint, not a host of Apollonian symmetry but an asymmetry of bright clashing colors and styles, flowers and bare feet, erratic dancing. A handful of young men and women, more serious than the rest, huddled near the lion statues at a large metal garbage bin with clipboards and a bullhorn and a military duffel bag. A nearby group unfurled and hoisted up a banner that said, "FUCK NIXON. END THE WAR." Other banners, randomly made without prior coordination, slowly opened. "MAKE LOVE, NOT WAR"; "GIVE PEACE A CHANCE"; "WAR PIGS LEAVE US ALONE."

Ziggy stood in the crowd, quiet, anonymous, invisible. He felt for the letter in his top pocket, as he had done all week, neurotically checking to see if it were really there. Why had he not told Jaz or Rag or anyone else? He couldn't explain it. He had always been open. And he was as close to Jaz and Rag and the Co-op gang as human beings could get. Now, with the letter of induction in his hand, he was almost overwhelmed with emotion at how close he was to these friends. He thought of that new Melanie song:

> We were so close, there was no room;
> We bled inside each other's wounds.

Ziggy figured he couldn't analyze songs any better than he could analyze art or literature. He couldn't make out if the song was about the crowd Melanie found herself in when she sang at Woodstock or about soldiers bonding in the Viet Nam war. But he could relate to the closeness idea. Being so close to someone that you could bleed inside each other's wounds.

Ziggy looked out over the small crowd of hippies, looking for signs of that same feeling. And he saw everything: awkwardness, sharing, joy, bewilderment, vulnerability. What were the next lines of the song?

We all had caught the same disease
And we all sang the songs of peace.

And then the uptick toward the crescendo:

Some came to sing, some came to pray
Some came to keep the dark away.

He could see the "came to sing" and "songs of peace," but didn't get how the disease and the dark fit in. But back to his own case. Why had he kept this to himself? Why was this, of all things, his and only his? Inside him. His defining moment. And he wasn't even sure, as he stood here, whether he would go through with it. How do you know what's right? How do you know who's right? You might be living your life one way and then realize that the other way was right. Maybe Uncle Frank was right. Ever since high school, Zig had identified with the draft-dodging Uncle Leo, but maybe that was just a kid being a kid, wanting to step outside the accepted box and test the boundaries. How could you really know who's right? It all seemed arbitrary. But arbitrary or not, Ziggy would know in an hour which path he'd taken. Inertia was not an option, not for long. Either you burn your letter or you're in the army. He'd come to burn. And now second thoughts were racing through his head, racing through his heart. He couldn't concentrate. How could you ever know? How could you find a true reference point? Suddenly he remembered being a small child holding his mom's hand in the park. She was talking to someone. The two grown-ups cast an inquisitory look down at him. "He's a good boy but fidgety," he remembered her saying. He chewed on his lower lip and almost cried, thinking that this was one of his earliest memories.

111

A murmur went through the crowd like a wave, and a man jumped up on one of the stone lions. His garb was not as brightly colored as that of most of his listeners. He had black boots, patched jeans, a jean jacket over a white T-shirt, and a square jaw. Another man, at the base of the monument, spoke through the bullhorn: "Man, it's nice to see this gorgeous crowd. We're changing the world beat by beat. One big family. And let's welcome now a brother from New York. The man that led the sit-in against the war at Columbia and fought the segregated gymnasium in Morningside Heights, our big city brother, Joe Katz."

With that cue, the man on the lion repositioned his weight on the statue, thought twice about it, threw off his boots, and stood with one bare foot on the lion's back and one on the head.

"It's a beautiful day, brothers and sisters. April flowers, green grass, the lagoon, all you beautiful young people. I wish we could all just relax and dig it. But we got work to do first. Are you ready to fight with me?"

A purr of approval rose from the crowd.

"Are you gonna let some stuffed shirts in Washington take you out of paradise and put you into the hell they built for you?"

The purr rose to a clamor, as outrage augmented the first wave of approval. Katz gazed over the horde until the force of his gaze led to mutual shushing and a resumption of relative silence.

"If Nixon wants to ask you to trade this in for horrors and murders of war, I have one thing to ask him. Where's your fucking M-16, Mr. Nixon? Where's the mud and blood on your face from the front lines? When you and Agnew spend a few days out there in Khe Sahn and Con Thien, when you come back pale and trembling and tell me that you saw your friend get his fucking head blown off, that

112

you watched the man you shot die calling for his children, then and only then can you even fucking ASK me if I want to fight to defend your cronies and their way of life. Until then, don't even fucking ask me." He paused to wipe his face with a handkerchief and the crowd roared. A woman in a Persian sari, deep purple with a silver, star-spattered print pattern, handed him some water. He took a drink and then went on in a more measured tone.

"Look around you, brothers and sisters. We're here with Mother Nature's paradise at our fingertips. All we want to do – all we need to do – is share this paradise that's all around us, share it with each other, share it with all the beautiful people in Viet Nam, north and south, in Europe and in South America. We'll even share it with Nixon and Agnew if they want it. But if they don't want it, if they'd rather send us off to die in the name of the powers that be, we have to – and this is important – we have to say 'fuck you' to the powers that be. Burn their flags, burn their rulebooks, burn their draft cards. Push back hard. It's not the way we want it, but it's the only way for us to reclaim paradise. And it IS our generation's destiny to reclaim paradise."

At that, he leaped to the ground, took out what looked like a draft card, lit it with his lighter and dropped it into the metal garbage bin. There was a pause, and then another young man, with his long hair tied up in a knot above his head, came up, lit a card and threw it into the garbage can. The crowd cheered approval. Ziggy was impressed, emboldened. He took the induction letter from his pocket and began reading it. But as he read, doubts crept back in and his heart began to race again. How do you know, really? Joe Katz could be a phony, too, no different than the cops hanging back at the edge of the crowd right now, some uniformed, and some, Ziggy presumed, under cover. Katz

113

had made a great speech, but how do you know what's in someone's heart, or what's right, or if there is such a thing as right? He felt his chest tightening and he was conscious of himself trying to inhale.

In the midst of Ziggy's angst, a Nordic-looking kid in a Mexican poncho, leaned in against him, crowding him, breathing in the air that he, Ziggy, was trying to breathe.

"Hey, man, that's not a draft card," the kid said.

The voice sounded far away to Ziggy, from another world. What was he saying? What did it mean?

"That's not a draft card," the kid repeated. Ziggy was confused. Was he having a flashback? What was this kid saying? And why is he pushing in on my space? Or is it just me? Ziggy thought of the song again: "We were so close, there was no room ..."

"This is a fucking induction letter, man!" the kid said excitedly. "These other guys with draft cards. They don't even know if they're going to be inducted." He hugged Ziggy and patted him warmly on the back. "You got balls, man. These other kids haven't even seen the Man. But the Man's pulled you over eye-to-eye and you're telling him 'fuck you' to his face. You're the inspiration these kids need."

The kid turned away from Ziggy but threaded one arm through Ziggy's arm. "Hey," he yelled over the crowd toward Joe Katz and his crew. "This guy's a fucking hero." Now he held Ziggy's arm behind the elbow as if ready to thrust him up on a pedestal.

Not now, Ziggy thought. I can't deal with this shit right now. Who am I to be a fucking hero? Not now. "Lemme go," he said weakly, unable to find his voice. He pulled his arm back.

"But you're a fucking hero." The kid snatched the letter and held it high overhead. Ziggy snatched it back. The kid was baffled, hurt.

"What the fuck is wrong with you?" the kid said. "You're a fucking hero," he added half-heartedly, and he tried to take Zig's arm again.

"Get the fuck away from me," Zig said, and pushed the kid hard. Someone pushed the kid back into Ziggy. There was a scuffle. But before it could happen, someone stepped between Ziggy and the kid with an air of command, the kid walked away, and others went back to their business. The mediator turned out to be Saul, who had come to the event to drum up business for his own anti-war event later that evening.

Zig was breathing heavily.

"It's cool, Zig," Saul said. "Let's sit." And they took a few steps back from the crowd and sat in the grass.

"Fuck that guy, Zig," Saul said. "You do your own thing. If you want to split, split. Not everybody's ready for a public showdown with the Man." They sat silent for a moment.

"You cool, Zig? I got to go back with Clay and Martin. We're spreading the word about the SAW meeting tonight."

Zig nodded. "Thanks, go ahead. I'm cool."

Saul walked off, but Ziggy was not finished tearing at himself. What did Saul mean by that? Ziggy picked at a scab on his shin until it bled. He couldn't stop thinking: "Is he saying that I'm not ready to face the Man? Or is he being supportive, saying it's cool for me to make my own choice?" Ziggy watched the tiny stream of blood run down his shin. Fuck that. He didn't need Saul's permission. He didn't need anyone's permission. He took a deep breath. Now or never. Impulsively, he strode toward the front of the line that had

115

formed by the garbage can. The passing scene was a blur –
moving pictures of human flesh – a guy with a brown fringe
jacket strumming a guitar, a black woman in high boots and
a khaki trench coat cradling something in her hands, flower
headdresses, bare skin and laughter, granny dresses and
smells of pot and patchouli, the warm sun reflected from
color-popping fabrics. Zig felt it all as a hallucinogenic
backdrop to his heartbeat focus. People spinning as in a big
game of ring-around-the-rosy, but Zig's game was moving
through their game, and it was his turn.

Now Zig was at the front of the line. He could smell
the burning paper in the garbage can. And the faces around it
seemed lit up. Then he was the center of attention. Joe Katz
walked up to Ziggy and embraced him. He couldn't turn
back, even if he wanted to.

"Brother," said Katz quietly, "we need more people
like you. Not a draft card but an induction letter. You're the
real deal, man. It's people with courage like you that will
lead the way." He embraced Zig again. The crowd had
noticed the respect Katz gave to Ziggy, and gathered around.
The guy with the bullhorn took note.

"Among all these beautiful people," came the voice
through the bull horn. "Sometimes real leaders emerge. And
this guy is one. An induction letter. Back in the face of the
Man." The crowd rumbled, building toward a crescendo of
adulation. Ziggy felt someone pull his arm, then there were
pats on his back and his head, he started to lose his footing.
Now the spinning was inside his head. Katz was whispering
something.

"Hang tight, brother. They'll need a few words."

Then the voice through the bullhorn. Zig couldn't
make out the beginning of the sentence. But he heard the last
part: "… give us a few words."

116

"Wait!" thought Ziggy. "Are they talking about me?" The faces in the crowd that had circled closer and closer were looking at him. Suddenly, his mouth was incredibly dry. He could not process the whole of the event. But he knew one thing: his focus, which had rendered all else a background blur. It was like the crowd wasn't there. Katz wasn't there. Zig was in his own space. He took the flip lighter from his pocket, lit the induction letter, and dropped it into the can. He saw the yellow flame and the black crusts of burnt paper curling inward, inward, to nothingness. Then, in a jolt, he recognized the crowd's presence. And Katz.

"... a few words" the bullhorn voice persisted. But it was too late. It was impossible. Ziggy was swamped in a sea of people. Cheering, wailing. Were they jubilant? Angry? Moved? Ziggy had lost all perspective in the crush of flesh. His head bumped another head hard. A glassy-eyed boy was at his feet, high, too high, he was being trampled. Then someone was pulling him out. The crowd continued to swirl and close in. Then cops coming through. Ziggy was disoriented in the chaos. Someone took his arm.

"Go limp," he heard Saul's voice in his ear.

The person who had taken his arm pulled. Ziggy resisted for a second. Then he heard Saul's voice again, but the voice was fading: "Stay limp, man, stay limp; we got your back."

Ziggy went limp this time. The person pulling him seemed to relax. Now Ziggy was being sort of dragged, sort of carried. He passively moved his legs and feet, but remained limp. Then he was inside. Somewhere inside but he couldn't tell where. A car. Why was he in the back seat of a car? Then a siren. A police car. It was a police car. Things came back into focus. The cops had wrestled Ziggy into the car, but the crowd had followed and now they swarmed around the car. Someone started a chant:

117

"Let him go! Pigs go home! Let him go! Pigs go home!"

The cop in the driver's seat cranked the engine but it was futile. The car was a fragment of driftwood in ocean of hippies. There was nothing to do but keep the doors locked and wait for backup. Something hit the window. Was it a rock? Ziggy saw the cop flinch. Another pop at the window. This was it. Ziggy felt the adrenalin that comes with danger but also felt the calm intensity of focus that comes when that danger is infinite in proportion – not just the threat of harm but the threat that everything is coming to an end. Here, as he sat in the police car with this person – who was this person? He had not been born a cop. He had been a kid like Ziggy, and in the game of life he ended up in this uniform, sitting nervously in the car with Zig. And now he and Zig would go down together. Another rock. Two rocks. A cat's eye crack in the glass.

"Let him go! Pigs go home!" The chant was closer, more threatening.

Zig gazed out of the window with unnatural calm, knowing the end was near and he was passively fixed in the back seat. He saw a character in slick black hair and leather jacket emerge from the crowd and rest his hips against the front fender of the police car. The character carefully took his shoes off and climbed onto the hood of the car. And as he climbed from the hood over the cherry lights to the roof of the car, Ziggy noticed that it was Saul.

"Hey, hey you," Saul called to a wiry-haired kid who was charging the car. Noticing he was being singled out, the kid stopped, unsure of what to do.

"Hey everybody," Saul went on. "Y'all need to back off a little. The cops are on the wrong side of the movement, the wrong side of history, they're pushing the wrong way, we all know that. But we can't have violence. These

118

particular cops are just doing their job." An undecided whisper crept through the crowd.

"These guys are our adversaries but they're our temporary adversaries. The system is the real problem. When the system comes down, these individual cops will shuffle off the old baggage and become part of the new. So do what you gotta do. Resist. But no bodily harm."

While the crowd steadied itself to hear Saul out, a well-heeled police commander – not in uniform but in a custom-cut Italian suit – had come through the crowd and up to the car window. He had a bald spot but his hair was impeccable, his hands smooth with an expensive gold ring and clean nails, his eyes a soft russet brown. His demeanor – calm, polished, genial, and yet authoritative – allowed him to cut through the sea of hippies as gracefully as a skillfully handled yacht slips through the waves. He tapped the driver side window.

"Murphy, open the window." Officer Murphy complied.

"The back window." Murphy rolled down the back window separating the commander from Ziggy. The commander studied Ziggy's face for a moment with no trace of hostility.

"Hey kid, I'm Commander Angelo Lombardi," he said pleasantly.

Ziggy had come back down to reality. He sat alert now, not belligerent but too guarded to reply or offer his own name too freely.

"Look, kid, I don't like what you're doing and you don't like what I'm doing. But neither of us wants a riot. Neither of us wants people's heads bashed in. You don't want your friends hurt, and my cops got families to go home to."

"They're not my friends," Ziggy said inexplicably. Lombardi paused and studied the features of Ziggy's face.

"You sound like a reasonable guy," said Lombardi. "I'm a reasonable guy, too. I'm going to open this door, you're going to walk out of here, and while these people are cheering like hell, my officers are going to pull back to the perimeter, and stay out of the way, so long as no violence breaks out. You got that?"

Ziggy nodded.

"You ready?"

Ziggy nodded again. He noticed something sad between the lines of Lombardi's face. But there was no time. Lombardi opened the door and helped ease Ziggy out, as if Ziggy were a shriveled old man. And at that moment getting out of the car, Ziggy felt that he indeed understood what it was like to be a shriveled old man. Lombardi straightened Ziggy's shirt, which had become crumpled in the fray, and then Ziggy was standing alone, unsupported, in the midst of he knew not what. Lombardi turned and strode off at a full pace, as if the crowd weren't there, and the crowd instinctively parted like the Red Sea.

Despite the sensation of floating separateness, of trying to keep his footing, Ziggy was not alone. He was swarmed and tossed upon shoulders and carried through the crowd. He needed to get out. He was tired, disoriented, nauseous. He had never until now noticed the smell of all this flesh. The blood drained from his face.

Just then, Murphy's police car slowly started backing toward the tree line. Attention and cheers momentarily turned toward the car. At that instant, Saul stealthily swept Ziggy toward the edge of the crowd and took him out of focus. The two young men were soon beyond the tree line. Saul sat with Ziggy in the grass, silently, as Ziggy began to relax. Then, without comment,

120

Saul touched his shoulder, stood, and blended back into the crowd.

Ziggy was grateful to Saul and suspicious of Saul. And guilt-laden for being suspicious. He stood and breathed deeply. In a way, he was free, freer than ever, an enormous burden lifted. But Saul had seen him on the inside. Saul had now seen something about Ziggy that no one else had seen. There was a sense of exposure, of vulnerability, of not knowing. In burning that letter, Ziggy had done something that an hour ago he would have considered a badge of honor, moral heroism, a demonstration that he, Ziggy, who had never done anything of public significance in his life, could take bold risks for a higher ideal. And yet now he slunk off through the park troubled in spirit and picked his troubled way toward St. Roch.

* * *

The scene awaiting Ziggy at the Duck was no great comfort. On the front porch steps sat a young man with a button-up shirt and a fair-haired Johnny Unitas crew cut. He was scratching the earth at the side of the steps with stick and seemed deep in thought. Jazmine sat next to him, also deep in thought. She had been in the kitchen before he'd arrived, thinking. The tan acid had definitely got her thinking about her life. It was weird. The more she felt that other time and place, the more she saw into her own life. She was losing traction in the Marketing program. That was now clear. She could see there was a deadening aspect to it. She was an artist at heart. You could see it in her studies, always pushing toward the art side and away from the analytic side of the discipline. She would inwardly blush when Cool Breeze would make comments about how the Establishment's marketing people had co-opted the Scene.

Sure, Pepper could throw something back in his face about how the Scene needs its own media, its own journalists, its own fact finders on the beat. But Jaz couldn't think like Pepper. She just felt a little ashamed that she was in the Marketing program. Of course, Cool Breeze and Pepper, had they thought for a moment that their banter was disquieting for Jazmine, would have changed the subject to Woodstock or Women's Lib or the puppet shows at Washington Square Park. Jazmine was sure of their love and friendship. But still she was a little ashamed. Then there were other times, times when she knew that she didn't want to sink, that the Marketing program was her life line to a job and stability and the things people needed to live. You couldn't just live like a hobo hippie forever. Could you? Well, she would soon be in or out. No in between. You either get the work done or you're out of the program.

It struck her that Rebecca was at a similar crossroads. Well, in an upside-down way. She already had a stable situation. She could live out her days as William's ward. But it was deadening. Her plan to run away with Jeremiah was risky. Jazmine couldn't quite figure out the risk, but it was definitely risky. Maybe you had to be there, in the Middle Ages, to really understand the risk. So much unexplained. What about the grumbling old Guda? And the horse! Yes, Darian's chestnut mare. And the chestnut mare at the park. Or was it a chestnut mare at the park? There was definitely a horse. Did it really matter if it were the same horse? Or the same color horse? Weren't all horses sort of alike anyway? She thought of her psychedelic experience with the tan acid. Color was just a language. Images, too, like horses, just a language. Or that was one way of looking at it. That they were made up of language. Another way of looking at it was that everything was atomic bits of colored glass. The tan acid had given her that, too. Somehow this

122

comforted her, ensured her that there was nothing ominous about the recurring image of a chestnut mare. After all, all horses, like all things, were the same atomic bits sparkling and rearranging and flying around in the cosmos at the speed of light. She sat down, lightheaded. This was starting to feel like a flashback. A streak of enlightenment in the head and a rush of anxiety through the veins and muscles of the body. She heard a knock at the door and shuddered. The force of the knock brought Darian into her mind. And William, popping nails into the coffin. She looked around as if she needed to hide something. But what? The adrenaline that had flushed out from her heart through the trunk of her body and out to her arms and legs subsided. She collected herself and opened the door. There stood her brother, Tom, whom she had not seen in over a year.

"Hey, Jaz, took me a while to track you down," Tom said drowsily. She straightened her long lemon-yellow T-shirt over her cutoff jean shorts, stepped through the screen door to the porch, and hugged him, choking back emotion. "Tom," was all she said at first. And kept hugging as she took a few deep breaths. Then they sat on the top step.

"What are you doing, Jaz? You need your family. Look at this place." Jaz looked around the small front yard of the Duck, the cracked sidewalk running down the street, houses, some with porches, some just steps, a scrawny azalea here and there. In the street, two black kid were kicking a ball with an older white girl who seemed to float on wide sunstripe bellbottoms. Her hair was unkempt and she was clumsy in her satiny bellbottoms – possibly stoned as well – and the kids were enjoying it.

"What?" Jaz blurted, unsure of what Tom meant by his comment. "You mean the Co-op?"

123

"Co-op," Tom scoffed sarcastically. "You call it a 'co-op,' but it's just bunch of bums in a house. Calling it a co-op doesn't change it, Jaz. There's no future here."

He gestured up and down the street. "And this," he said, as if his meaning were self-evident. Jaz was too tired to respond, but she leaned against his shoulder. She did miss Tom, although she was glad to be away from that toxic house. And she couldn't really say that she missed her mom. It wasn't that she hated her mom. She hated Ken, yes. But for her mom, she felt nothing. Tom, though, she kind of missed him, even though he was such a square. She smiled, and her smile seemed to set Tom off.

"The house is a dump, the neighborhood's a dump. Hippies and losers. Look around, Jaz. These people are going nowhere. Isn't it obvious?"

"Where is there to get to, Tom?"

"What do you mean, 'Where is there to get to?' I'm worried about you, Jaz. A decent job, a nice house, a good neighborhood with good schools for your kids. That's where there is to get to. Here, these people, they're going to be junkies and losers ten years from now, with no jobs, trying to figure out how to stay on the dole. C'mon, Jaz. Think a little."

Jaz couldn't say he was wrong. But she couldn't say he was right, either.

"I like it here," she said. "These people are my friends."

"Look, I'm not saying they're not nice, but they're losers. Where are they going? Think about your future, Jaz. ANY future."

"They love me. They're good to me. A thousand times better than mom and Ken. You think my future should be like theirs?"

124

"No, look, Ken's not a teddy bear, but he kept a roof over mom's head. And ours."

"What do you mean, 'ours'? You were out of the house and in that community college when the creep moved in."

"I was there all the time, Jaz," Tom protested. "Trying to look out for you. What choice did mom have? She was falling apart. Ken's a jerk but a provider."

Jaz bristled at what seemed like Tom's continuing defense of Ken. "Ken did nothing but serve himself. Provider? Why do you think he provided? He's a total asshole." She aspirated in disgust. "If only you knew."

Tom was a little taken aback by the force of Jaz's response. They sat silent for a moment.

"Did that fucker ever touch you?" he asked suddenly. Jaz watched a silver beetle with closed-up wings trying to climb the bottom step. What were the wings for? Couldn't it fly up the steps? Apparently not, as the commotion of its eyelash legs twice tried to hoist the body up the cement, after which it abandoned the project and wobbled toward the grass.

"No," she lied. She wasn't even sure if it was a lie. That was the problem. Ken never "assaulted" her, whatever that meant. Eyed her up, yes. She could tell. Any girl could tell. And when he walked by, he'd sometimes brush against her and once, just once, when brushing against her, he laid his hand on her butt, spoke a few soft words, and continued on his way. She had been too shocked to process what words were spoken. She did remember pulling away briskly. And feeling helpless. What could she do? It wasn't like he raped her. Was she overreacting? Whatever he did, it was sexual, it was dirty, but it wasn't something she could explain to other people. Not even to her mom, who was already shaky anyway, probably from prescription drugs. No, the violation was too subtle. You couldn't go to court and say, "My stepdad's hand brushed against my butt in the kitchen and I think it was on purpose." The thought of making a public nuisance of it was too much for her anyway. It was something she would just have to carry inside. Ken must have sensed from Jazmine's reaction the risk to himself, because he was on his best behavior after that. Jazmine, for her part, damn sure kept her distance till she could get out and hitch to New Orleans.

As Jazmine pondered how many girls have to go through this shit, Ziggy walked up unnoticed by the reuniting siblings. Jaz did not look altogether well, and the crewcut stranger sat scratching a stick in the dirt.

"I'll kill him, Jaz, I swear I will," Tom said.

"Who?" said Ziggy bluntly.

"Oh, hi Zig," Jazmine said. "This is my brother, Tom. We were talking about my mom's boyfriend, Ken."

"Oh, hey Tom. Sorry to barge in."

Tom eyed Ziggy, thinking from the deferential comment that he may have found an unlikely ally, but before he could test the waters with Zig, Pepper bounced up a little more cheerily than usual.

"Howdy, y'all," Pepper said.

"Pepper. My brother, Tom," said Jaz. "You're a ray of sunshine today, Pepper."

"Just got laid," Pepper said buoyantly.

Tom tensed up and Jaz kept mum.

"Male or female?" asked Zig formulaically, without the jovial humor the words would imply.

"Male."

"Hoss?"

"Nope."

Jaz thought she might lighten things up a little and relieve Tom's tension.

126

"I hope that cowboy tone of yours doesn't mean you slept with Tex."

"Even I have standards, Jaz. No, just a fling. My guy done took off to go back to San Antonio. But Hoss and Gina can join in the after party. He gave me a bottle of good wine, not that cheap shit chianti you keep in the Duck."

Tom couldn't hold back completely.

"So you slept with this guy, he gave you a bottle of wine, and now you're going to go drink it with your boyfriend?"

"Not exactly," Pepper added. "More like my girlfriend and her boyfriend."

"Pff," said Tom in disgust.

Pepper was incapable of being intimidated, but she could sense some family thing going on between Jaz and Tom. She took off her bandana and shook her red hair loose. Her blue eyes burned their ice and fire into Tom for an instant, and then she opted for decorum.

"See y'all," she said and cut a path to the Island.

Zig was feeling less decorous at the moment.

"So if that's her thing, Tom, why do you care?"

"Because society is held together by rules and commitments and morality. You start throwing them out the window and next thing you know it's chaos."

"So where has society's rules gotten us?" queried Zig rhetorically, then answered himself. "Haves and have-nots, wars, machines, the rat race, people cheating on each other behind their Ozzie and Harriet front. Better to try a commune. Better to try open love for a while."

"A few unemployed bums in a house – that's what you call a commune? Down with jobs but up with free love? Like women in love with women? Men with men?"

"Why not?"

"Because ... gayness just isn't right."

127

"If you don't believe in gayness, don't date a gay guy. And let everyone else decide for themselves." Zig surprised himself a little. He'd never actually stuck up for the gay brothers and sisters like this before. But it felt natural, an effortless extension of everything else he believed.

Tom meanwhile, could see that Zig was not an insider ally after all, but he didn't come here to fight with Jazmine's friends either, so he tried to tone it down.

"Look, I'm not here to fight. I love my sister and want what's best for her. The rest of y'all can do what you want. Her, yeah, I'd like to see her married, stable, house in the suburbs."

"Trap, trap, and trap," said Zig, perhaps pushing for the sake of argument beyond his present grasp. "All your old morality is a trap. All that one partner, one track thing, that's what drives the cheating and hypocrisy. If I love somebody and she loves another guy, then I love him too, he's part of the family."

"To each his own," said Tom laconically.

"Look at Ken," Jaz insisted. "That's what Ziggy's talking about. The old stiff morality you're talking about. That's where all the Kens in the world come from."

"I don't know about all the Kens in the world," said Tom, back on track of the previous discussion. He looked at Jaz sharply. "But this Ken. Do I need to kill him or don't I?"

Jazmine took a breath. "No, Tom, you don't have to kill him. He didn't do anything. He's just an asshole, that's all."

Chapter 9

Jazmine sat at one of the large rectangular tables in the university library on Monday morning with another stack of books. Not marketing books. She had all but quit the marketing books. These were books about the Black Death that swept Europe, the Wars of the Roses, and the Carolingians. Sure, she felt guilty, she felt the sting of Tom's words, but the tan acid was taking over. She could hear in her mind the thumping bass line of Jefferson Airplane's "White Rabbit" again. Is this how obsessive-compulsive behaviors start?

She toggled back from daydream to books, naturally drifting toward the German side of things. Pope Leo, the Magyars, King Otto and the Holy Roman Empire. What kind of German king names his empire after a city in Italy? Then her finger froze and she felt a chill on her neck. Was this her white rabbit? It was weird, that's for sure. She pressed down to keep her finger from trembling. There was that word: "Michaelskloster." No way she could make that up. She closed her eyes and tried to catch her breath. She – no, Rebecca – had thought of that place. No, Jeremiah had spoken of it. "When the Lord Bishop arrives from Michaelskloster," he had said. She opened her eyes and read the full sentence: "They replayed the rites of Walpurgisnacht on the ruins of the Michaelskloster monastery, which was abandoned in the 16th century." Walpurgisnacht was little more than an echo in her head, but Michaelskloster – that's definitely where the Lord Bishop had been in her vision or dream or other life, or whatever the hell it was. She was dizzy. This was exhilarating, fantastic, mind-blowing. Also terrifying and alienating, because it was her body, her being, and possibly her sanity at stake. It's all well and fine to watch *The Body Snatchers* or *Rosemary's Baby* on the big screen, but you don't want to be the one who's living it.

She slammed the book shut. No more. Not now. She looked around for Saul. He was here last time. But why would she look for Saul? And why did a sharp-featured man with curly black hair flash through her mind? Why was her lower lip tingling? The tingling conjured up an image of someone preparing for her death. Everything was so different when you looked at it differently. She shook her head in disbelief. "God's Bones, but I know thy craft," she said, and smiled at herself for saying it. Troubled by her own smile, she thought quickly of abandoning the tan acid. No, it was like the Marketing program. Good or bad, she would put her mind to it and drive this thing through. She would not fall victim to the million things that knock you off course. She would not take the easy way out. Her mom had taken the easy way out, and look at her. Zoned out on her daily medications and depending on Ken because she's too screwed up to take care of herself. Jazmine would not be like that. She was halfway into this thing and she was damned sure not going to leave everything hanging. Anyway, something personal was at stake with the tan acid, something about her own deep identity, her lost identity.

Ziggy had been pacing the Co-op yard, pinching off rosemary bits, chewing a viscous chip of aloe vera, thinking. He needed a plan. No more fooling around. He sat at the picnic table and took out a notepad.

1. Find Beachbum and warn him to clean up all drugs.
2. Investigate draft dodger status. Will they come after me?

He had to think about that one. Would the feds come after him? Can they really go after everyone who doesn't show? Is it just something that will get you later in life? Uncle Frank would know. But no, he couldn't talk to Uncle Frank directly. Saul might know. He's really into this. He would know the general habits on the feds on draft dodgers. And, fuck, it's like he has a whole research team. Yes, it would have to be Saul.

1. Find Beachbum and warn him to clean up all drugs.
2. Investigate draft dodger status. Will they come after me?
3. Jaz. She seems slippery. Keep an eye on her with this tan acid.

He had to think about # 3 too. She went into this willingly. And she's going deep. It can't be bad to go deep, deep down into identity and reality. But it's taking a toll. It's risky. And she may not be in the best place to see when she's crossing the point of no return. She could *lose* her identity over this, too. Someone just needs to keep an eye out. Not her brother, Tom, though. Zig couldn't see into Tom's heart but he didn't need to. He could see clearly enough that Tom would be no help keeping Jazmine grounded. No, Tom would say his piece and go back to his world. Jazmine's life, her soul, her whole being was in this world with Zig and Rag and Pepper and Tex and the Co-op gang. It was like someone shook the clouds away and Zig could see clearly that he would have to keep an eye on Jaz to make sure she didn't slip too far and lose balance. This might mean keeping an eye on how far Ragman is willing to go, too. No, Rag's cool, cautious. Rag would not let it go too far. But he might let it kill her schoolwork. "Drop out, turn on, tune in," and all that. No, Zig would make sure she stayed in school. At least finished this semester. It's too much to give up for a pipe dream. She at least needs to finish her classes. But why

131

Zig? Who made him king? No matter. This is no time for second thoughts. Time to stay in action.

As if on cue, Hoss came stumbling out of the Island and headed toward Zig with his acoustic guitar in hand.

"Hey, Zig, you sweet, beautiful monster." As often happens in the best of encounters, the nearer Hoss got, the more his running commentary shifted from self-expression to an interactive awareness of his audience.

"Hey, Zig, you look strung out. You need some pot brownies."

Zig couldn't help but smile.

"You still cooking pot brownies, Hoss?"

"Yeah. I tried to quit after all that shit came down with the college, but I couldn't help it. I didn't last two weeks. I just love chocolate too much."

"You didn't have to quit eating brownies, Hoss. You could have just quit the pot."

"Have to say, Zig, that angle never crossed my mind. Got some fresh brownies though. Ain't kiddin' about that." Now seated, Hoss strummed an exploratory chord. Zig stood up.

"No, Hoss, I got to go."

"Your thing, man," said Hoss sociably. "The music's here when you want it." He strummed another chord and paused to twist a tuning key.

Pigeon Town was perhaps the most run-down part of Uptown New Orleans. Indeed, one suspects that disputes about whether it was or was not in Uptown had as much to do with politics as with geography. There was no dispute about this, though: Beachbum's apartment in Pigeon Town was a dump. It was one side of an old shotgun house – chipped paint, shutters with missing slats, uncut grass. Zig knocked. No answer. He knocked harder and then walked down the alley alongside of the house. It was not uncommon

132

for Beachbum to be in the kitchen, at the very back of the house, listening to music or smoking pot or just tuning out anything beyond the small radius of his visual field. Zig tapped on the window when he got as far back as the kitchen. No answer. Beachbum had so mastered the skill of tuning out reality that this was still an indefinite clue of his absence. But a couple of guys were sitting at the house across the street. The house looked abandoned last time Zig was here. Indeed, it still looked abandoned. Maybe these people had moved in, or squatted. Pigeon Town was a place where the normal rules of urban living had never gotten traction. A house might be abandoned one day, occupied the next by a friend of a friend who said it was empty, and occupied by a still different group the next day with a different but equally dubious claim to residence. These two figures looked careless enough, the skinny one unshaven but with a baby face, and the big doughy one with windswept hair who kept his hand in his pocket. Probably a couple of the petty thieves stereotypical of Pigeon Town, thought Zig. He chuckled to think of the corpulent loiterer trying to get in and out of a window. And the baby-faced guy. Zig thought he'd seen him before but couldn't put his finger on where. Anyway, no point making a ruckus at the side of an empty house. Zig did not need any more attention from the Man in his present circumstances. He walked glumly back to the front of the house. Shit, he'd forgotten his notepad and pen at St. Roch, but it was urgent that Beachbum know what's going on. He rummaged his pockets. Still no pen. But he had that dumb Saint Francis card with his face pasted on it. He stuck it under the door so Beachbum would know he had come by. As he turned down the sidewalk, he threw a nod at the two characters across the street. The hulk just looked down but the baby-faced fellow nodded back. The nude

133

beach at the lake, hanging back by the palm tree. That's where Ziggy had seen him.

Zig continued over to the university, where he could hang out with Jaz for a bit before going to work at Polo's. He found her on the front steps of the library. She stood with her backpack on when she saw him cutting across the great, green expanse of the quad. He put his hands on her waist and kissed her cheek.

"You look great!" he said. And he meant it. She looked better than ever for some reason. It made Zig a little self-conscious about his greeting. Did it seem a lover's greeting? An old friend?

"I went by Beachbum's but he's nowhere to be found."

"That's too bad," Jaz said, and she reached out and momentarily squeezed his hand.

"I'm walking over to Saul's. You want to come?"

"Why Saul's? I thought you were just going to relax and then walk over to Polo's with me?"

She started walking, and Zig mechanically followed alongside. Whatever path the conversation took, she knew that Zig would walk with her to Saul's. Zig took mental note of how the tree-shaded streets and nicer houses, some stone, some wood, stood in contrast to Pigeon Town.

"I found something in the library today," Jaz said. Zig tensed up without knowing why.

"So why Saul's?" He immediately felt foolish for asking twice. It sounded accusatory.

"He said his people are from Germany."

"You found something about Germany in the library?" Shit, Zig thought. The tan acid. I don't like where this is going.

They didn't have to knock on the brown oak door. Saul was sitting cross-legged on the top step, surrounded by

134

leafy vines of unknown genus and species, like an archetypal figure in a primeval forest. The smell of freshly cut grass hung in the air.

"Hey, Jaz," he said, like he was expecting her. Zig watched him closely but saw nothing amiss. Saul sat friendly, casual, self-assured.

"Saul, that day at the library. You saw me with that stack of history books. You said your people were from Germany."

"That's right."

"You ever heard of Michaelskloster?"

"No, but Germany's a big place."

Jaz felt like an idiot. But she had so much riding on this. She was almost in tears at her foolish emotional investment in what anyone could have seen was a dead end. She sat on the lower step. Zig sat next to her.

"What's wrong?" Saul continued.

"Nothing. I just read something about it today, and … and I thought I heard of it somewhere before."

"Hey, if one story bothers you, go to the next one. Don't stick to the book that bothers you. Write your own story if you have to. Self-indulgence doesn't pay."

Ziggy put his hand on top of Jazmine's. "No worries, Jaz. It's all good." He could feel Jaz respond to his touch, relaxing. But he could see her respond to Saul's words also, a more dynamic response. The comfort in Zig's touch was counterpointed by the challenge in Saul's words. Zig kept his hand on Jazmine's but addressed Saul.

"Hey, that day by the cop car. You broke your own rule, Saul."

"Oh? What rule is that?"

"The crowd was going to wreck that car. They were gnashing their teeth to get at the cops, but you were the champion of non-violence. 'Go limp,' you told me. And

135

then, 'Back down, everybody. Keep it peaceful.' You even took your shoes off so you wouldn't damage the car."

Ziggy wasn't even sure if his tone expressed hostility, a taut and testy male-to-male comradeship, or just plain curiosity, but he went on.

"I didn't get it. I still don't get it."

Ziggy thought back to what he had said to Angelo Lombardi when they had him in the cop car. Lombardi had said something to Zig about his "friends" in the crowd. "They're not my friends," he remembered tossing back at Lombardi. But what did he mean by that? Was it passive-aggressive pushback against Lombardi? A childlike clarification – after all, Ziggy really didn't know the other kids out there? Or was it his betrayal of the movement, like St. Peter denying Christ at the gate?

"Good observation, brother," Saul said to Ziggy. "Your senses were no doubt heightened by the intensity of the scene, with the cops coming down on you at close range."

"What cops? What did you do, Ziggy?" asked Jazmine, stunned.

But for a moment, the two men engaged each other, and Jazmine was outside the scope of their focus.

"But wrong interpretation. Yeah, I was very careful to get you limp and prevent a beatdown with the cops. I was very careful to respect that car. But it's all strategy. If peaceful resistance gets you through today's scene, do it. Live to fight another day. That day was not a fight we could win. Either you were going to get every bone in your face broken, or this crazy mob was going to kill a cop. That's a lose-lose situation, brother. Live to fight another day. You dig?"

"Yeah, I dig," Zig acknowledged. He had to admire Saul in a way. But he added one more push: "I thought for a minute Ragman's peacenik ways were rubbing off on you."

"No." Saul paused and gazed across the lawn. "Rag and I might not be as far apart as you think, though," he added enigmatically, giving all three a moment's inconclusive pause, before Ziggy brought things back to a point.

"Look, Saul." Ziggy was more confidential now. "I need to ask you something about that. About the feds and how things work."

Saul looked at Zig as if measuring him briefly.

"Ok, come on. I got a call coming any minute, but we can talk in the back." He paused and added, "Welcome to the Den, brother."

Jazmine now realized that she would have to walk through that tunnel of a house again, the house that had left her so distraught. But as soon as the realization hit her, there was another realization that she felt no trepidation at the prospect. "Damned be all these lunatics and tramps," she said to herself. "We's all the same devil's vermin." And then Saul's words echoed up in the well of her mind: "If one story bothers you, go to the next one."

In the first room, Lonnie and the close-cropped redhead still sat at their work. Jazmine was taken aback. Maybe this would not be as easy as she had thought – or as whoever it was had thought – a moment ago. The jigsaw puzzle seemed no closer to being finished, but the man and woman seemed much older. Jazmine could see that gray hair had pushed out much of the red on the woman's head. Lonnie still wore his suspenders but his body was shrunken and no longer filled his corduroy shirt. Was Jaz just seeing them in her own way? From some timeless point of view? Through some symbolic economy more real than our surface

137

way of seeing? Either way, the sight of the stooped and brittle Lonnie, grinning and holding out his little mirror with powdered coke and razor blade, and the wrinkled face of the redhead, was disturbing. The redhead moved her bony fingers across the puzzle. "Got one," she said dryly. Jaz felt paralyzed by the whole scene. She could not take her eyes away. She could not move. "Look at me, Jazmine!" she heard Saul command. She looked at him. "Don't mind the freaks," he said gravely. "Now keep walking." Saul took her elbow and moved her through the beaded curtain. Zig was oblivious, attending to his own concerns, unfazed by the weirdness of the Den.

The Sheik was at his piano but did not even look up to acknowledge the passers-by. He was studying the piano keys like a condemned man studying his own executioner. He had transitioned, it seems, from flamboyant extrovert to angst-ridden introvert. He poked a few keys incoherently, as a child might who had never seen a piano. Jazmine wanted to console him. But she passed with her team through the next door and into the War Room.

The room was empty except for the straight-laced girl, who sat lounging at Martin's desk, with one leg thrown over the arm of the chair. Zig and Saul rehashed the draft card scene at the park, how Ziggy had burned his induction letter, while Jazmine sat on a bench and gathered it in as a new revelation.

"No, you're cool for now," Saul said to Ziggy. "They're not going after draft-dodgers right now." Ziggy was relieved, but he wanted to say something that would show investment in the cause and not just in his personal situation.

"That's good for everybody, I guess. Maybe your anti-war things is turning the tide."

138

Saul laughed. "No, brother, don't get your hopes up. It's just a tactical move. They figure they can get the same guys through drug laws and lock them up more surely."

The phone rang at Martin's desk and the girl jumped up startled, answered the phone, and passed it to Saul.

"Ziggy, come here," Jazmine whispered, as if she were cutting in. Ziggy stepped over to the bench.

"Ziggy, how are you?"

"What do you mean?"

"You burnt your fucking induction letter?"

"But Saul's right," Zig said with some heat. "Those fucks have no right ..."

Jaz put her finger on his lips. "Shhh, no, no, baby, I'm not blaming you. I wouldn't know how to judge you if my life depended on it."

It was true. Jaz was incapable of being judgmental. This, thought Ziggy, is either the source or effect of her perfect purity. But he knew that. Why did he react defensively? It was stupid.

"I know," he said. And he closed his eyes and rested his forehead against hers.

In that moment of calm, they could hear isolated phrases from Saul's telephone conversation across the room. "For storing ammonium nitrate" ... "check the BOM" ... "never buy two items from the same source" ... "then burn it."

When Saul hung up, Zig asked him point blank: "Burn what?"

Saul was at the map on the center table and did not look up.

"The bill of materials."

"What bill of materials? What ammonium nitrate?"

"Ziggy, if I wanted to fuck with the ROTC building, I'd burn it, not blow it up. You know how easy it is to start a fire? But that's not what we're burning. We're burning the lists of names we're not supposed to have. The BOM is code for the lists."

It sounded credible, but Ziggy was not persuaded.

"You expect the cops to believe that story?"

Now Saul looked up and turned his face to Ziggy's. His words were as direct as his gaze.

"Ziggy, that's the story. True or false, it doesn't matter. You and I and Rag are on the same side, brother. We need each other. How do you think we know about the feds' resources on drugs and draft dodgers? Think of that as the BOM." Ziggy had to admit that Saul had a point there. He was indebted to Saul for info received. He was implicated. Maybe we do all need each other.

Saul turned to the War Room girl and said, "Pull the second and third files for tomorrow." Then he guided Ziggy and Jaz to the door behind the calendar that led to the alley and opened it. Jaz stepped out, but Saul caught Zig's arm and looked at him calmly, earnestly, eye-to-eye. "True or false, brother, what you hear in the War Room stays in the War Room."

Jazmine and Ziggy walked mechanically in the general direction of Polo's Pizza. Ziggy thought he should say something, but he didn't know what. He stared dumbly at the broad elephant ear leaves. The saw palmetto brushed his scab, the one he had obsessively picked at the draft card burning.

"Jaz, did you notice how he said 'you and me and Rag'? Chauvinistic bastard didn't even include you."

"I know," Jaz said as they crossed the streetcar tracks on St. Charles Avenue. "I know it's weird, but don't jump to judge. It's just the way some guys are chivalrous – men on the front lines, women safe, that sort of thing."

"Yeah, sure, Jaz, but those are the guys who end up controlling and abusive."

"Just don't overreact," was all Jaz said, but Zig's comment triggered something. Is that what she found attractive about Saul? Is it that controlling thing, the thing that Ken had, not to mention a half a dozen guys she'd flirted with in high school? She knew in a way that the whole dynamic put her down. Zig was right; it was a controlling thing. And yet somehow it had gotten into her psyche as the norm. It was like a game that she knew how to play. It was invigorating, and yes, there was an irrational attraction. "We take comfort in what we know," she thought to herself, even if it's not good for us. That's why people get stuck in self-destructive cycles. That's how things pass down to your kids and your kids' kids. Was there no escape? How could she, a struggling creature grasping at straws to get through the next day, break such a thing. She thought of Rebecca. Rebecca didn't have it, that irrational attraction. Zig may have thought of Jazmine as pure and good, but to Jazmine Rebecca was the exemplar of purity. That was her way out. She pictured Rebecca in the little house. She tried to picture her at the table with the sprigs of herbs, but she could not keep out the image of coffins. "Aye," she thought with a sneer. "Here's your innocence, my little lamb. Here in this box. You and your gamecock be damned for your nasty innocence."

"Fucking Guda," Jazmine said out loud.

"What?"

She'd forgotten Ziggy was there, and fumbled at his question.

"Nothing, Zig. But I'm gonna skip Polo's. All this crazy stuff with Saul has me tired out."

Ziggy went on his way toward Polo's. He knew Beachbum would not be there. Saul was right. It made sense

141

that the cops would carve their path through the drugs. That's their fucking stock-in-trade. He'd make it right with Beachbum. But would it end there? Why Beachbum? Why not through Beachbum to him, and to Ragman? He remembered what the kid at the beach had said about taking Rag down. "Clean, man, just be clean," Zig said to himself.

There's a little Catholic church in the Faubourg Marigny, in Spanish colonial style with bricks weather-washed by time. Two square turrets adorn the front exterior corners. Stormy and Rose Petal were just emerging from the rounded arch doors, having lit a devotional candle to the Blessed Virgin and dipped their fingers in holy water, rituals that awed little Rose and soothed her mother. It's not that Stormy was a practicing Catholic, certainly not an exclusive Catholic, but she found all spiritual ways of attunement soothing and could never figure out how some people professed to distinguish true creeds from false. She could not wrap her head around such distinctions, and so she wrapped her soul in a motley quilt of grace composed indiscriminately of any and all spiritual traditions. For Stormy, a blessing was a blessing.

On this Monday afternoon, they emerged from the rounded arches to find Jazmine sitting on the church steps.

"Funny seeing you here," Stormy said.

"I just needed a place to think," Jaz said.

"Don't we all, girl."

Rose Petal held her doll out to Jazmine and showed Jaz the hard plastic hand.

"Ho-wee water," said Rose Petal, and Jazmine could see in her small round face true awe and reverence. This is what it's all about, she thought.

"Come here," Jaz said to Rose Petal, and grabbed the bouncy little body and hugged it for dear life.

142

Chapter 10

Ziggy walked more slowly than usual toward Polo's Pizza. A group of frat boys were sharing a pitcher at a picnic bench by a corner bar. A bum sat on the curb a few feet away from the property, drinking from a can still wrapped in a paper bag.

"Spare a dime, brother?"

Zig walked past. No time for that. He felt his shirt pocket, not for money but as a late reflex to reach for his induction letter. His conscious mind then caught up with the reflex. Of course there was no letter. But there was a pencil-thin joint, the last joint he had from the bag of weed they had dug into before the Big Lake Fest. Zig turned back and handed the joint to the bum, eliciting a gap-toothed grin.

"God bless you, brother. You're a saint."

Zig continued past the small commercial strip that served the dire needs of college kids, mainly little cottages that stood recessed or jutting toward the street: pubs, dress shops, burger joints, the plate glass window of the Christian Science Reading Room.

"Shit," Zig thought to himself. "I forgot to ask Jaz about that Michaelskloster reference." All that theorizing for nothing. Jazmine's experience as the old woman, Guda, shot down the simple reincarnation theory, and the DNA thing. She couldn't have DNA memory of two unrelated people. Got it. But what if she really discovered some spot in Germany? That means Pepper was wrong. The Freudian thing is out. She might dream up struggles from her personal past but she couldn't dream up something that happened a thousand years ago in a country she'd never been to. So maybe it is the akashic record. But Rag made the akashic record sound so dreamy and euphoric, like Enlightenment

143

itself. Jaz was having specific memories that were not all bliss and ecstasy. What is Rag thinking? Zig put the question to himself. And then he thought, with an inward turn, that it was all like a painting or a novel, and he was doing something like art or lit criticism. He, Ziggy, hahaha. No, not really. He was looking at a real world problem and taking it apart one step at a time. Maybe he had a newfound sense of focus, but nothing more.

Ziggy stepped into Polo's. The inharmonious hodgepodge of Italian checker tablecloths and psychedelic paraphernalia – lava lamps and macramé, lucid dreamlike rock concert posters from Bill Graham's lunatic press – always cheered Zig up. But what was Rag's thinking on the tan acid? Zig felt more than ever that the critical point was not in Rag's thoughts but in his own words. The comment he'd made to Ragman at the Big Lake Fest: This is not about philosophy or social justice or Age of Aquarius visions. This was about Jazmine. It was personal.

* * *

The akua ma doll was breathing. Jazmine reached around the edge of the blue sheet to feel the Russian birch. That was her ground, her comfort, her rock. It was Tuesday, April 21. She watched the dark flat head of the akua ma. Poor thing had not much body to speak of. The body was not much more than two wooden cylinders in the shape of a cross. She would have to talk to Stormy about that, Jaz thought incongruously. But the flat round head was real. The stylized face: eyes, eyebrows, nose. Sure, it was carved and crafted by Stormy, but that made it no less real, no less a living thing. The small string of beads wrapped around the cross body heaved in and out. Jaz was aware that no one else could see this, but that did not nullify the reality of her

144

vision. Now the room was heaving. The burgundy curtains, the rich, root beer wood of the walls, the Madonna's gold-leaf halo, resonating with the akua ma in infinite passion. The passion of Christ, compassion, passion, compassion, passion. Jazmine's mind flickered across the sounds.

Then she remembered. She was twelve. She was dying. Her father, Meister Conrad, was preparing for her death. Then Berold arrived. This was before her delirium broke. Yes, now she remembered. He must have still had one drop of that magic sap of the dwarf palm. He must have put it on her lips. She had had that one vision before coming out of her delirium. But what could such vision mean?

Two old women bearing refreshments. But this was not the rich green forests and pasturelands of Germany. It was all dry, rocky, low mountains. The vegetation consisted of aromatic, low-growing scrubs. The smell of fennel and dill and marjoram.

The two old women rose from their resting place on the rocks to continue their journey. One stood, straightened her light tunic, and adjusted the shoulder pin. She picked up a basket carrying figs and olives and dried fish. Then she handed a vessel of wine mixed with water to her partner.

"Here is thy amphora," she said as the other took the vessel.

"Efharisto, Eudoxia."

"Parakalo, Ioanna."

For a time, the two women wended their way up the slow ascent of the crags. Despite the strange roughness of the terrain, Rebecca noted familiar reference points: the tinkle of goats' bells, the sight and smell of oregano, clustered like soft-needled seaweed here and there along the footpath. She pinched off a sprig of oregano and held it to her nose.

"Take care, Ioanna," came her partner's warning. "We're in His territory now, and these His fruits."

"Oh, Eudoxia, 'tis childish credulity to think He sees everything."

Eudoxia took no notice of the remark but continued toward a break in the rocks.

"Well," Eudoxia said finally, "at least the fiend will be pleased with our small gift. But the god himself will not like it."

Rebecca felt herself prickle.

"Pff," said Ioanna. "The great god may be in his cups, or a-courting in the character of some bull or swan."

"Beware your profanity," said Eudoxia.

As the two neared the break in the rocks, Rebecca felt in her heartbeat signs of expectation building. The break itself was where the mountain sheered into giant monoliths of rock, with pathways running between the granite walls of fifty feet high or more.

At the first turn into the jumble of monoliths, Eudoxia bent and set down her bundle.

"Shall we turn back before it's too late, Ioanna?"

"No, Eudoxia." Ioanna laid her hand on Eudoxia's. "I know you want to protect me from divine reckoning, but my heart tears apart for the fiend, as you call him. He that saved the other from the Titans. He that brought us fire."

"Aye, fire. To make us like the gods."

"And why not make us like the gods, Eudoxia?"

"Aye, why not?" was the other's response.

As the path grew steeper, foggy patches began to impair their visibility. They turned through another pass among the stone monoliths, and Ioanna's heart faltered. Rebecca felt the pounding in her own heart. A great apprehension, but of what she knew not.

"Let us turn back," said Eudoxia.

146

Ioanna set down her amphora and peered into the fog. Nothing yet could be seen. She gathered her strength.

"No, Eudoxia, let us go on." And the two climbed up to the next turn. Here, Ioanna set down her amphora and fell to her knees in the climax of fear and trembling that she knew would come at the sight of the beast. No, not a beast, not a fiend, but a god himself. More worthy than Zeus, the other, for whom he had fought so valiantly. Ioanna forced her eyes to view the dreadful scene. There he hung, gigantic against the rocks. His body, twenty feet in height, his chest the breadth of five full casks. His buttocks rested against a shelf in the rock, not quite seated but supported enough for his legs to stretch out wantonly. His ankles and wrists were bound in iron and chained to the rock, and the mass of black curls on his head and chin were grizzled from the fog. His torso was torn and bloody on one side where the vultures had been feasting. Ioanna gathered her strength and her amphora and approached that part of the gigantic torso.

"Poor, pitiful creature," she said. "So noble, so godlike, so broken."

She dipped a sponge in the amphora and took a small jar from a clasp purse. She rubbed a little bit of balm from the jar on the sponge to salve the wound.

"And he that put you here a tyrant," she said bitterly.

"Would you then call Zeus a tyrant," came a voice from behind her back. It was a female voice but it did not sound like that of Eudoxia. Ioanna turned. Several feet away, where Eudoxia had been just a moment ago, stood a female creature, human in form but not human, Eudoxia but not Eudoxia. A glitter of stars was in her hair and shoots of light emanated golden from her head and upper body. She held a black spear with a leaf-shaped blade. Ioanna recognized her at once.

"Dione! Concubine of Zeus! What trick is this?"

147

Rebecca saw compassion in Dione's face. She felt lightheaded.

Passion, compassion, passion, compassion.

"Dione, for thy daughter, Aphrodite's sake, spare me. Take my goods, what gifts you will, but spare my person."

The compassion in Dione's face resolved itself in fierceness. Rebecca recoiled, turned away. She was twelve. She was dying. Her father, Meister Conrad, was preparing for her death. Then Berold arrived. He had rubbed something on her lip. It soothed the pain, but with a current that ran from her lip through her body and into her heart.

Jazmine resisted the current running through Rebecca's body. She let Rebecca turn back, but she, Jazmine herself, turned forward, forward to the monster, to the goddess. "Into the roots of consciousness," someone had said. But who had said it? Jazmine couldn't remember.

"For myself," said Dione with imperial stoicism, "I wish naught against thy person, Ioanna. This concerns not your person. This concerns the Law."

"I meant no harm," Jazmine said to the deity.

"Aye, but harm is done. Thou may to Hades or to join the Pleiades in their starry heaven, but here thou must die."

Jazmine saw the black spear turn. She saw the goddess loosen her grip and tighten again to get a better purchase on the shaft. And then it was done. The black spear thrown. The leaf-shaped blade entered Jazmine's soft torso. She could feel the splitting of flesh and organs – not as pain but as wild curiosity. She fell back against the tree-trunk thigh of the shackled beast who had garnered her pity and sealed her fate.

"You fear me, Dione," she heard a female voice say. And then she realized it was her own voice. "But I bring

148

only balm and gentleness. The hero will come stronger next time and Prometheus will be unbound."

Dione responded only with a bow, turned, and hobbled away, once again taking the form of the aged Eudoxia. "'Tis pity, aye, all a cursed destiny, she and I and the gods themselves. All the world's vermin. What good fire? What good the knowledge brought to mortals by the beast? We all be damned by what we know. Ay, 'tis pity, and yet, fools all, we take comfort in what we know." She turned a corner between the giant granite slabs and disappeared into the mountain fog.

Jazmine awoke and reached down for the Russian birch. Someone was crying. It was her. She was crying. She was a girl in a headband crying. She outstretched her fingers and reached them to her forehead, her hairline. No headband. No, she was Jazmine, coming down off the tan acid, surrounded by her friends, Ragman and Ziggy and Pepper. Ziggy knew now not to ask questions. He gestured Ragman and Pepper away.

"Hey, Zig," Jazmine said.

It was so sweet, so innocent, so like a creature just seeing the world for the first time, that Zig almost forgot about the tan acid. He put his hand under her head and stretched his fingers into the copious flow of her black hair.

"Can you get up now, Jaz?"

"Sure."

She sat straight up, stood, then sat back down, realizing she was not quite as strong as she had supposed.

"Let's go to the Magic Mushroom, Zig, and get some of that Kenyan tea Claire's been hyping."

They walked quietly down to Frenchmen St. Cool Breeze was rocked back on a kitchen chair outside the shop, with his hands behind his head. A melodious female voice and acoustic guitar was pouring out of the shop and seemed

149

to float up into the gills of the painted mushroom along with
the smoke from the eternally mellow monk's pipe.

"What's playing?" asked Zig.

"Joni Mitchell's new album," said Cool Breeze.

They paused to relish the sweet vocals.

> They took all the trees
> And put them in a tree museum
> Then they charged the people
> A dollar and a half just to see 'em

"You're like the senior dude in hippieland, Cool
Breeze," said Zig. "Why are you listening to this depressing
stuff?"

"How can you call Joni depressing?" asked a
shocked Jazmine.

> Hey farmer, farmer
> Put away that DDT now
> Give me spots on my apples
> But leave me the birds and the bees

"Right there!" exclaimed Zig. "That doesn't seem
like the Age of Aquarius."

"Dig, Zig," said Cool Breeze, smiling, pleased with
the sound of those two syllables together. "Age of Aquarius
came and went in 1967. Joni's right, man. The Corporate
State is poisoning our fruit. Viet Nam war heating up. Nixon
cracking down at home."

"Well, it still sounds sweet," Jazz said glumly.

> Don't it always seem to go
> That you don't know what you've got
> 'Til it's gone

150

They paved paradise
And put up a parking lot

"Dig, though," said Cool Breeze. "Joni's right on time. Tomorrow's Earth Day."

Zig and Jaz shared a blank look.

"April 22, 1970, man. The first Earth Day. They're going to do it every year. Joni's got her finger on the pulse as usual."

Joni's finger on the pulse seemed to have shifted as soon as Cool Breeze spoke, as the final stanza of the song become suddenly personal:

Late last night
I heard the screen door slam
And a big yellow taxi
Came and took away my old man

Don't it always seem to go
That you don't know what you've got
'Til it's gone
They paved paradise
And put up a parking lot

Jaz changed the subject: "Is Claire here?"

"Nah, she and Bitzy baked some cookies and went to an after-school market in Bywater. By the time they're finished trading and carrying on, we'll probably have a house full of goodies."

He pulled a harmonica from his top pocket and blew a note.

"Wish Hoss could show me how to play this thing," he said. But he seemed happy to blow his atonal melody, oblivious to the discrepancy between his gloomy views on

151

the general state of things and the remarkable amount of domestic bliss that seemed to grace the Mushroom.

"Y'all got some of that Kenyan tea?" asked Jaz.

Cool Breeze took his harmonica from his mouth, moistened his lips with his tongue, and replied: "Go behind the counter and look by my dog-eared copy of *Fat Freddy's Cat*. Take a couple packs on the house."

Jaz went in, and Cool Breeze started to raise the harmonica to his lips, then thought twice about it, and dropped the device back into his pocket.

"Like to offer you a toke, Zig, but you can't be too careful in my line of work." He gestured toward the only other business that had opened this far out on Frenchmen Street, a small newsstand with newspapers and magazines for all tastes, but particularly well-stocked for the nascent gay scene in the Marigny. There was one table and two chairs in front of the stand, and a lone customer sat at the table apparently deeply absorbed in his paper. He was short but compact, with a bull's neck and the arms of a bodybuilder. Cool Breeze was suspicious of him, and Cool Breeze had good instincts when it came the Establishment and its minions. Zig thought he had seen the guy before. The man took a sip of his coffee and looked up but did not look toward the Magic Mushroom. Another fellow came out of the newsstand, talked to him briefly, then turned and walked down the street away from the Mushroom. Neither had looked toward Ziggy and Cool Breeze, but Ziggy definitely knew the second man. He could not believe it, and it came to him like a chill running up his spine, although he didn't even know why, but there was no doubt. The skinny kid with the baby face. He was clean-shaven now, but it was him. The guy who had first appeared in the group by the palm tree at the nude beach, and had then reappeared by Beachbum's house with the big doughy guy. Now things started

152

cascading in Ziggy's mind. The bodybuilder, the one who now sat thirty yards away at the newsstand, with his nose so studiously buried in his paper – he was one of those cops by the Falstaff bar near Uncle Frank's house. Now Ziggy recognized the thin lips. Those thin, malignant fucking lips. So he was a cop. And the baby-faced kid was working with him. Those were cops watching Beachbum's house. And why are they here, scoping out the Mushroom and St. Roch? This isn't about Beachbum. Or it isn't just about Beachbum. Fuck!

Jazmine came out of the shop, happy with her Kenyan tea in hand. As she and Ziggy walked back to St. Roch, Ziggy figured there was no need to tell Jaz any of this. She was not in danger. Of the whole Co-op group, Jaz was most likely to be studying at college and least likely to have any personal dope on her. Anyway, she was flipped out enough lately.

Upon arrival at the Co-op, the scene was not fit for reflection. Pepper sat agitated on the front porch steps.

"What's wrong, Pepper?" Jazmine asked.

"Fuck me!" was Pepper's response.

"You want some tea? It's Kenyan."

"Yeah, sweetie, thanks."

Ziggy retired to the picnic bench in the communal yard, where Pepper and Jaz joined him shortly with a bottle of the cheap chianti Pepper had so recently cited as an example of the Duck's low tastes. It may or may not have indicated lack of refinement, but it apparently suited Pepper's present mood better than Kenyan tea.

"So I don't know what to do about Gina," Pepper was saying. "She was still thinking about me being with the San Antonio guy, like she's been holding it in for the last two days. What the fuck am I supposed to do? I can't hide things?"

153

"No, you're right," Jazmine sympathized. "You're right not to hide things."

"I just want to let it all hang out, but then Gina gets so controlling. It's like she doesn't want me to do shit without her."

"But Pepper, how can she be jealous when she sleeps with Hoss half the time?"

"I don't know. Ask her. She fucking knows everything."

Oddly enough, Jazmine got to do just that a few minutes later. Pepper grabbed the chianti by the neck and stormed off to the Island, and Jaz cradled her tea cup between both hands. But Pepper's entry into the Island precipitated Gina's exit, and soon Gina was crying softly with her birdlike body perched next to Jazmine.

"Pepper's pissed," Jazmine said.

"I know," Gina said. "But I don't want to hear about her balling this guy or that guy."

"But Gina, you sleep with Hoss."

"That's different. Hoss is one of us. We know Hoss. I wouldn't care if she slept with Hoss. Sleeping with Hoss is not abandoning anybody. But to know that she's out there, without me, without Hoss, just out there in the open for strangers to fuck."

"You're smothering her, Gina. Pepper's one that can't be smothered."

"I just want her to love me like I love her."

"And stay close to home."

"Yeah, and stay close to home."

"So you don't care if she sleeps with Hoss. You just don't want her out there where you're not in control of her."

"Exactly," said Gina, as if that were her vindication.

Jaz tried not to smile. Gina was so blind to her own control issues. But who could blame her? We all have our

154

shit. God knows Pepper has her shit. And poor Hoss. Jaz could never imagine Gina or Pepper or anyone getting mad at Hoss, but then Hoss would be utterly useless when faced with these emotional distresses. It's not that he wouldn't care; it's just that he would be incapable of anything but hand-wringing bewilderment. He'd probably offer them a pot brownie, meaning well from the bottom of his heart.

But Jazmine could see the irony that Gina missed. Her art for self-sabotage. How her fear of abandonment became a self-fulfilling prophecy. She'd try to prevent people from leaving by grasping so tightly that the very grasp drove them away. Even her "liberation" was an exercise in irony, as she took comfort in Hoss when at odds with Pepper. But Pepper was the liberated one here. Gina wanted to grasp, Pepper wanted to keep everything open. But Pepper's liberation only works in a vacuum. Mix with someone a little less open and stress fractures show up. Mix with someone equally open and then the truth of Gina's position comes out – you really do lose cohesiveness, lose intimacy, and it's just a chaos of one night stands and STDs. So how do you limit your number of partners without being controlling? Who knows? But at least Gina has Hoss for now. He's a good man to take comfort in. Not much of an emotional IQ for relationship nuances but a heart of gold nonetheless. And Gina would never need to take comfort in Pepper because no one was ever at odds with Hoss. Still, it was weird how something could mean two different things at the same time. Having two lovers was an expression of free spirit for Pepper; but for Gina, it was just a failsafe backup in case of abandonment. Is that what sexual liberation was all about? Multiplying dependency under the guise of free spirit? No, Pepper was right, too. Pepper was not dependent. Pepper did not want anyone in a cage. That side of it was also true.

"It's just a little bump, Gina," Ziggy said. "I know it hurts like hell now, but y'all will be alright."

"I know," Gina said. "I just need to let it out."

Zig put his hand on Gina's. "Yeah, let it out."

Zig felt for her, but he was having his own inner struggle with the topic. Just two days ago, he had defended Pepper when Tom criticized her lifestyle. He had defended free love. He, Ziggy, not one to argue, but he'd put it on the line for Pepper. And now she and Gina were proving him wrong.

"I thought y'all were all so happy together," he said, more to himself than to Gina.

Jaz could read Zig's mind. See his confusion. Poor Zig. She saw a flaw in him for the first time. He thought free love meant indiscriminate sex, and indiscriminate sex without complication, and now his hippie idealism was shaken. Little does he know, she thought, that his hippie idealism is not unjustified, but he needs to get his expectations in sync with his idealism. She liked the sound of the phrase – "get his expectations in sync with his idealism" – that should be written down somewhere. But here she was, Jazmine, finding flaws in Ziggy. It was weird. She was serious back at Saul's Den when she told Zig she was incapable of judging. When she met other people, people who were judgmental, it always mystified her. It was like she was born without that piece of her brain. But here she was. Maybe she could see flaws without being judgmental. Maybe that's what she needed to learn about herself. Maybe that was her gift.

The back screen door of the Duck slammed, and Ragman stood on the back steps in a white T-shirt, stretching his arms out toward the horizon line.

Jazmine thought she saw Ziggy jump. She also thought Gina did not need a gathering crowd at this moment.

"Come on, Gina, let's take a walk to Schiro's."

Rag approached the table as the two young women took to the grassy alley between the Duck and the Island.

"Rag, I need to talk to you," said Ziggy, all focus now.

"Shoot," said Rag.

"There's shit happening out there, Rag, something building."

"Like what?"

"Suspicious guys. Cops hanging around. Plainclothes cop was watching Beachbum's house the other day. I thought it was about Beachbum. But today, the same cop shows up watching the Magic Mushroom. Wherever I go, cops, troublemakers, something."

"You selling drugs, Zig?

"No."

"You know how many people smoke pot, Zig. They're not gonna stake you out for that. They might bust you on a whim, but they're not going to invest manpower. Unless there's something else."

Well, Zig thought, there was the induction letter. No use tiptoeing around it. Better to just blast it out there.

"Burning an induction letter at a public scene. Does that count as something else?"

He braced himself for some sense of shock. Maybe Rag would feel betrayed that Ziggy had kept this secret from him. Maybe Rag would think he had done the wrong thing, had drawn the wrong kind of attention to the whole Co-op scene. Ziggy thought again of his words to Lombardi – "they're not my friends" – and how he later felt guilty, like they were the words of one who had denied his own people.

But Ragman's face showed no emotion, no surprise.

"Yeah, Zig, I know about that. But there too. Do you know how many people skip out on the draft? And how many people actually get prosecuted? Maybe if you were Muhammad Ali. But you're small potatoes. I'm not saying it's nothing. Sure, it might bite you in the ass if you apply for a government job, but …"

"But wait," Zig cut him off. Zig was losing Rag's train of thought. He could only focus on one thing right now. "How did you know about the induction letter?"

"Saul told me."

Ok, Zig thought, this is something new. Saul had said something too. He couldn't remember what, but it vaguely hinted that he, Saul, and Rag were growing closer, that they were in on something together. Was Ziggy imagining this? Maybe he should feel Ragman out on this.

"I'm not so sure about Saul," Ziggy said. "Something's not right about him."

Ragman smiled. "You sure you're not jealous of Saul hanging out with Jazmine."

Ziggy was stunned but also confused and a little hurt.

"No, Rag, I wouldn't … I mean, yeah I don't want Jaz to get into a bad scene, but that wouldn't give me this sort of misgiving. Anyway Jaz is free to do what she wants."

Zig found himself avoiding eye contact, but Rag was close in, fixing him with those hazel eyes.

"Zig, you don't know your own mind, but it's cool, it's coming, man. You got such a deep moral compass. You don't know that either, but as your compass comes into your mind, into your conscious mind, you're what the new age is going to be all about. I'm out there. I know I'm on the radar. My days are numbered. You're under the radar, Zig. Under the skin too. You don't need philosophy, Zig. You're a natural. You see the personal side, the human value in everything. You don't see yourself that way because you think everybody's like that. But everybody's not." Rag stopped short.

Ziggy felt several emotions pass. He was agitated by the intensity of Rag's gaze; he felt the weight of Rag's compliment; he still wasn't sure how Rag's relationship to Saul figured in. But he definitely did not want to talk about his feelings for Jazmine, whatever they were. And he didn't want to talk about himself. So he turned back to Saul with concentrated attention.

"But, Rag, what if Saul's the rat? Somehow behind this weird thing building."

Rag pulled a needle-thin joint from his pocket and rolled it between his thumb and forefinger.

"Have a toke, Zig?" he asked.

Zig was beat. He put his elbow on the table and rested his forehead in his hand.

"No, Rag, I don't want a toke. Not now."

It was Rag's turn to reach out in comfort. He patted the arm that held Zig's head. He gently squeezed the narrow wrist.

"Saul's no rat, Zig."

"How do you know?"

Rag lit the pin joint for his own benefit, took a deep drag, then exhaled.

"I know."

But Ziggy wasn't so sure.

Chapter 11

Just as it had one week ago, on that Wednesday morn after the hippies had danced and drunk and sung their hymns of planetary awakening through the night in the Co-op yard, another Wednesday sun rose over the still houses of the Faubourg Marigny. The neighborhood was quiet. Equally quiet was the solitary figure who had seated himself on the levee at the river end of the Faubourg. The dark green of the levee grass yielded to wilder vegetation where the river eternally lapped at the banks. A drift of morning fog still lay over the river itself, making dreamwork of the gigantic sea-going ships as they jutted in massive fragments out of the fog and into the visual field. The seated figure seemed compact, folded into himself, but he was not disturbed when a second figure, long-limbed and sinewy, approached and sat next to him. Neither felt obligated to speak, and they sat for a minute, as great blue herons darted in and out of the dream marked out by the fog line. Then the second figure pulled his wavy black locks into a pony tail holder and spoke.

"What you thinking about, Rag?"

"Jazmine."

The two let the quiet morning absorb them again. Ziggy was aware of how few words needed to pass between them, bonded as they were like brothers, and was aware of the proximity between this silent connection and the so-called meaning of life. He was reminded of that song again: *We bled inside each other's wounds.*

"You know Owsley?" asked Rag.

Zig continued to gaze at the lush marsh vegetation at the water's edge, but his lip curled slightly at the conflicting associations the name raised for him.

"Owsley. I think he's either a comic book villain or the LSD-maker in California."

"The LSD-maker," Rag said, without noticing or seconding Ziggy's smile. "The guru of all gurus on the chemistry side. The electric kool-aid acid tests with Ken Kesey and the Pranksters and the Grateful Dead. It was all

160

Owsley's acid. The whole Haight-Ashbury scene blossomed on Owsley's acid."

Rag's tone indicated that this was serious business. Ziggy felt guilty for having smiled at it all.

"I have to go see Owsley," Rag continued, with lips taut and jaw tight, as if he were going into battle.

"I know, man," Zig said. "The tan acid. It's not working out."

"So close," Rag said.

Ziggy heard something unusual in Rag's voice: longing or wistfulness, something sad.

"So close," said Ziggy, upbeat. If the words as Rag had uttered them reflected a missed opportunity slipping hopelessly into the past, Zig used them to the opposite effect, as if they were on the cusp of a breakthrough. "Easy in, easy out, gets you under the fake stage set of everyday life. This could still be the turn-on everybody needs, Rag. The Age of Aquarius."

"That's what I thought, Zig. But you yourself straightened me out."

"Me?"

"It's not about the Age of Aquarius you said. It's about Jazmine. What's it doing for her? What's it doing *to* her?"

Zig was once again chastened by the thought. It was Rag's turn to feel a little guilty as he saw Ziggy's face fall. He jiggled Ziggy's elbow.

"It's OK, brother. I just have to go see Owsley and sort out where to go from here. On the chemical side, at least."

"So California?"

"No, Denver. He's at Tim Scully's setup in Denver.

"How long you gonna be gone?"

"Just a few days."

161

They heard the deep boom of a steam freighter horn on the river, and they could hear the water lap and stir at the banks. Then the fog lifted suddenly, and in a moment they could see short stout brightly colored tug boats zipping between the enormous ships.

"What about Saul, Rag?"

"What about him?"

"Even if he's not a rat, like you said, he's still trouble. Jaz heard him talking about burning a recruitment center or …"

"Or an ROTC building," Rag added.

"You know?" said Ziggy in shock. "And you're not going to do anything about it?"

"What do you want me to do?"

Zig hadn't really thought about that. "I don't know," he said morosely.

The young men sat watching the gulls gather behind the tug boats.

"But things are getting heavy," Zig added.

"Then why don't you do something, Ziggy."

"Me!?" Ziggy hadn't thought about that either. "I don't know. I guess I'm not ready yet."

"Well then I guess we have to let Saul do his trip," replied Rag.

At this point, Ziggy noticed a vehicle that had pulled over at the side of the levee: a Chevrolet carry-all, stop sign red. It looked like a pickup truck in the front and a station wagon in the back.

"Hey, Rag, is that Mr. Anthony's carry-all?"

Rag came out of his reverie, turned toward the vehicle, and smiled.

"Yeah, that's Mr. Anthony. He's driving me to the airport in that thing, but then he said we can keep it as long as we need it. Since his daughter went to Italy, he just putts

162

around in her Rambler Classic with the carry-all truck just sitting there."

Ragman stood and waved to Mr. Anthony, but Ziggy remained seated.

"What about Saul, Rag? It's this Sunday, man, just a few days away. The same day the Kesey and the Pranksters are supposedly coming through. What if you're not back?"

"I'll definitely be back," said Rag, eye-to-eye with Zig, decisively. Then he turned and sprang down the levee like a mountain goat.

Ziggy laid back on the grass. The sun was full out now. One of those fine April days in New Orleans, not too hot, not too cold, but some element of change in the air. Had he been too aggravated with Ragman lately, pushing him too hard? Did he sound belligerent? Was it *he*, Ziggy, who was becoming like Saul? No, he was cool. Rag was cool. But Ziggy could not so easily shake his uneasiness. Ragman knew too much. He knew about Ziggy's letter of induction. How? From Saul. He knew about the scheme coming up to burn the ROTC building. How? From Saul. "Let Saul do his trip," Ragman had said. The more Ziggy thought about it, the more troubled he was. What did Rag mean – "I'll definitely be back" – was he in on it with Saul? Maybe Rag really thought Saul had the answers. After all, it was like Saul said. We're all on the same side. We'd all rather go non-violently into the next age. But we have to react to the enemy's terms. Violent oppression requires violent resistance. What if Rag really did go that way? Would Ziggy follow him? Or would he stick to the core ideals of the Co-op. The outdated, hopeless fucking ideals of non-violent revolution. But once upon a time – at the Tree of Life – Ragman had argued eloquently for those ideals.

Stretched out, hands behind his head, Ziggy watched isolated clouds floating past and smelled the earthy smells coming up from the river bank. He heard another horn blow and recognized it as the sound of the Algiers Ferry. In a half-slumber, he heard the lapping of the water but it was no longer the river. It was a pond, a secret pond from thousands of years ago, when gods and goddesses laughed and roamed fields of giant clover to the monotonous throb of primeval honeybees. It was night. The lapping of water continued. The stars were the same then as they are now, but the constellations were different. A young woman was with him, at the pond, listening to the lap, lap of the night water. Was it Jazmine? He couldn't say. She dipped her hand in the water as if to study an undersea plant or fish, and he dove in to do something but then he couldn't remember what. And when he came up, the constellations had changed into Virgo and Scorpio and big and little dippers. The old cosmos was gone. That quickly a new age had begun, a human age of quiet hunger and missed connections. Dark and silent, he and she retreated into the ferns and mosses and heavy branches, the moon more lovely and distant than ever. He felt her hand still wet with the possibilities of that lost moment.

A steamship whistle blew and Ziggy started. An hour or a year or a thousand years might have passed since Ragman left with Mr. Anthony. Clouds had begun to retake the sky. Ziggy saw a figure coming up the levee, dazed, disheveled, holding herself with her own arms, like a bundle, black hair outstretched as if it were floating on water. Was he dreaming? She stopped suddenly and sunk into the grass. She seemed confused. That orange top. It was Jazmine. Ziggy came full awake at once and rushed down the slope of the levee.

"Jaz, what is it? What's wrong?"

She looked at him with glazed eyes. "Jeremiah," she whispered.

"Who? What? Jazmine?"

164

"Who?" The question floated in her mind. Who was she looking at? Who was holding her by the shoulders? Ziggy. It was Ziggy. Oh God, now she remembered.

"Tex," she said.

"Tex what, Jazmine? What's wrong?"

"Tex is dead."

It was as if a thunderbolt hit Ziggy. He could not move. He could not think. Then his mind started racing.

"What do you mean, Tex is dead? He can't be dead. He was sitting in the yard teaching himself that Otis Redding song yesterday."

Jaz was coming back to life. "That was yesterday, Zig. "Today they found him. Somewhere. In the French Quarter."

Ziggy's mind was spinning. Could it be possible? Could it be a mistake? From the corner of his eye, he saw another figure drifting down North Peters Street. As he peered across the distance, he noticed that the day had become gray and dreary, the sun concealed by a fresh heave of clouds. The approaching figure seemed lost, and she was calling: "Jazmine, Jazmine." The figure turned up the levee. It was Pepper but her red complexion had turned to ash. In the presence of two people who loved her, Jazmine let herself glide back down into oblivion.

"Pepper," said Zig. "Tex. Where is he?"

Pepper was all ash and steel.

"Gone," she said.

"What the fuck," was all Zig could get out.

Pepper sat. Ziggy sat next to her. Pepper gently pulled Jazmine down to rest in her own lap, and worked her fingers through the rich sable locks. Pepper visibly normalized her breathing, and everyone started to relax just a little.

165

"It's true," Pepper said. "He was sitting at the bar at the Drunken Monk drinking a Jack and Coke." She breathed in, then out. "Then he just dropped off the stool."

"People just don't drop off the stool," said Ziggy, in genuine confusion.

"Quaaludes," Pepper said. "OD'd on Quaaludes."

"I didn't know Tex did Quaaludes."

"Tex was always out there making noise and mixing it up with people, but he kept shit to himself too," was Pepper's response.

"How did you … did you see him?"

"I heard and ran over from the voodoo shop. There he was on the floor. People staring. I held his hand and he looked at me. Then the EMS guys got there."

"Did he say anything?"

"No, but I could see it in his eyes. He knew what was happening."

Ziggy and Pepper thought about that for a minute. Jazmine had closed her eyes and wrapped herself in her own thoughts.

"Funny thing," Pepper finally said to Zig. "One of the EMS guys was the square that Tex almost got in a fight with that day about the saints cards. The bald guy with the bowling ball head."

"Did he know who y'all were?"

"Yeah, he knew. He seemed to work harder than anybody else to get Tex stable and into the ambulance. Then he looked at me before they drove off, and I could see what he already knew – that he could try, try, try, but Tex wasn't coming back."

"Why was the square downtown with a suit that day?" asked Zig. Somehow an EMS guy in a suit downtown did not make sense. And if that didn't make sense, none of this made sense. Zig vaguely felt that if he could unravel one

166

thread in the tale as bogus, then the whole story could be bogus. Tex could be back at the Co-op blasting Neil Young's "Cinnamon Girl" or Sly and the Family Stone through the windows at maximum volume, driving the neighbors crazy.

"I don't know," Pepper said. "Court case maybe. Applying for jobs. Who knows."

Of course, Pepper was right. What did it matter why the square was downtown in a suit? Tex was dead. It finally registered for Ziggy.

* * *

The next day, Thursday, was a dead day. Both houses of the Co-op stumbled through in a timeless daze. The sun rose and set over the empty picnic table in the yard. The moon rose stark and indifferent. Nothing happened because it was as though nothing existed. As if nothing had ever existed.

Despite the siren call of oblivion, Friday was a painful recall to life and to the bizarre human rituals surrounding that final passage upon which Tex had preceded his Co-op fellows. The funeral home had a Mediterranean tile roof and a flat, sprawling sandstone exterior. Broad stone steps between potted palms led up to the archway of the entrance. A pristine, gold-carpeted common area had rounded arches on each wall with name tags indicating the private wakes of the various deceased. It was a little out of element for the St. Roch crew, but Tex's family in Mississippi had arranged everything, and quickly too, since Tex's younger brother was to be deployed tomorrow with the Army 1st Cavalry LRPs.

"Aaron Hodges," read Tex's name tag. It was weird, Ziggy thought, that Tex had a real name. Aaron Hodges. Tex Whittaker – where in the world had "Whittaker" come from

167

– was also Aaron Hodges. It sounded like a different identity. Was the person in the coffin Aaron Hodges or Tex. How could we be sure of anyone's identity, even our own? Stormy and Hoss sat in a corner across the room from the casket. The casket, a mahogany box with silver trim, also struck Ziggy as weird. He was leaning on Jazmine. She had come through as the strong one today. Gina had the flu and Pepper had stayed home to watch Rose Petal.

A stoical woman with iron-gray hair sat closer to the casket. Tex's mother, thought Zig. Next to her stood her younger son, equally stoical, with a posture and expression obviously inherited on the maternal side. The father seemed a quiet man but more emotional, barely holding it together. Who were these people, Zig wondered. They loved Tex as much or more than anyone in the St. Roch crew could claim to do, but they did so from some alternative universe, completely unrelated to his world, the world of Jazmine and Pepper and Ragman. Had anyone told Ragman? Did anyone even know how to reach him in Denver? Ziggy couldn't think about it.

Mr. Anthony had arrived in a simple, outdated, but dignified suit. His battleship-gray eyes had an elegiac look, but he was the only one who seemed to know what to do. He walked the rounds, comforting people and making of them a cohesive group. Then he sat with the Hodges family.

Ziggy's stomach was in a knot. He certainly did not know what to do and was grateful for Mr. Anthony. At least most everyone looked reasonably dignified. Just then a black man walked in, and the knot tightened in Ziggy's stomach. It was not that he was black. The hippies were oblivious to race in this context. They were saved from racism, as Stormy had intuited back in '67, not by political savvy but by political innocence. Untutored into this or that posture of political belligerence by liberal or conservative ideologues,

168

they simply treated everyone equal by default. What alarmed Ziggy was rather the black man's get-up. He was short, about 5 foot 6, but with his tight 'fro that shot straight up about 6 inches, with his purple velour jacket with wide lapels, with the squeally laugh that came out as he introduced himself to Hoss and Stormy, Zig feared that he might cut a comical figure and somehow scandalize the Mississippi family. Jazmine must have feared the same, because she instinctively took the moment to go introduce herself to Tex's family. Ziggy was relieved. Jazmine was the perfect interface for the Co-op group. Long-haired male hippies might elicit fear or contempt from the small-town Mississippi folk, and Hoss would probably offer them a pot brownie in heartfelt condolence. But Jazmine was sweet, cool, she knew how to act. That purity of heart would cut through any demographic wall.

Alone and self-conscious, Ziggy approached Hoss and Stormy and the new mourner.

"Hey Zig," croaked Hoss. He was trying to tone down the normally robust volume of his voice but at the same time pull it back up from a whisper. So what he achieved was a croak.

"Meet Catfish." Catfish's smile flashed a gold tooth, a somewhat common accoutrement Zig had noticed among African-American friends, although whether its significance was historical or merely aesthetic was a mystery to him. Ziggy could now see that under the purple jacket was a T-shirt that featured a dark image of a B-52 bomber with the words, "Fly the Friendly Skies of Laos and Cambodia."

Catfish grasped Ziggy's forearm with affection. Ziggy grasped back and the two men stood for a moment in a symbolic arm-to-arm embrace.

169

"Ziggy. I be damned." Catfish's smile would not let up. "Tex told me about you. He loved you, man. He said you were his flower child king."

Ziggy blushed at the compliment, but he could already tell he liked Catfish.

"Catfish was in Nam with Tex," Hoss said.

Ziggy was taken aback.

"I didn't know Tex was in Viet Nam."

"There was that side to Tex," Stormy chimed in. "I knew that white boy redneck kept too much to himself." She stopped suddenly. Her playful interjection had reminded her too much of her own affection for Tex. She held in her tears.

"Yeah, Zig," Catfish continued, as if he and Ziggy were old friends, and indeed in a sense they were, although they had never met.

"Some vets don't like to talk about it. Tex and I were at Lo Ke when the Vietcong 9th Division attacked. Then lots of small-scale stuff north of Saigon. It's the small-scale stuff that freaks you out though. More than the big battles. The small-scale shit is so intimate. That's the shit you remember."

"That T-shirt," Stormy said. "Is that in memory of the small-scale shit?"

Catfish busted another great big grin. "No, babe, I'm out. But this is a gift from my cousin still in. You know that United Airlines jingle: Fly the Friendly Skies of United?"

Stormy nodded.

"Laos and Cambodia are neutral. Off limits. Nixon can't send us there, right?"

"Right."

"So the air force guys in Nam getting shot at. They must all want to fly the friendly skies of Laos and Cambodia, right?"

"Right."

170

"Wrong! Hahaha. The guys over there know we're bombing the shit out of Cambodia. The more Nixon says we ain't, the more we know we are. There ain't no friendly skies in Laos and Cambodia. That's the joke. Hahaha."

Zig and Hoss and Stormy saw the irony, but it didn't seem so funny to them. Maybe you had to be on the inside, like Catfish, to really get a laugh out of it. Maybe you had to earn that laugh.

"Why didn't Tex tell us any of this?" pondered Ziggy out loud.

"You're a good brother," Catfish said to Zig, feeling the confidence between them. "But it's a special bond when you're over there together. I know you guys have a special bond in the Scene you're in, too. I can dig that, man. I'm with you guys. But when you're in Nam together man, it's not like any other bond."

Things were getting a bit somber, and Catfish poked at the guitar case that Hoss had brought in just in case.

"Play us a tune, brother,"

"I don't know," Hoss croaked sheepishly. "I mean, this is not my gig. I don't know if everybody would like it." He gestured to the Hodges family.

"Well shit," said Catfish, and walked straight toward the family. Ziggy was apprehensive. He already knew and trusted Catfish completely, as if he had known and trusted him for all time, but he didn't know how the family might take to the black man with the stand-up 'fro and gold tooth, wearing a purple velour jacket and a vaguely irreverent T-shirt at their son's funeral, and now approaching them with foolhardy self-assurance.

"Excuse me, ma'am," said Catfish to the mother. "I know y'all don't know your son's local friends too well but they loved him with all their hearts. I know they're not family, mind you, but their love was real. Do you mind if his friend over there plays a couple of quiet songs on the guitar?"

The mother nodded and sobbed. Stoical or not, she could not speak just now. The younger son did not know what to say.

The father stepped in with a cracked voice. "God bless you, young man. You and all my son's friends. Y'all pay whatever respects y'all want."

Just when it looked like he was home free, Catfish turned to the younger son of the family, the one holding to his poker face, the one who would wake up one day soon in Viet Nam.

Catfish held out his hand.

"Robert Jasper Hill, 28th Infantry Division," he said sharply.

The younger son took his hand and beamed, eyes filling with tears.

"Your brother was a good man. A great man to serve with. You're about to join a band of brothers like you never knew you had. Take every day to make them proud."

The young man nodded, still biting back tears. He looked about to break. Catfish wrapped his arms around him with a force that belied his 5 foot 6 frame. The two hugged for several seconds, then Catfish stepped back.

"Th-thank you," the boy said weakly. Then with a final restorative handshake, the boy stepped back and Catfish joined the hippie contingent across the room.

Hoss took the guitar from the case as if it were a fragile artifact. He strummed a chord, then hit the lovely, soothing string of notes that set up the lyrics of a Melanie song. Stormy stepped in with the vocals:

> Beautiful people
> You live in the same world as I do

But somehow I never noticed
You before today

Ziggy gazed out the window, letting the sentiments of the song wash over him. Speckled black birds pecked in the green expanse of grass that extended out from the building to the busy street, which seemed far away.

We never met before
But then
We may never meet again

Out on the street, in the distance, a black sedan pulled up and let a well-dressed older couple out at the curb. Then Ziggy noticed other cars, of various makes and models and conditions, picking up mourners or letting them out. A skinny kid was getting into a broken-down Plymouth. Something odd. The skinny kid looked back toward the funeral home window. Beachbum! It was Beachbum! Ziggy started for the door but stopped immediately. The Plymouth was already gone. But Beachbum! Why was he here? And if he was here for Tex, why hadn't he and Jazmine and the group seen him?

Ziggy was in a cold sweat. Jazmine returned to join the hippies, calmly, steadily, but Ziggy could tell by her look. She too had seen Beachbum through the window.

If I weren't afraid you'd laugh at me
I would run take all of your hands and
I'd gather everyone together for a day

"Come on," Jaz whispered. "Let's take a walk.
She took Ziggy's hand and they slipped toward the door. There was nothing to say. They were both thinking

173

confused thoughts about Beachbum, but neither could articulate a meaningful question. Neither could say anything that the other was not already thinking. Ziggy felt that Jazmine had it together, that she had taken charge, and he was comforted. He needed that right now. Jazmine too felt herself in the lead. She could feel Ziggy relax into her charge. She could feel his comfort and was happy to be able to offer it. But was it really she who offered it? She felt as if she were pointing Ziggy homeward in his confusion, but she herself was being directed. They stepped through the threshold to the common area and Ziggy stopped. Was it a premonition? The paralysis of emotional exhaustion? Whatever it was, Jazmine could not bear it.

"I need to walk," she whispered, and her whisper brought Ziggy back to life. They walked together, each leading the other around the gold carpet and somber red walls of the common area, the classical flower pots and pedestals. They could still hear Stormy's sweet, raspy voice.

> I'll pass buttons out that say
> Beautiful people
> Then you'd never have to be alone
> 'Cause there'll always be someone
> With the same button on as you

But Jazmine could not take it. The oppression, the sheer atmospheric weight of the common area. She had to escape into one of the other rooms. Not Tex's room. She needed to get to some privacy out of the common area but she also needed anonymity.

> And if you take care of him
> Maybe I'll take care of you

Jaz tugged Ziggy's arm as they passed the threshold to another private room with an ongoing wake. He resisted.

"Zig," was all she said. He could feel the desperation in her voice. His resistance, his trepidation, gave way before her need. They tiptoed in.

The mourners in the room were surprisingly like the mourners in Tex's room. Some well-groomed older folks, some younger hippyish types. But the hippies here seemed edgier, hungrier. Jaz tugged, and she and Ziggy glided slowly toward the casket. Jazmine mentally noted that the casket, unlike Tex's casket, was not mahogany but solid onyx brush silver. "Tex's casket." The very words in her head felt strange. She saw the white fabric from inside the coffin folded over the edge of the open half, forming a white trim on the outside, framing the ... person inside. "There is a body in that box," she thought. She wanted to stop. She felt Ziggy's urge to stop. And yet her body followed its own urge forward. Slowly, with dignity, she and Ziggy moved a smooth, continuous pace along the wall. She felt her eyebrows, her forehead tighten. Someone was in that box. She should not be here. This was not her place. Her hand was cold and sweating in Ziggy's. But he was with her, and it was good. She looked away as they came up over the open casket. She felt Ziggy's hand tense up in hers. She turned. She knew that face. The face in the box. Or she thought she knew.

"Who is it, Zig?" she whispered.

"It's the lanky kid from the beach. The one who talked about Rag and then went all weird. He's not wearing his black frame glasses."

Odd, thought Jaz. That a dead body could wear or not wear glasses.

"But that's him," Ziggy continued.

And then it hit Jazmine.

"Beachbum was here."

Chapter 12

Saturday morning a late April chill was in the air. Jaz sat on the rag-tag couch in the Duck, holding her knees.

"How you holding up?" Ziggy asked. Jaz saw his silhouette framed against the door to the kitchen, the light source behind him. Was he a man, a god, a monster? She needed to choose. It was her choice.

"You're a god," she said. "And I'm here to comfort you." The words sounded strange and she had said them without thinking them. Ziggy tried to take it in stride. He flexed his bicep.

"Sexy, romantic, and ready for revolution," he said.

But Ziggy's words reminded Jazmine of that day with Tex. They brought her back to herself, or what she thought was herself, and she started to cry softly. Zig sat next to her, touching her.

"What is it Jaz, is it Tex?"

"Yeah. No. I mean the Tex thing is part of it. I don't know who I am any more."

"Look, Jaz," Ziggy said firmly. "We're going to get through this. Step 1: No more tan acid."

Jazmine panicked at the thought. "But the tan acid … I think … I don't know … I might need it to find who I am."

Zig could feel both sides of the argument, pushing for and against the tan acid, but he was absolutely clear on which side carried the day.

"I'm serious, Jaz. No more tan acid. Not now. You have to get your shit together."

"But Ragman said …"

"Forget about what Ragman said." Zig was resolute. "Ragman's not here."

"Ragman's not here?" muddled Jaz.

"Don't you remember? He went to Denver."

"Oh yeah," Jaz said. Was she really losing her mind?

Zig put his face close to hers. "No tan acid. This is not about Rag. You and I will get through this, and then you're free to do anything you want. But first we gotta get through this. OK?"

"OK," she said mechanically. "Let me rest."

Ziggy laid her down on the couch. He paced as she dozed. He tried to think. "Fuck, fuck, fuck," was all he could think. He went for a walk. He started toward the newsstand near the Mushroom. Maybe he could browse the magazines or pick up something to distract himself. Maybe a Freak Brothers comic book. No, on second thought, he didn't even want to risk the very small chance that the narcs, or whatever they were, were there. He had enough on his plate. Schiro's. He turned toward Schiro's Grocery for a coffee. Make that a decaf. The friendly houses jutting back and forth, the sparrows hopping beneath an avocado tree, and all the lush April greenery in the Faubourg Marigny calmed him. He could see a few people loitering around Schiro's. So what. Good. He needed to be around people. Strangers. As he stepped in, there was an open area with a pay telephone to the left of the door. Two guys were hanging around there: one with long sideburns and a turtleneck sweater, the other with a polo shirt. He felt eyes looking at him but didn't care. He looked through the small magazine rack. He heard voices. Then he realized they were talking about him.

"… one of the nigger-lovers in that yellow house."

Shit, Ziggy thought. I can't deal with this right now. But I can't let it pass either. He took a deep breath. "Pocket the insult." He remembered the phrase from Gandhi's autobiography, which had made the rounds through the hippie community not long ago. In his moment of hesitation, he caught a sudden movement in the corner of his eye. For a fraction of a second, he thought of it as some kind of giant mythological flying creature swooping for a kill. He looked. Mr. Anthony had left the cash counter and had one foot out of the door when he heard the insult. The boxer's reflexes took over. He had the kid with the turtleneck pressed against the wall with his hand on his throat. Mr. Anthony must have had his thumb and index finger right in those soft spot pressure points under the rear of the jaw, because the kid seemed too terrified even to twitch, as if a wild animal had him by the throat. But Mr. Anthony was no wild animal. He also had the old boxer's presence of mind. He gestured the kid in the polo shirt to leave, and the kid seemed more than happy to take the hint and desert his cohort.

"Them people's my friends," Mr. Anthony said. "You got that?"

"Yes," came the squeak through the turtleneck. Then Mr. Anthony gestured and the kid ran out to join his Judas friend. Mr. Anthony continued out of the door and watched as they slunk away. Mr. Schiro chuckled from behind the counter and the double chin beneath his pear-shaped head shivered like jello.

Zig could not see the humor. Everything was too intense right now, too self-directed. He stumbled back out into the sidewalk sun, thinking. What is going on? What should he, Ziggy, have done? Not long ago, he would have labored over the question. But now he could not even afford that self-indulgence, not with so much going on, with Jazmine, and Tex, and Beachbum. Shit, Beachbum! The hints Uncle Frank had given him about the bust! "A week from today," he had said. That means yesterday, Friday, should have been the bust. But they were all at the funeral. What happened to Beachbum after that funeral?

Then Ziggy remembered the carry-all. He had the keys to the carry-all. In a moment he was driving down St. Claude, then Rampart St., and up St. Charles Avenue toward Pigeon Town. There was Beachbum's house. If possible, the paint looked even worse, the grass wilder, than last week. The place – both sides of the double unit, really – looked deserted and shabbier than ever. The viny resilience of nature seemed to be overtaking the place, as it would one day overtake all the struts and frets of human industry. Ziggy looked across the street. At least the baby-faced spy and his doughboy friend were not gawping from their perch. Ziggy knocked, pounded, trod through the weeds down the alley. Nothing. No sign of Beachbum. No sign of a bust. Maybe Beachbum had been tipped off. Maybe he hadn't been home.

Ziggy had no idea of where to look but pursuit seemed necessary. He puttered off in the carry-all aimlessly and then turned toward Polo's Pizza. Long shot, but he had to drive in some direction. He parked in front of the used record shop, where a few kids were browsing the $1 box on the sidewalk. Inside Polo's, he wondered why he'd even come.

"Hey Rachael," he said to waitress weaving her hips slowly between the mostly empty tables. "You seen Beachbum?"

"Beachbum's long gone," Rachael drawled.

Of course Ziggy already knew that. He looked over at the counter. The counter where Jaz had walked in that day, where he showed off his pizza dough spinning to impress her, where Beachbum honked that stupid snorting laugh. Through the telescope of time, Beachbum seemed like such

179

an innocent kid back then, oblivious to how swift things, and people, fall.

Zig went back out and sat in the carry-all. Where to go? Nowhere. Maybe the nude beach out at the lake. Everything seemed a long shot. Everything seemed arbitrary. The same kids dug through the same records in the same box right there on the sidewalk. But further down the sidewalk, Ziggy's eye caught something. A skinny kid turning the corner from the college drag into the neighborhood. THE skinny kid. Beachbum.

Zig cranked the hoarse engine of the carry-all and lurched forward with a squeak of the wheels. He eased up to the corner and turned. There was the skinny kid up ahead. Ziggy edged up beside him.

"Hey, Beachbum."

It was Beachbum alright, but all the innocence of that night at Polo's Pizza had been drained. He had a worn, glazed, heroin look.

"Hey, Beachbum," louder.

"Who wants to know?" said the skinny kid in Beachbum's body, without looking.

Ziggy slammed on the brakes, parked the carry-all, and got out. He walked in front of Beachbum, cut him off, held his shoulders so he couldn't move.

"Beachbum, do you know who the fuck I am?"

"Ziggy," said the zombie, "Do you think I'm an idiot. I know exactly who you are."

"What does that mean, Beachbum?"

"Stay away from me, man." Beachbum broke loose and the two walked side-by-side.

"You think I'm out to get you, Beachbum?"

"Everybody's out to get me."

"You're sick, man. You're fucking sick. What are you high on?"

"Pizza, pot, heroin. What does it matter? Why do you care?"

"Beachbum, listen to me. Whatever you're holding. You gotta get rid of it. Have you seen any cops yesterday or today? Or anyone suspicious?"

"What do you know about the cops?" countered Beachbum. "Maybe you're the suspicious one."

"Beachbum, listen. I heard you were on a bust list. Don't worry about where. Now what are you holding?"

Beachbum's eyes half-closed and he swayed as if he might fall.

"Fuck," exclaimed Ziggy. He led Beachbum back to the carry-all and wrestled him into the passenger seat, which was quite easy since he encountered no resistance from his charge. Ziggy paced quickly around the truck front to the driver's side and got it. He looked over. Beachbum had a vacant smile on his face.

Ziggy started driving. Where? Anywhere. Just go. Vaguely toward St. Roch. As they cruised down St. Charles Avenue, Beachbum, still smiling vacantly, leaned his head out the window to feel the wind ripple across his face and hair. Sweet oblivion. That was the only thing left for him to appreciate.

Bubble lights came up behind Zig. Ziggy's thought his heart would explode. Do not have a breakdown, he told himself. Not now. He pulled over and the police car whizzed by. Ziggy stayed parked.

"Beachbum, I swear to fucking god, what are you holding right now?"

Beachbum smiled at Zig.

"Packet of smack."

"Let me see it."

"Not right here, Ziggy, you sweet, beautiful thing. I got nothing right here."

"Nothing at all."

"Nothing."

Beachbum pulled his pockets inside out in a symbolic show of honesty. Ziggy would have to trust him on that for now.

"Beachbum, why did you quit Polo's?"

"What you said, Ziggy, my man. Cops looking for me."

"You're not thinking straight, Beachbum. Quitting your job doesn't magically make the cops go away!" Ziggy was getting frustrated. Cool down, man. Cool.

"Get the fuck away from me and stay away," was Beachbum's reply.

OK. What to do? Don't get Beachbum worked up. Zig eased back into the traffic lane and started for the Co-op. Crossing Canal Street, onto Rampart and then St. Claude, approaching the Faubourg Marigny.

"You want to go to the Co-op, Beachbum?"

"No."

"We'll take care of you but first we have to get rid of your stash. All of it, no matter where it is. Now if it's at your house, tell me. If it's on you, tell me."

"Nothing on me," said Beachbum. And then he started to panic. "Nothing, man. I got nothing here. Where are you taking me?"

"Shh, shh, Beachbum." Zig slammed on the brakes. He'd almost run a red light. Someone behind him blew the horn. Beachbum jumped out of the car and started running back toward the traffic. Ziggy put the car in park. Beachbum wobbled across the sidewalk and turned a corner into the French Quarter. Zig opened his door to get out. The car behind him blew the horn. Then another car blew the horn. Shit, the light was green. Ziggy got back in, slammed the door and drove onward, disillusioned, self-loathing, toward the Co-op. He had to get to the bottom of this. He was at the Co-op only briefly before he decided what he had to do. He would go back to Beachbum's house. If no one was there, he'd sleep there in the dark and wait for Beachbum – or whomever. He took a padlock and a dish towel to crack through a window, if necessary, to get in.

That night, an early season heat wave rolled in from the Gulf, breaking against the houses and street lights and drunken R&B joints of the city, washing over the junkies and squares, the noble dreamers and desperate angels and uncertain hippies, sweeping all chill from the air and leaving only salt humidity behind. Predictably, Beachbum's house was desolate. Ziggy tapped and cracked a window and slid out the pane. He cut his palm, but no big deal, he scooted in and held the towel over it for a minute. No problem. There was no wound. From that point forward, he tossed and turned on a scruffy mattress on the floor, confused, concerned, but not beaten. Never beaten.

* * *

The sun rose in a near-summer swelter. Sundays did not see so much activity through the mid-morning hours, and this Sunday the city seemed reluctant to stir and face the premonition of summer. One could hear, though, the creak and swing of van door on a side street near the college. A man wearing white painter's bib overalls, hard hat and boots pulled a five-gallon bucket from the rear door of the van. He looked for all the world like a one-man construction crew. But he was not a construction crew. He was Saul. He carefully stocked each element of his supplies in the bucket: a small hammer to crack through the windows, hard plastic fuel bottles of kerosene, a sack of rags to toss on the floor. Railroad flares to light the curtains. He smiled his stingilygiven smile. He had impressed even himself with the compact but comprehensive stash of supplies. Two blue jays darted around a mimosa tree in a courtship ritual in a grassy yard by the truck. Saul marveled at the chips of flying color, blue and black and white. The beauty of nature. He sat back down in the open trunk of the van, giving himself a moment's break to enjoy the scene, and to think about things.

In a neighborhood not far away, Ziggy was as disgusted as Saul was exhilarated. No Beachbum, no spies, no peep of life at the Pigeon Town shotgun. The quiet was eerie. This was not a good quiet. This was not the quiet of tranquility. He stretched his long arms and legs. He ratcheted his fingers through his hair. He went to the sink to throw water on his face. No water. Shit, even the water was turned off. How did all this happen so quickly? Who knows, but Ziggy could feel a point of no return being crossed. He got into the carry-all, cranked the throaty Chevrolet engine, and steered into the street and back toward Carrollton Avenue. This was not his normal route, but there was a coffee shop near the curve of the streetcar line there where he could get himself together. Then he would go back and get Jazmine. Beachbum may have faded away, but Saul was making his presence known somewhere. Ziggy would get Jazmine and they would go to the ROTC center. Maybe they could talk some sense into Saul. Maybe they could work something out. It was risky, but maybe they could be of some use on the scene. Dodging was definitely not the answer. Ziggy knew that now. He saw the façade of the coffee shop and pulled out of the traffic lane.

Back on his side street staging area, Saul threw his work gloves into the bucket and slammed the swinging doors at the back of the van shut. Back to business. He crossed the street to the campus and started walking the route through

184

the buildings toward the ROTC center. Sunday morning on campus was always dead quiet. But Saul was uneasy. The quiet was not complete. Sound came through the distance, voices. What the fuck! Well, maybe just a few frat boys puking their way home from an overnight party. No reason to believe anyone would be around the ROTC building. No reason to believe anyone would be watching. And who gives a shit anyway? He was doing this for them, wasn't he?

Saul rested the bucket on the ground momentarily. Then he saw a familiar figure about forty yards ahead around the turn of a building. Ragman. Saul picked up the bucket, thought better of it, switched it to the other hand, and walked steadily on. The figure of Ragman gestured, encouraging Saul forward. But the frat boy voices did not go away. Saul was confused, but followed Ragman's gestures. When they were close enough to speak without shouting, Ragman spoke in a low tone: "Ready, man. More ready than you think."

Saul thought it best not to converse, or indeed to make any unnecessary noise that might attract attention, so he just turned the corner by the building with Ragman and stepped onto the last leg of the route to the ROTC building. Now he could see the building itself. But the voices had grown to a chorus. Something was happening. Saul did not like the odd grin on Ragman's face. Whatever was happening was happening *at* the ROTC building. Saul set down his bucket. No, he picked it up again. He had to see what was happening. Something like snowflakes or foam had settled on and around the base of the ROTC building, and a small group of students had gathered. No, it wasn't foam. It was flowers. Someone had dumped truckloads of flowers – red, yellow, blue, white – at the base of the building. It was like the ROTC building itself were sprouting, growing out of a topsoil made of flowers.

185

Saul looked at Ragman. "What the fuck, Rag?! We were going to burn this fucker down!"

Ragman smiled benignly. "Just couldn't do it, brother."

Between perplexity and despair, Saul stared blankly into his bucket of supplies, as if he might find there some solution to his perplexity.

"But Rag. What the fuck?! Flowers?! Really?! Where the fuck did you get truckloads of flowers?"
"I still got a few friends."

Saul hung his head. He did not even know where to go with the conversation.

"Don't worry, man," Rag said. "I owe some big favors for this. It wasn't easy."

More students drifted up, relishing what seemed to them a quite spontaneous happening in the general drift toward a new age of new values, of peace and love and flowers. In any event, it was a cool affair for a Sunday. The voices gained volume and coagulated into song. Someone spontaneously showed up with a guitar and started picking. They went into the anti-war song that Country Joe and the Fish had sung at Woodstock.

> Now come on all of you big strong men
> Uncle Sam needs your help again
> Got himself in a terrible jam
> Way down yonder in Viet Nam
> Put down your books and pick up a gun
> We're gonna have a whole lot of fun

The gathering crowd, laughing, dancing, was more than ready to join in the chorus.

And it's one two three

186

What are we fighting for?
Don't ask me, I don't give a damn,
Next stop is Viet Nam,
And it's five six seven
Open up the pearly gates
Well, there ain't not time to wonder why
Whoopie! We're all gonna die!

Saul was still torn between quiet disappointment and seething rage.

"Come on, man," Rag teased. "It's not that bad. Fire up a joint and mingle in. Flowers, not guns, man. These kids are doing your dirty work for you."

As if "dirty work" were a cue, Saul was tempted to spit in Ragman's face. But he just glared. Then he picked back up his bucket and stormed off toward the van.

Jazmine had spent the hours after Ziggy went off to Beachbum's Saturday night gathering her own scattered energies. She avoided people. She sat in the yard when no one was there. She moved to the kitchen when the yard was taken. She needed perspective. Her life was good. Despite some sliding, she was still getting decent grades in the Marketing program. As soon as the thought completed itself, though, she blushed. She was proud and ashamed at the same time. Academic success was no mean feat, but there was the other thing, the hippie thing. She felt like she had been swept up into something larger than herself, something that could change the world. And somehow her marketing studies was a Judas kiss to that beautiful social revolution. But that wasn't why her energy was scattered. Sure, there was some unresolved tension there, but really, she knew it was the tan acid. Her identity was breaking apart, compartmentalizing, becoming like those many atomic bits of stained glass she had seen on her first trip. But she was

187

coming to know herself better also. Scattered as she was, she could feel a sense of enlightenment, although she couldn't quite get her arms around it. What was this tan acid experience? Definitely not just visions of history. The German stuff, yes, but Olympian gods the size of mountains? Does that blow the akashic record theory? The Greek stuff – or some of it – was not lives lived past, present, or future. It's mythology, for God's sake. Maybe that part was personal unconscious. Maybe Zig was the most right of all when he asked why it couldn't be both – an opening up of the personal unconscious and of some historical consciousness. She liked the thought of Ziggy being more right than brashly assertive Pepper or quiet genius Ragman. She let herself smile, then went back to thinking.

Stormy and Rose Petal came into the kitchen. Jazmine went to the bathroom. She looked in the mirror. She could feel – and she could see – the toll taken on her own body and mind. Maybe she should not reveal the full toll? After all, she hadn't even told anyone about the vision of Prometheus and the rock. No one had asked. Why tell anyone anything? She could trust that Rag would not go foolishly forward until things were sure. No need to tell him on that score. Zig would worry. He was such a carefree guy – or he used to be – but Jaz was not blind to the protective instinct that she sometimes elicited in him. But was she really protecting Ragman and Ziggy from anything they didn't know? Maybe there was another reason she kept the Greek thing to herself. Maybe Rebecca was right. A woman must keep some power to her own bosom. Jazmine may as well admit it. But that weird thing about Rebecca's lip? Jazmine looked back to the bathroom mirror. She pinched her lip to see if it would bleed like Rebecca's. She felt dizzy.

Ziggy had reached the Co-op on St. Roch Sunday mid-morning, still planning to team up with Jaz and run over

188

to the ROTC building. But when he walked through the door, he could tell something was going on. Something that would scuttle his plan. Voices in the bathroom. Pepper stepped from the bathroom and greeted Ziggy.

"It's OK, Zig, she slipped and cut her lip on the sink. It's no big deal."

This unusual introduction gave Ziggy a definite idea that it was a big deal. He opened the bathroom door and nearly cried. It was only two stitches in her lower lip, but the cross stitches of black thread struck him as gruesome, as a marker of the undeserved cruelty of the universe, a dark-side duplicate of the sad black lashes over her eyes.

"It's OK, Zig. I feel better now," Jazmine said calmly. Ziggy wrapped his arms around her.

"No more tan acid," he said.

"Rag's back in town," Jaz replied.

Zig no longer saw the relevance of that datum in this context.

"No more tan acid," he repeated. And that was all he could say.

"OK, Zig," she said, and kissed his cheek.

"I do feel better though. Pepper and I are going out for a late breakfast. You wanna come?"

"No thanks. I got my own thing. You sure you OK?"

"I'm sure."

Ziggy wondered how so much could happen at once. Was it some secret rite of passage, some plan laid for them by the gods? It was a coincidence, that's for sure. But why not? Things can't stay childhood-smooth all the way through. Something's got to fuck up. But it would not fuck *him* up. He needed at least to get to the bottom of the Beachbum thing. He would go to that Falstaff bar by Uncle Frank's. The so-called cops would be hanging out there for Sunday sports in their idiot male bonding rituals. He would just ask them point blank. What could he lose? He wasn't holding any drugs. At least let them know they're not going to pull shit with no push-back. He may be right, he may be wrong, but Zig went back to the carry-all and cranked her up.

The Falstaff Beer sign looked all forlorn with no one sitting at the picnic benches. Zig got out of the carry-all and paced around the exterior of the small building. What to do? That they were open was clear. Voices from the interior rose and fell. Ziggy stepped in. It was dark, and it took a few seconds for his eyes to adjust. Two middle-aged men sat at the bar talking to the bartender, who nodded to Ziggy as if in greeting.

"Can I get you something, young fella?"

"No. Just looking for a friend."

"Bad bunch of friends you got if you looking for 'em here," quipped the barman, gaining a weak chuckle from his two patrons.

Ziggy swung the door and stepped back out. When his eyes readjusted to the sunlight, they were there at the picnic table: the mustachioed guy and the weightlifter guy. Zig stiffened, then relaxed. He walked slowly and casually to the table, and breathed deeply as if he were lazily taking in the day.

"Nice day," he said. They nodded.

"Get y'all a beer?"

"Sure," they concurred.

Ziggy went back in and ordered three Falstaffs. The bartender popped open the longnecks and put them on the bar.

"Found your friends already?" he chatted.

"Sort of."

Back at the picnic table, Ziggy passed out the beers.

190

"Something's on your mind," said the taller mustachioed man. "This isn't just about the beer, is it?"

"No," said Ziggy, and he took a long draught, thinking calmly of where to go from here.

"I got this friend. Everybody calls him Beachbum."

The two men perked up.

"I know the cops hang out at this place." He looked squarely at the two cops drinking their Falstaffs.

"And you know we're cops," said the squat weightlifter. "No secret. No problem. But we can't help you with your Beachbum friend."

"How do you know I need help?"

The weightlifter cop turned to his mustachioed colleague.

"Go get us a shot."

When he and Ziggy were alone, he leaned in.

"Be careful what you ask, my friend. What makes you think I know about this Beachbum kid?"

Ziggy looked at the thick shoulders and bull neck, and they triggered not fear or respect but indignation. He kept his cool though.

"I just figured a plainclothes cop staking out the Magic Mushroom talking to a plainclothes cop staking out Beachbum's house might know something."

The cop pulled a big sip of Falstaff through thin lips. Then set his bottle back on the wobbly wooden table.

"You're smart, kid. Don't be too smart."

Ok, Ziggy had gotten his attention. Now for a new tack.

"Look man, I'm not here to fuck up your scene. You gotta do your job. But Beachbum's a good kid. A good kid with a bad habit but still a good kid. He needs a second chance."

"Do you know where he is?" asked the cop.

191

"I don't know. I really don't. I tried to wrap the little bastard up for detox but he slipped away."

The cop smirked and it dawned on Ziggy. The cop knew where Beachbum was.

"We're not going to bust your friend," said the cop.

"This isn't about Beachbum, is it?" asked Ziggy.

The cop sipped his beer without speaking, but he nodded as if to confirm the obvious.

"What is your fucking deal?" Ziggy's measure tone slipped somewhat. "So a bunch of kids get together and try to stop the war and experiment with drugs a little bit. They're just trying to make the world better for their own generation man. What's the big deal?"

The cop just sat coolly and sipped. Ziggy was afraid he'd said too much. But he'd learned something too. The cops had already gotten their hands on Beachbum. And the result was that the bust was off. This sent Ziggy into his own trails of thought. He stood to leave.

The mustachioed partner came out of the bar just then but without any shots. Sneaky bastards, thought Zig. They plan everything, don't they?

"You can plan and plan and plan," Ziggy said. "But people's gonna rise up for a better planet anyway. You're right. This isn't about Beachbum. This is bigger than Beachbum. And it's bigger than whatever you're working on. This is about the future for your kids and their kids. You want them torn up in fucking wars and hitting resistance everywhere or something more free and beautiful?"

The cops were now closed up, expressionless.

"Think about it," Zig said.

"Thanks for the beer," said the bull-necked cop.

Zig got back into the carry-all and thought about his next move. The interview yielded no action but did provide information. This afternoon, too, was the Merry Pranksters

192

thing at the park with Ken Kesey and his gang. Maybe a little break from the heaviness would be good. Juice back up the spirit of revolution. Yes, he needed that. They needed it.

Ziggy started the carry-all and maneuvered out of the parking spot. Then he recognized someone walking down the side street toward the bar. A slick, suave someone, but not with the same suaveness as the mustachioed cop. Something more rebellious. It was Saul.

Ziggy did not stop the car, but his thoughts raced as he drove on. Saul! Saul was in on it. That's one way of explaining everything. Best not to go back and show his hand right now. He would think on it. He would visit Jazmine. He would see Ragman at the gathering to greet the Pranksters.

Chapter 13

On a grassy field near the Tree of Life, near the lagoon with its waterfowl splashing in the unseasonable warmth, sat the fabled vehicle of the Merry Pranksters, an old school bus fantastically painted, giant geometric blobs of bright color, every space a day-glo wormhole to the outer limits, churning psychedelic designs across the exterior sidewalls. F U R T H U R read the bold calligraphy across the front of the bus above the windshield. The roof was nearly covered with what looked like an extended luggage rack, where the Pranksters would sometimes ride in the wind as the bus lumbered its transcendental journey of disruption and awakening across the country.

Ken Kesey had gathered this misfit crew way back in the early 60s. While studying at Stanford, he had volunteered for a CIA-funded study of LSD and other hallucinogens. In the hands of a madman like Kesey, though, the experiments had some unintended consequences. Instead of generating new tools with which the CIA could conduct its covert activities abroad, people like Kesey took the psychoactive drugs to the street to destabilize the Establishment of conformist America. He and the Pranksters had turned their entire lives into a bus journey of outrageous, confrontational street theater, fueled by mind-blowing drugs and the desire to break the deadening norms of the world's malaise. Cool Breeze would no doubt argue that the Pranksters were over the hill by 1970, but a medium-sized crowd of well-wishers turned out in Audubon Park nonetheless, eager to get a glimpse of Kesey or Neal Cassady. They lazed around in small groups, chatted, picked guitars, danced, smoked a clandestine joint here and there. A small contingent of Hell's Angels that sometimes accompanied Kesey cut circles around the bus on their Harley-Davidsons, and the roar of the open throttles was a bit rough for the flower children in the field, but the overall picture was still that of a fairly typical hippie love-in.

Ziggy had caught up with Ragman at the park, and the two stood toward the back of the small crowd. Ziggy was trying his best to tune back into the Scene, to recapture his own idealism. The image of the psychedelic bus definitely helped. It was beautiful, a perfect portal for the journey into a new age. This wasn't your everyday swirly painted VW bus. The people who painted this one were channeling something, some messianic force from the primitive regions of the collective unconscious. You could tell. The Harleys, on the other hand – Ziggy was especially susceptible to their disruptive power at this point in his life. And it was not the kind of disruption he needed. Disrupt the Establishment, yes. Confront the Man with the errors of his ways, yes. But the

194

thunderous ratcheting up and down was not good for Ziggy's focus. And then he saw Angelo Lombardi. Just like last week at the bonfire. So what? Of course the cops would be on hand in some fashion for an event like this.

"You recognize that guy, Rag?" Ziggy gestured.

"No."

"So I guess Saul didn't tell you everything."

"He didn't give me a photo album, if that's what you mean," laughed Ragman.

"That's Angelo Lombardi, the police commander that got me out of here last week."

Rag took a second look and saw in Lombardi a sharp, well-groomed figure with powerful eyes. The figure looked back, unmistakably, at Ziggy and Ragman.

"He's no toy to be played with," said Ragman.

"I know, man, that fucker thinks just like Saul. Last week he was all nice. It's like he pretty much told me. It wouldn't serve him right then and there to arrest me and start a riot. It's like Saul said: 'Live to fight another day.' Do what serves you today, and then come back and crush the bastard when the terms change. I can see myself back in Murphy's police cruiser now."

"That's not where I see you," said Ragman.

"Oh, and where do you see, O great Nostradamus?"

"In Montreal with your Uncle Leo. Getting ready for the next stage."

As expectation built around the Prankster bus, Jazmine was returning to the Duck after her late breakfast with Pepper. But not only with Pepper. Hoss had taken Rose Petal and Bitzy to see a traveling petting zoo set up in the tiny neighborhood Mickey Markey Park – just a couple of goats, according to Claire, but it would be all the natural world to Rose Petal. Ragman, they say, had come back, and Ziggy went to meet him at the Pranksters happening. So with

195

all the guys gone, it became sort of a women's day out. Stormy and Gina had angled in with Pepper and Jaz for breakfast. Then they all stretched out on the levee. Jazmine could feel strength coming back into her body, but something was not exactly right. She felt it as a gnaw in the stomach and a tingle in the lip.

"Gina," Jaz started. "Do you know about the tan acid?"

"I heard something," Gina said. "But I assumed you'd tell me if the time ever came."

Jazmine liked that about Gina. She had her self-defeating control issues, especially with lovers, but she could also really respect boundaries with friends. It was weird. Once you crossed a certain line of intimacy, Gina's control issues took over. But as long as you were outside that line, she could be as trusting and respectful and anyone could imagine.

"The time has come," said Jazmine. Pepper and Stormy sat up now, alert, as they pondered the implications of this widening of the circle. Now all four young women sat facing each other in the grass. For a while they sat in silent communion, each pouring her own thoughts into the center of the circle. Jazmine felt a new elasticity and vigor of mind, telling her that she needed one more trip for closure. It didn't matter much at this point anyway. She only had one blotter tab of tan acid left. She'd heard nothing from Ragman since his visit with Owsley, but it was clear he would not be making any tan acid for a while. Probably good that he and Ziggy were off on their own. She felt the unique strength of the combined women around her. One tab left. What harm could it do? It would give her closure.

She lay once again on the powder blue sheet. On the Russian birch table that she and Ziggy had bought together. There were the images that had become a whole new comfort zone in her life. The gold-tinged Madonna, the burgundy curtains, the women now lighting the candles. The candlelight now flickering on the akua ma dolls. Stormy's akua ma. She felt a connection to the akua ma dolls, deeper and more archaic than she had previously. Jazmine felt a gush of love for Stormy. Maybe she needed Ziggy and Rag out of the way for this. So she could feel this special purified flow of love with Stormy, now branching out in liquid form to the other women. Sure, she loved Ziggy, too. That was pure too. But this was different. This too was necessary. She wondered if Ziggy ever felt that way with Ragman or Hoss or Tex. Oh God, Tex. Tex was dead. She gripped Stormy's hand while Pepper and Gina massaged her feet. Under the weight of Tex's absence, filled with the presence of Stormy and Pepper and Gina, the room really felt like a shrine for the first time. Jazmine closed her eyes.

"Rebecca," called a voice. She was facing a man with short-cropped curly black hair, beady eyes, and a prominent – almost a hook – nose. He was in the prime of life – thirtyish maybe – but had a stern ruggedness that made him seem older. She recognized him now. It was William. The moment seemed uncanny. A repetition. Had Rebecca been here before? She saw the edge of her own face. She saw her own hand reach out into the space of the village, goats and peat, earthy smells, tunics, forest green and tawny brown.

Back at Audubon Park, someone in the driver's seat of the bus – everyone noticed at once that it was not Neal Cassady, the legendary driver – pivoted the mechanical assembly that controlled the door, and the door slapped open at the bottom step. There was a momentary pause that seemed an eternity. Then out stumbled a sturdy man in his mid-30s with curly tufts around the balding crown of his head. Like Ragman, he had been a high school wrestler but he preserved more of the muscular thickness of that stereotype than Rag did. So this was Ken Kesey. He seemed dazed, perhaps by the sun and unseasonal heat. The crowd gradually came to a hush. Kesey rubbed his eyes and looked around, worked his jaw like he was going to say something, then turned and climbed back into the bus.

"Is that Kesey?" came a voice behind Ziggy.

Ziggy turned to see a square with a buzz cut and sport coat and black frame glasses oddly paired with a staggering hippie covered in beads and tie dye.

"That WAS Kesey," the hippie responded to his square friend. "That was like Groundhog's Day, man. Like the dude saw his own shadow."

"Six more weeks of winter for hippiedom," wisecracked the square. And the two wandered off like honey-sopped lovers, as perhaps they were. Ziggy had lost interest, as he was taken aback by what he saw at the perimeter of the gathering behind them. The same fucking guys. The ghosts in the machine. The characters that had been haunting the edges of his life for two weeks. Baby face and the dough boy.

Ragman also had not paid much attention, not to the Kesey fiasco nor to the odd couple. He was wrapped in his own thoughts. The tan acid. Owsley had shot it down. Just like the STP Scully and Owsley made back in '67. They had to shut it down. Too many bad trips. Owsley didn't like the tan acid either. Bad chemistry for the brain. Was it good for enlightenment? Maybe. Every guru, grifter, and day tripper wants enlightenment. But what if enlightenment means total disintegration of personal identity? Then we pull back. That's the whole scene. Pushing for enlightenment, fulfillment, then pulling back, pushing, pulling. It's like cosmic breathing. Everywhere two forces. The urge to change, to grow, to unfold. And the urge to remain the same

198

eternally. The tiger wants to be a tiger forever. Every hunt shows it. Every nap shows it. The rock wants to be a rock forever. It cultivates utter stillness, solidity, that it may hold its place forever. Every object, every thought, every moment, an equation of force and resistance to force. Extroversion, the becoming of the objective universe. Introversion, the becoming of the subjective universe. That horizon line where they fold into each other, that's where it's all happening. The more you study the physics of the universe, the more you see it's all a subjective trip. And if you follow the inner journey all the way, it flips and becomes the physical cosmos. Cosmic consciousness. The term itself holds the fullness of the objective world and the fullness of the subjective world together. Do we need the tan acid to know all of this? No. But maybe we need it to feel all of this. For example, he, Ragman, was thinking all this cosmic stuff, conceptualizing it, but he wasn't experiencing it. He wasn't feeling it. Maybe we need something like the tan acid to feel it. But Owsley was right. The risk was too high. Maybe in some later generation. Some later cycle. Cycles within cycles. All different sizes. We're at the beginning of the LSD cycle. LSD as a political tool. A tool to re-envision the whole structure of society. That's the beginning of the cycle. But soon, maybe 15 years, the whole drug scene will become deadening. Someone had said that. Leary. It was Timothy Leary who said that in a California lecture near the beginning, three or four years ago. The cycle will come to the end. The liberating force at the beginning of the cycle becomes the deadening, destructive force at the end. Look at Christianity. Liberating at the beginning. Now part of the deadening Establishment. Wow, though, it took 2000 years for that one to play out. Cycles within cycles. But it's cycles. That's important. It's not all linear. History isn't chronology. The movement toward enlightenment, it's not

199

chronological. It doesn't go left to right. Maybe chronology is the objective way of looking at it. But cosmic consciousness is an involution. Wow, have to think about that. The vanishing point on the event horizon where subject becomes object and object becomes subject. Where things move and flow, but not forward or backward, not chronologically. Force and resistance to force. We're all contributing to that force or resistance. We're all doing our own little trips, but we're in a collective trip too. Our collective trip might be bearing fruits in the so-called past or the so-called future. It's not a chronological trip. Like the tan acid. Abandon it. But it brought us all into a single thought process. At least we had to put our heads together and interpret what was going on. We had to think each other's thoughts. It was a site where all our separateness flowed together. We were all contributing into that one pool. Maybe that's the objective way of looking at it. We were putting it out there. Subjectively, we were taking it in. We were all experiencing the same thing from different orientation points. How much of this had Jazmine herself intuited? Ragman thought about the narratives Jazmine had shared. She was actually tripping on the tan acid. Maybe it was different for her. Maybe she was part of an entirely different set of characters, unrelated to the Co-op scene. I mean, of course she's part of us, but maybe she's on another axis of space-time too. She's got her Co-op brothers and sisters. Then she has her other brothers and sisters. Another set of helping hands passing forward and backward through time. Walking each other home. Cycles within cycles. The Establishment might not crack in this cycle. But it will crack. Then watch a million angels break free in splendor.

"Rebecca, where were you at the matins? The Lord Bishop has come and gone. And you and me and Jeremiah with work to do."

200

Why did she shudder at the reference to "work"? What work? Oh yes, the boxes. She had to get her materials together – linseed oil and alum and walnut rinds – to stain the boxes. Maybe that was it.

"Yes, William," she said, giving him the comfort of complaisance he sought. But she didn't feel it.

She walked back through the village with William, she more servant than ward, he more master than guardian. Guardian indeed! She pictured him kicking the chickens out of his way, but in reality he just walked steadily past fowl and fen, past the smithies and workshops and timber-framed houses. The tumblers still tumbled and the bagpipes piped in the town square. Across the square, the small rectangular church where she had parted from Jeremiah not more than an hour ago. A happy hour, too, as Jeremiah had sealed the arrangement with the Mohametman boy. She had seen the witch, Guda, observing them near the church. Perhaps she should have told Jeremiah. But no. She knew of Guda's jealousy. She knew what Guda knew. And she suspected not a little that Guda may have acted the serpent on the day they took Berold and her father. But no mind. To tell Jeremiah of that hatred and its source now would mean revealing everything. No, she reminded herself: In this world a woman needs to keep what power she can. She smiled to think that Guda followed the same politic, that Guda had kept Berold's secret as well as she, Rebecca, had done, that Guda was saving that power for her own use. But to no avail. She and Jeremiah would be far hence.

Jazmine, for the first time, felt herself painfully splitting from Rebecca. It felt like organs within her own body splitting and tearing. Where had she heard that? Pepper. Yes, Pepper had said that about her own LSD trip. But now, for Jazmine, it was like she and Rebecca were organs in a larger body – no, a single organ in a larger body

201

– and she could feel it tearing. Jazmine wanted to tell Jeremiah everything. Throw open all the doors and windows. She had been inside of Guda and knew the danger. But where was Rebecca when she, Jazmine, had been inside of Guda? No matter. She feared Rebecca's secrecy. Sure, she could see the correct politics of Rebecca's position. But Jazmine was starting to see that the matter of human connection was deeper than politics. She wanted openness with Jeremiah. With Ziggy. With everyone. In her naivete, she wanted Rebecca to go back to Jeremiah and share her soul.

But the weight of the historical moment was too heavy upon Rebecca. She must move in the only space the world had granted her. So she brushed aside the occasional voice she had become accustomed to in her head, and continued her own fantasy. Tonight, Jeremiah would get the sweet sap; tomorrow she would be free. Unbound from her affliction, she and Jeremiah could flee and risk all. They might even join the Lord Bishop's train themselves. No one could quarrel with his protection. But if not, they could fly south, to the Bodensee and beyond. Then might she discover the secret of which Berold spoke. She dared not think of the fantastic vision in the rocky crags from which she had recoiled. She dared not think of what Berold meant. Her body a secret. But first to fly.

William and Rebecca now approached the house. She could see the herb garden in front, where last night she and Jeremiah had embraced and spoken of the Mohametman. But there was something else. A nobleman on a horse. Darian, pacing.

"You there," called Darian to William. "Are you master of this house?"

"Aye." William was cautious. Tight-lipped.

"And that hag thy beldam?"

"My mother."

"And the young man, thy brother?"

"I have no brother."

Darian had been circling in the chestnut horse. Now he stopped and eyed William.

"Th'art a rustic lad. What is thy trade?"

"Coffin maker, m'lord."

Darian eyed still more keenly.

"Well, coffin maker, hast thee apprentice?"

"Aye."

"And lives the apprentice here with thee?"

"Aye."

"The aged dam, thy mother, spoke of him familiarly."

"I know nothing of that, m'lord."

"And what hath thy apprentice to do with my father's servant boy?"

"I know not."

Darian smiled at the apparent coyness of his quarry.

"Well, thy apprentice, of whom thou know'st so little, hath an appointment with one of my father's train this afternoon. See to it, my know-nothing rustic, that your friend make his appointment. I wish to engage the fellow myself about a matter that he may find less pleasing. Aye, but see to it. For if he fails, I will return in haste to arrest thee and thy beldam and thy entire household as a nest of heretic magicians to be burned at the stake." Here, Darian turned and eyed Rebecca. Then he slapped the mare's haunch and trotted off.

Rebecca had been watching this interview in some alarm, but thought it best to hold her tongue and bide her time for some opportunity to act.

"Damn these filthy noblemen who take all and give naught," excoriated William. "And damn Jeremiah too for his foolishness."

Rebecca and William had reached the perimeter of the herb garden.

"Ready thy stains. I'll tend to the poultry pen," said William, and he trudged to the side of the house.

Rebecca opened the door, but her heart forsook her. Something was wrong. Gammer stood at the end of the hall, at the threshold to the workshop. She had an odd visage, something Rebecca had not seen before, not so much malignity as madness. She gestured a bony finger for Rebecca to come forward. She cackled under her breath. It seemed to Rebecca an otherworldly crackling of logs in a fire.

"Come, come, my sweet lamb," the old woman coaxed. The strangeness of her attitude was much for Rebecca to bear. But Rebecca paced unsteadily toward Guda and the workshop. Then she stopped. She felt that she could not go on.

"But Guda," she stammered. "William, William says there's work to do."

"Aye," said Guda, as benignly as the devil in waiting. "Aye, work. I'm here to help you with the boxes. Come, child."

What could Rebecca do? She moved toward Guda, taking small steps for fear she might collapse.

"These boxes be all our homes one day. Come on, child."

After what seemed an eternity, Rebecca reached the old woman. She looked into the workshop. Several unfinished boxes stood about in disarray. Two lay horizontal, a near finished one and behind it one finished.

204

"Come, child, what's in the box?" Rebecca could tell she was being toyed with, as if Guda were a cat and she, Rebecca, a torn mouse. But what smell is this? Earthy. Citrus and leather. And cornflower too. Reminding her of something lost in subterranean byways of her psyche. Something heavy with love and loss. She felt herself moving as if in a dream. Jeremiah. Where was Jeremiah? She needed Jeremiah. She stopped suddenly, unable to move.

"What is it, my little game hen? Hast thou seen a fox that thou'rt confounded thus?" The old hag would not be silent. Her voice seemed far away. The axe on William's tool shelf! Blood on the blade!

"Let's move this one my child." Guda stepped to the near finished box. Guda took her end of the box cover and nodded to Rebecca. Rebecca was in a dream that she could not stop. They lifted the cover and set it aside. The box was empty. Of course the boxes were empty, thought Rebecca. Why torment herself with imaginary fears? Whence this childish dread?

"Push, dear, push." Guda instructed and the two women pushed together until the empty box sat flush against the wall.

Guda stepped to the finished box.

"Now this one, lamb," she said. And she rocked the box slightly to get a better grasp.

"Ooh, by Christ's nails, 'tis a heavy one." There was that otherworldly cackle of smothered laughter again.

"What's in the box, dear?"

Rebecca could not answer.

"Let's take this one out to the field where the crows gather."

Rebecca still could not speak. She could not stop the dream. Citrus and leather. And the spicy smell of cornflower. No, the cornflower was coming from the field. Guda had left the back door open.

"But p'rhaps she wants a peek first," said Guda with exaggerated politeness.

"Yes, one peek won't hurt," continued the witch.

Guda took her end of the lid and nodded to Rebecca. For a moment, Jazmine pulled back from Rebecca and pictured the walls of her own St. Roch shrine, and the faces of the St. Roch women around her, faces wilting and melting like wax. She gripped the Russian birch and steadied her perception against the drug. She regained control and became Rebecca again. She lifted with Guda. Two tries and the lid moved up and over at an angle from the interior.

Jaz felt dizzy, nauseous, but she could not tell if it were the tan acid or Rebecca's horror. The body in the box had suffered one blow to the head, the skull cracked and bloody. But the face? Why Ragman's face? Ragman's brown hair bloodied, Ragman's wide-set eyes and high cheekbones. Jazmine was losing control. Losing her stomach, her mind. Now Ragman's face was melting, as Jazmine had seen the other faces melt. It's a trip, a dream. I'm tripping. I'm dreaming. Perhaps the entire world was melting wax. She heard Guda's voice from far away.

"Here's your innocence, my little lamb. Here in this box. You and your gamecock be damned for your nasty innocence. Aye, the gander come into the house a-whistling, and now the house become his box."

It was true. It was Jeremiah in the box. Yes, of course it was Jeremiah. She saw his face clearly now, its soft features forever quieted. He wore a white linen tunic with the chest open. The scar on her lip tingled. Rebecca again joined Guda in lifting the box, the dream she could not stop. Jazmine must have been at a distance, in the field behind the house, not far from the one called St. Mary's field, because

206

she saw Rebecca and Guda laboring to bring the coffin toward her in the field. She felt Guda's rage and pain and self-loathing. Guda's own history that had brought her to this pass. The tempestuous years of love and rage with her man. Her rage displaced into protectiveness over William. William's independence, and the betrayal she felt at his willfulness, and at all who touched him, her mind long pastured on phantasms of betrayal, bringing her to the brink, aye past the brink, of madness. So here the hag was, observing Rebecca with hatred and curiosity and sympathy, yes sympathy.

"It had to be this way, dearie," she said to Rebecca. "It had to be this way all along. Now you're all healed. You're my child too now." She took Rebecca's hand. "He in the box, he bewitched you with those bright eyes. But my William shan't suffer that he should live. Now you can be one of us, dearie. It's all better now. Calm thy troubled heart." She sat Rebecca on the box and stroked her hair, while Rebecca watched the cornflowers blowing in the wind.

Jazmine was watching, as it were, but was not invested in the scene in the same way that she had been before. She was reading it like a narrative, a novel. Passion, compassion, passion, compassion. All of history as a novel. And yes, the great mythological foundations too. Of course there was a time when history and mythology were one. She was feeling trippy, like Jazmine on the tan acid and not the suffering Rebecca. She could feel infinite compassion for Rebecca but from a place of detachment. In fact, weird though it was, she could feel that the detachment was the prerequisite of the infinite compassion. She felt part of a wave. As if her body itself were the place where history and mythology were curling into each other. She felt her head floating away from her body. Panic. More nausea. She retracted and regained her cool. Ok, Jazmine's life,

Rebecca's life. One big novel. Of course there are patterns of images and symbols that run through the different episodes. The boxes, the trippy drugs, the bodily weirdness. Foreshadowings. How novels create expectations and then give you the payoff later. But the boxes. What foreshadowings? Panic was creeping in again. She couldn't save Jeremiah. Passion, compassion. She couldn't save Rebecca. But what if this was all a narrative setup? Jeremiah had engaged to free her with the exotic oils and he was killed. Berold had shared with her the secret of the elixir and he was killed. In the luminous dream of the tan acid, she saw all our joys and struggles as one great novel – how had she not seen this before – and the architectonics of the novel pointed one way. Or a medieval altarpiece, a triptych. In the Greek scene, the firebringer she could not succor. But she had been tricked. The middle panel, Rebecca and Jeremiah. If only she had warned Jeremiah. But the third panel? Rebecca and Guda had moved forward with the box and dropped it in the field next to a hole sized for a burial, a hole Guda must have dug with superhuman strength.

"The crows be a gathering, my sweet. And your old beau's a wasting. Aye, he's nothing but a bundle of empty rags now, he is."

That was it! That was how the novel worked! How could Jazmine have not seen this also? The foreshadowings pointed to Ragman. The third panel of the triptych. Ragman was in danger and she was wasting time. She needed to get to Audubon Park while the Pranksters were still there. She couldn't save Jeremiah. She couldn't save Rebecca. At least not now and not in any normal way. But she could save Ragman. She could write the ending. She could feel the ending. She was surprised that she had the presence of mind, and the force of will, to pull herself out of the hallucinatory regression. "Easy in, easy out," she thought to herself. To come up with a strain of acid like that, Ragman had to be a genius.

The genius himself was at that moment standing by Ziggy observing the forlorn inactivity at the Prankster bus and thinking of Jazmine, of Beachbum, of Ziggy. It was the one thing he feared most. Hurting other people. Putting them at risk. He remembered how, as a kid, he'd invited Carl, his black friend from school, to a playground in his white neighborhood. Carl had resisted. Even as a child, Rag instinctively knew that segregation was stupid. Carl knew it too, but perhaps Carl had reason to be more prudent. Rag, in his childish idealism, pushed and pushed until he had Carl convinced. It would be fun. Everyone would play. They would play tag, marbles, football, yo-yo. They would like Carl because he could make his yo-yo sleep longer than anyone. It would be a new day. But when they arrived at the playground, things did not go as planned. The white boys teased and mocked. Rag teased back and encouraged Carl through a few yo-yo tricks. Carl became a little more comfortable as he showed his stuff, and Rag beamed. But only for a minute. The peer pressure cruelty of pre-teen boys, combined with the times, took hold. The boys turned on Rag and Carl. Carl went home bloodied and crying. Rag was bloody too, but too disillusioned, too filled with self-loathing, and with loathing for the world, to cry. He never forgot it. He would never put anyone at risk again. He would play, he would learn to drive, he would go to sporting events and horse around. But he would not trust himself, nor anyone else. He was cynical for years, even brutal at times. But then LSD reawakened something dormant in him. The visionary came back. He felt like he saw what all the crazy visionaries saw – pagans and Platonists, Egyptians and Mayans, John of Patmos and John the Baptist, and the Swiss alchemists too – they were all seeing the same thing

209

underneath the glazed coating. And all the less crazy visionaries – Gandhi and Martin Luther King, John and Robert Kennedy – why do they all get killed before they deliver the full goods? Is it coincidence? Is it something structural about enlightenment? About the collective trip we're on? LSD did that for Ragman. Opened his eyes again to the possibility of enlightenment. To a collective power, too, in the Scene of his generation. There was a collective visionary thing happening. Would it be snuffed out like Gandhi and MLK? It had to be. Even if it didn't, it would turn bad. Cycles within cycles. You have to use the key to open the door but then you have to throw away the key. LSD, too. It can open a door but Ragman knew that one day he – we – would have to throw away that key. He didn't know if he could do it. But Ziggy could do it. Pass the torch. Ragman looked at the simple goodness in Ziggy's face, standing there in the orbit of the Pranksters. Ziggy didn't know it, but he was more ready than Ragman. Ragman had put Jazmine at risk. He had been careful at St. Roch. He had protected Rose Petal well. But he had put Jazmine at risk. The one thing he feared most. But Ziggy had stepped in. Ziggy had put a stop to the tan acid. Good old Ziggy. Ragman felt spent, but he felt good to know that Ziggy would pick up the torch and carry on. He felt it in his bones. And it was good.

Jazmine was trying to calm herself back down, to concentrate on her breathing, as the streetcar rumbled down St. Charles toward the park. She felt a little guilty about Stormy and Pepper and Gina. She had felt the bond so strong going into that final trip. In fact, she couldn't shake the thought that her unique bond to her fellow women of the commune had opened her up to the trip itself. How much of it was the tan acid and how much the vision that comes from such bonding? She had no clue. But the trip had played out, she felt, into a personal journey. When she saw those faces – Stormy and Pepper and Gina – melting like wax, it was like everything divided into an x-axis and a y-axis. The x-axis was her life with these beautiful women of St. Roch. The y-axis was more personal, but not exactly personal. This axis was driving from Rebecca through her to Ragman. It was inexplicable. But it was there. This was something she needed to do personally, not collectively. She had calmly suggested that the others go to join Hoss and Rose and Bitzy at Mickey Markey Park. She would rest and see them later. Yes, that part was not a lie. She would see them later.

She looked out of the window, trying to find a focal point. Oak trees lined the avenue, wagging their gray beards of Spanish moss. A squirrel chattering in a tree. Now she got it. The house. The box. Jeremiah had not been warned about the house. He could have been warned today at the church. Wait, was it today? Or a thousand years ago? No matter. Jeremiah had not been warned. He could have brought Rebecca the secret, the sap, the fire of her knowledge. He the bringer, she the doer. Her body would unfold that knowledge like a flower onto the world. But Jeremiah had not been warned away from the house, the box. Perhaps it was not time yet. And the house became his box. Rag could still be warned. Yes, Rag would be safe. Rag was humble. Rag resisted the Promethean urge. He had the power but he was not anxious to use it. Rag was patient, calm. His was not the power of disruption.

Ziggy and Ragman had given up on Kesey and the Pranksters, but theirs was no quiet after the storm. Ziggy could not believe what he was seeing. Lombardi had joined baby face and the dough boy at the edge of the crowd. The dough boy had pulled something from his pocket and the three were studying it. A card of some sort. A saint card. Could it have been Ziggy's saint card, the one with his

211

cutout on the front? Could it have been any other? Doubt was soon put to rest, as another figure joined the probe. A skinny guy, skinnier than baby face. A ghostly, heroin skinny. Beachbum. Ziggy shuddered. Beachbum had reached a new stage of zombiehood. A pure ghost, a silver knife slipping through the hairline cracks of reality. As if he would reach the vanishing point any minute. And then he did. That fast, Beachbum was gone. It was like a supernatural scene had occurred, and when it did, it was the most natural and predictable thing in the universe.

"Rag, did you see Beachbum over there, by Lombardi and those guys?"

Before Ragman could answer, they were both startled by the sight of Saul's lieutenant, plodding through the assemblage of hippies, squares, and curiosity seekers. Martin sidled up and spoke conspiratorially. Panic was in his eyes.

"Did you hear about Saul?"

Zig thought about what he had seen leaving the Falstaff bar, and he turned on Martin.

"Yeah, that Saul's a rat. Yeah we heard, he's probably on his way right now with the weightlifter cop to join McHale's navy over there." Ziggy gestured to Lombardi's team.

Martin toughened his stance.

"Saul's no rat. Yeah, he knew about the weightlifter cop and the bust plans. Saul knew a lot of shit. He knew the cops turned Beachbum too. What do you think he did all day? Saul had a thousand eyes."

Ziggy was taken aback by Martin's righteous indignation. He was also getting nervous about Martin's use of the past tense. Rag must have picked up on it, too, because he cut in.

212

"Martin, you're talking about Saul like he's dead. I saw him this morning at the ROTC building."

"No, he's not dead, but he might as well be. After that debacle at the ROTC building, he flipped out." Martin glared at Ragman, and it was Ziggy's turn to cut in.

"But Martin I saw him going to meet the bullnecked cop at the Falstaff bar. It must have been after the ROTC thing."

"Yeah, well, like I say, he flipped out." Martin paused before going on. He licked his fat lips and continued.

"He stabbed that cop."

Ziggy was stunned. Ragman was stunned.

"But his own rule," stammered Ziggy. "Deal with the battlefield you're on. Live to fight another day. How could he break his own rule?" Ziggy felt something akin to the vertigo he'd felt when he'd heard about Tex. And felt that tic of denial again. Resisting the crossing over the point of no return. If he could show that what Martin was saying didn't make sense, then it couldn't be true. But Martin brought it home.

"Yeah, the cop's got a punctured lung. Not expected to make it. Saul's in custody."

"Do those guys know?" Ziggy gestured at Lombardi's crew again.

"Fuck!" said Martin when he saw the crew. Like a snail, he went back into his furtive posture and slunk away. Neither Ziggy nor Ragman tried to stop him. Ziggy thought it best not to make any more of a scene. But Ragman – something different was holding Ragman back. Ziggy had that shuddering feeling again. He saw something in Ragman's face. A shock, a paleness. Ragman had not looked back at Lombardi since baby face and the dough boy had come along. Now he looked at the burly dough boy with saints card. With ghastly horror, he looked.

213

"The saints card?" blurted Ziggy, trying to figure out the root cause of Rag's alarm.

"I left that under Beachbum's door. I knew they had it. That's what I meant about Murphy's car." Rag was shaking his head.

"It's not the card," he said under his breath.

"Fuck!" said Ziggy. "You didn't know about Beachbum! How could you? You were out of town when I found him, when I lost him again. You couldn't have seen him in and out of Lombardi's crew over there. I'm sorry, man. It's bad, I know."

"It's not Beachbum," said Ragman.

Now Ziggy was truly baffled. But he noticed that Ragman continued to look at the huge man towering over the others in Lombardi's group, holding the card.

"But … ?" Ziggy couldn't think. "But you said it wasn't the card."

"Not the card," said Ragman. "Look at the hand holding the card."

What the fuck, thought Ziggy. So the mammoth has fat fingers. But wait! Something odd about the fat fingers. And it dawned on Ziggy all in one stroke. Hair bristled on the back of his neck. The thumb. Ziggy had to look twice. Half of the hulk's thumb was missing. His mind reeled back over a field of associated images that had built up since he had joined the Co-op. The Duck and the Island. A big guy. Disappeared soon after Ragman came. Jolly and sneaky. With half a thumb missing from an offshore accident involving a hydraulic jack.

"Fucking Biggles," Ragman said. "Working with the cops. Fucking Biggles. Behind Beachbum and everything."

Biggles made eye contact with Ragman and said a few word to his compatriots. They separated and began to move around the perimeter.

214

"Saul in custody. Biggles circling. This is it." Rag spoke like a prophet who had known all along that this day was coming. Ziggy looked at him, at what was happening, in wonder, like it was happening to someone else.

"Look, Zig," Rag buttonholed Ziggy and brought him back to attention. "They don't give a shit about Beachbum. Never have. Biggles will have these guys at the Co-op in hours. Now, with the Saul shit coming down, they got no more time on their side."

Ziggy looked back at the space where the Lombardi's group had been a moment ago, had evaporated. It was almost as if he tried to see them there and undo the pattern.

"Ziggy!" snapped Ragman, bringing Zig back to a focus. "There's a drug bust coming down. But their eyes are on me, not you. Go to the Duck, get your stuff and get out. I'll be there in a few hours. You must be gone by then. Get everybody out."

"But Rag ..."

"No buts. I have to go back to the house and clean up, but not for a few hours. There's too many people can get in trouble. I'll rig it so I take the heat alone. Don't look for me again. Whatever Jaz says, get out. Tell her anything. Tell her I left town already. She'll remember the circus people from the beach. The Red Queen's Naked Circus. Tell her I went there. They're back in upstate New York. Dutchess County. Tell her we're all meeting there. Get her there. Get out of this state."

"But Rag ..."

"Now!" Rag said with irresistible force. And he was gone.

Jazmine felt her knees buckle as she descended from the streetcar at Audubon Park and stepped across the long iron arc of the rails. But she held firm. She knew what had to

215

be done and she would do it, buckling or no buckling. And here, barreling towards her, like Beowulf swinging across the fen, was Ziggy. Now barreling past her. He did not see her. He was in his own world.

"Ziggy," she cried. He stopped, paralyzed. He did not turn. She took him by the shoulders and turned him toward her. When their eyes met, he came to himself. Jazmine put her arms around him, held on and said nothing for a few moments, then slid her hands down to his elbows and stepped back.

"Something terrible is happening, Ziggy."

"Jaz, how … but how could you know?"

"I know stuff, Ziggy, I don't know how."

This utterance brought them down to a reflective space, a quiet space amidst the rage of events.

"Do you know we have to leave?" asked Ziggy calmly.

Jaz nodded. She knew.

"But Ragman," she said. "Where is he?"

"Gone."

"Gone where?" Jazmine was starting to get worked up again. "He can't go back to that house. Not even for a minute." She tried to pull away and now it was Ziggy who took her by the elbows.

"Shhh, Jaz," he comforted.

"Where the fuck is he?" asked Jazmine with severity in her violet eyes.

"Shhh, he's gone." Ziggy remembered Ragman's words. *Tell her anything. Don't let her look for me.* And here she was in Ziggy's arms, struggling with him, with herself.

"Shhh, Jaz, it's OK. Ragman left town. He's cool. He's gone." Ziggy could feel Jazmine beginning to relax.

Now she had collapsed against Ziggy's chest in earnest. "Can't go back," she was whispering. "Not even for a minute."

Chapter 14

St. Roch was in turmoil, but it was controlled turmoil. Ziggy had gotten Jaz into the carry-all with a few bags. Everyone had been told. Everyone was out. It was cool. Stormy and Rose Petal were collecting the last of their things in the house. No one panicked around Rose Petal. Cool. Everything was cool. Now Ziggy just had to get them out and off to the mid-Hudson Valley and the Naked Circus. He would find and help Ragman. Fuck the Rag's directive. He was not going to let Rag go down alone. Jaz was in the passenger seat.

"Look, Jaz, I got to go to my parents' house in Metairie. You and Stormy and Rose go. I'll be up in a few days."

Jazmine looked a little dazed. Ziggy thought for a second that she had that faraway look that he'd seen in a few friends that had done too much LSD. An unnerving look. No doubt, LSD had its positive potentials – personally, to expand the consciousness, and politically, for collective re-envisioning – but it had its risks. The law of diminishing returns. This is what Ziggy saw in his friends who had done too much. And now he thought he saw it in Jazmine.

"You OK, Jaz?"

She broke for a second. "Oh, Zig, I don't know who's who anymore."

217

Then she pushed herself to regain composure. Ziggy saw in that push the strength that he knew was in there, in Jaz.

"Look, Jaz, stay grounded to Stormy. She'll keep things right. It will get better."

Ziggy leaned in through the passenger window and kissed her cheek. He wanted to say something more. She wanted to say something more. But there was no time. Anyway, he would see her again. Or so he hoped.

Nighttime came and Ziggy felt like a failure. He figured he'd find Ragman at the Magic Mushroom or at their spot on the levee. No, and not at Schiro's either. Of course not. What had Ziggy been thinking? Ragman wouldn't be anywhere obvious. He certainly wouldn't bring the spotlight to Claire and Cool Breeze. Ziggy had wandered over to the old ironworks on Piety Street, thinking maybe Ragman was rummaging the ruins for some demolition materials to bring down on the acid lab and whatever else he had at the Co-op. But all he found was a fantastic panorama of sheet metal and wood post beams and massive iron ribs and bones from some imaginary defunct whale. Cans and bottles and bits of discarded clothing on the floor. No Ragman. Ziggy spied on the Duck and the Island, marveling at how rapidly they'd been emptied. No Ragman.

He'd finally gone back to his parents' house in despair. They had a simple meal of roasted chicken and makeshift jambalaya. His mother, the very picture of worn-out kindness, opened the conversation.

"Why don't you go back to school, Arthur. You must be getting tired of that pizza place."

"I like the pizza place, mom." It occurred to Ziggy as he said the words that he'd worked his last shift at Polo's.

"Well, you eat some more chicken," she said in resignation, and wiped her hands on her apron.

218

"Don't know what you kids are fighting," said his dad, who had black curls like Ziggy, but they were cut short and square to match his stature. "First we had the depression, then the war, then Ike got in and it's been nothing but peace and prosperity. Look at us, we got a house in the suburbs. Who woulda dreamed it? Right when everything's good, y'all want to destroy it all. It don't make no sense."

"I know what you mean, dad, but it's not peace, it's Viet Nam. We don't want the same prosperity. Money and war and becoming part of the machine. We want to be free."

"You gotta fight for freedom, son," was all his dad said. Ziggy had had this discussion before. It was benign. His parents loved him. Of that he was sure. But they were too far gone into conventional thinking to understand. He knew that too. They had moved to one of the new 1960s suburbs in Metairie when the Civil Rights movement took hold in the city. Ziggy had never heard either parent say one bad thing about black people; growing up, he had played with the kids of the black men his dad worked with at the river front. Until today, the packages of homemade delicacies his mom sent to the Co-op would always have a special treat for Rose Petal. They were actually grateful that Stormy and Rose Petal were there, thinking, perhaps rightly, that the child would put some brakes on whatever hippie craziness was going on. But back in '65, at the prospect of imminent integration, with whatever volatility that might mean in home prices and neighborhood schools and street crime, his parents, like so many whites, had opted to the suburbs. They wanted security for themselves and their kids. Ziggy hated it. He went back into the city as soon and as often as he could. He could never accept the conventional life of his parents, and they could never understand why.

"Let him alone, Walter," chimed in his mother. "Kids gotta be kids. Let him sow his oats." Then she turned

219

to Zig: "Live your life, Arthur, just be careful. Don't let it go too far."

Ziggy moved around the table and kissed her on the cheek.

"Well, let's catch the baseball game on TV, Arthur. Tom Seaver pitchin' tonight. Did you see what he did to the Padres last week?"

"No, Dad, I missed it. I gotta go to bed anyway. Got some thinking to do."

"Good idea, son. Do some thinking before it's too late."

But Ziggy couldn't think, couldn't sleep. He tossed and turned, dozed and stirred until he didn't know if it was night or day.

Rag, meanwhile, had waited for the Co-op to clear. He was indeed perched up in the rafters of the abandoned iron works, where he could see over the rooftops, where he had seen Ziggy not so long ago. Ziggy, looking for him. But Rag would not reveal himself to Ziggy. Not now. He would not make the mistake of endangering his friend. His idealism was tempered by reality. He could see the troops slowly appearing around the corner, by Schiro's, by the newsstand. Not Biggles or Lombardi. No, these were the foot soldiers, the guys who did the dirty work of breaking down doors and dragging out whatever poor terrified junkies or pot smokers they could find. To do them justice, thought Ragman, they did sometimes pull bad guys off the streets. Even he, Ragman, could appreciate that. But the system just made bad guys worse. Bad guys were not born bad guys. Some of them could be turned. At least some of them. But these foot soldiers, thought Rag, too often they're dragging out innocent kids, idealist kids with the creativity to make a better world, kids just smoking pot. Or junkies who could still turn back with a little human kindness and treatment.

220

But no, the system would push them beyond all turning back. And the kids. It wasn't the pot that brought the foot soldiers down. No, it was the protests for social justice and against the war, it was the new definitions of family and community, that's what terrified the Man. He could see his world crumbling faster and faster between 1967 and 1970. Rag could feel compassion for those people, too. The ones who saw their world caving in.

The Co-op cleared, Rag stealthily descended his perch and crept back to the Duck through the back shed. He knew he was being watched, but he would play the creeping game, let them watch, gain a few minutes. All was still, with the dew still on Stormy's tomato plants, only the sound of crickets to disturb the silence.

There was not much to Ragman's lab. Nine ounces of pure LSD can make a million hits. All the LSD from the Summer of Love to Woodstock was made in a few labs working with an ounce or two of pure LSD. Ragman's lab consisted of a couple of tiny vials, some eyedroppers and paper for making the four-way windowpanes of blotter acid, not to mention various funghi, a little peyote, and a half a bag of weed.

Ragman heard something at the back door. Someone had moved the garden shovel, whether by accident or by design.

"Here it comes," he said.

Funny thing was, he'd never sold any drugs in his life. He was just a dime-bag-at-a-time weed purchaser like Ziggy or Hoss or anyone else in the Co-op. And the LSD? No one made money from LSD in the 60s. Rag, for sure, was not just a user but a maker. He was in on the research side with Owsley and Scully. But LSD in the 60s was not for profit; it was for humanity. Everyone practically gave the stuff away. Rag definitely gave the stuff away, to anyone who he thought could use it to open their minds and open up our collective vision. He knew that's what made him a threat, the fact that he was giving it away without monetary gain. An idealist out to change the world is far more dangerous than a penny-ante profiteer. And that's why he knew the cops would rewrite the story tomorrow. They would make him a profiteer. They would edit out any idealism. Ragman knew how they worked.

"Pepper would be proud of me," he thought, with a grim smile.

Another sound at the back. This time it was no accident. They were jimmying the door. Then a deafening boom at the front door. They were coming in. Ragman grabbed the small axe from the gardening tool shelf and rapidly destroyed the tiny office of his revolutionary dreams – the acid, the herbal materials, the notes. Yes, they must not get the notes. Give them as little as possible. Then they were inside.

Two front-line officers in plain clothes stood face-to-face with Ragman. The uniformed unit hung back. The house was dark, except for the panes dimly lit by an exterior light source. The two officers, badges affixed to their belts, focused intensely, guns trained motionless on Rag's head and chest.

Rag could see in the intensity of their gaze all he needed to know. They were confident in the justice of their cause, of their side. They saw Ragman as the kind of cancer that was spreading, contaminating, bringing down the world as they knew it. "Pharmakos," thought Ragman. The Greek word that means both poison and cure. To them, he was the poison. And Ragman saw all the way down. Below their intensity, below their confidence, their professionalism, was fear. Fear that their world was under threat. Fear of

222

everything Ragman represents. Rag could see them with unlimited compassion.

"Put the axe down!"

Compassion. Little do they know, Ragman thought. It's not me that's the threat. It's the people I leave behind.

"Put the axe down NOW!"

Unlimited compassion. This is the way the world moves forward.

Ragman dropped the axe and moved his other hand to cover his heart. He felt his own heart beating, the heart of all humanity, the heart of these poor, confused, and very professional police officers. The heart of a movement that never stops.

The solid bang of the axe hitting the floor must have triggered a trace of panic in one of these expert officers. He fired. And then the other fired.

* * *

Light coming in from the window indicated to Ziggy that morning had come. Then he heard his dad shouting.

"Arthur, get in here. Come see this."

That was not the way his father normally spoke to him. Ziggy pulled a pair of Jetsons pajama bottoms (a gift from Pepper, delivered back in the day with much extempore sarcasm) over his underwear and ran out to the kitchen. His dad was sitting at the table looking at the TV.

"Goddamn son, that's that damn commune right there!"

Hair bristled on Ziggy's neck. It was true. There was the top local news reporter standing in front of the Duck. With him – what the fuck was going on! – was Mr. Anthony.

"I understand, sir, that you are the landlord of the house?" Mr. Anthony, with his crumpled black sweatshirt

223

and scrappy appearance, looked uncomfortable next to the reporter with perfect hair.

"Yes, sir. They was good kids."

"You mean," corrected the reporter, "that they seemed good kids until today."

Like an old boxer in the ring, Mr. Anthony seemed to catch his footing at this jab from the reporter. He delivered the next line with calm certainty.

"No, sir. I mean I STILL say they're good kids. These kids were minding their own business and set up by the cops."

"But, sir, the drug lab ..."

"Don't play fool to your station master, boy. These kids was set up."

The television station cut to a 30-second commercial break. Ziggy knew that was the last he'd hear from Mr. Anthony today. He and his dad were speechless, and the reporter returned to the screen with a summary of the story.

"Once again, a notorious drug dealer known only as 'Ragman' has been shot by police. Charity Hospital has pronounced the suspect dead with bullet wounds to the head, side, and hand. The police believe the lab was filled with heroin and cocaine as well as LSD but the evidence will take some time to gather. Police suspect that the dealer was armed and dangerous at the time of the bust. Believed to be high on his own drugs, he destroyed the lab completely with an axe, leaving nothing for the forensic team. We'll bring you more as the story develops."

"Damn, Arthur," said Ziggy's dad. "That boy was crazy. I'm glad you outta there. Did you know he was that crazy? Destroying everything in a rampage like that."

Zig lashed out: "Of course he didn't want the cops to get all his stuff intact? He wasn't a 'dope dealer,' whatever the cops mean by that. He was part of something bigger.

Handing that stuff to the cops is like giving your secrets to the enemy."

Ziggy's dad was stunned – not angry, but confused. "The cops are the enemy?! Against an armed and dangerous drug dealer?"

"Come on, Dad. He wasn't armed and dangerous. And Ragman never touched heroin or cocaine. LSD – yes, OK. But the cops are just making up the rest. Why do you think it's taking time to gather evidence? They're planting stuff, building a narrative. Yes, the cops are the enemy."

Ziggy's mother had wandered into the kitchen, looking more woebegone than ever.

"Arthur," she said. "Listen to yourself. Is your Uncle Frank the enemy?"

Ziggy paused. The question shook him.

"No," he said glumly. "But it's different."

"Why?" asked his father, coming back in. "Just because he's your uncle?"

"No," said Zig, flustered. "I mean, sure, there's good guys who are cops. It's just the whole system. Attacking and grinding and crushing every movement, every time people try to change the system, everybody with a new vision of how to live together gets crushed."

Ziggy stormed into his room to stuff his backpack. He wasn't mad at his parents. He was mad at the world. His parents, on their part, did not know what to say. When he got to the front door, his mom said the only thing she could think of.

"Arthur, be careful."

She hugged him and he hugged back. He stepped in to hug his dad, too.

"I'm sorry dad. I gotta do my thing. It's the only way."

"I know, son," said his father. "Be careful."

225

Instead of heading east to the Gulf Coast, Ziggy went straight north on Highway 51, up the Mississippi River through the delta blues country, turning at Memphis and heading through the southern pine forests toward Nashville. At some spots he could hop on the new interstate system, but it was mostly still the older U.S. highways, the infrastructure of Jack Kerouac's *On the Road* and Alfred Hitchcock's *Psycho*. Ziggy had a sleeping roll attached to his backpack, but he hoped to nap during his rides and avoid tucking up under an overpass or along rail lines for sleep. He would consider hopping a freight train but he didn't know the routes. A freight-hopping hippie from California had once spent a week at the Duck, regaling the gang with tales of old hobos and freight yard dogs, but that guy had a timetable in his head. If he got kicked out of the Western Pacific freight yard, he'd walk to the Southern Pacific yard, knowing exactly when the next train was going his way and where he'd have to switch tracks. So Ziggy just stayed on the road and napped in cars as best he could until a middle aged steel worker in a beat-up Chevy Impala, despite being out of work, offered to take him into Nashville and buy him breakfast.

Nashville was more eclectic than Ziggy had pictured it. He wandered through Midtown and Music Row and Printer's Alley. Hippies were everywhere in the mix, mingling with country crooners holding down the fort and folk singers rattling up the social protest, filling in the ranks of college kids and strippers and agitators. But the night came on and Ziggy was tired. After a few games of pool, one of those college kids snuck Ziggy into the Barnard dorm at Vanderbilt. Great. He could use the sleep. But his eye was on New York when the sun rose.

After Knoxville, Ziggy forked onto Interstate 81, but the highway was still under construction and pullover spots for cars were tough to find. Walking along the dusty half-shoulder, he joined up with a Japanese hitchhiker heading from the Smoky Mountains back to DC for a flight home. The two young men considered hitching together through Virginia. No, they were stuck as it was, and it would be easier to get a ride solo than with a partner. The Japanese guy gave Ziggy a banana and, at some turn in the conversation, assured Ziggy that a hippie scene was blossoming in Japan, too – in the Zen communes of North Kyoto, in the Shinjuku district of Tokyo, where AWOL Americans blended in with Japanese art students and experimental playwrights and bohemian free-love beatniks. The two men then spread out, each to get his own ride, but the banana and the thought of the scene in Japan fortified Ziggy for the road ahead. He finally got his ride and finally made it through the spectacular Blue Ridge Mountains of western Virginia.

The last ride that took Ziggy into New York City was with a skinny, swaggering black guy going to Harlem to pick up some drugs to take down to Philly. Luckily, Ziggy had slept through the night in Pennsylvania, wrapped in a blanket like an enchilada in the back of a pickup driven by a young couple with a hog farm in the Susquehanna Valley. By the time he woke up, he realized he was too far north. He'd bypassed Bethlehem and Allentown. The couple offered Ziggy a bed on the farm, but his eye was on his destination and whatever might await him there. So he turned east and watched the sun rise over the green velvet Poconos. It was slow going as the day wore on. Now he found himself in a shabby Oldsmobile with an apparent drug dealer, and he was glad that he'd gotten some sleep. He'd feel better staying awake for this ride. The driver had a puckish grin, mischievous but disarming, and threw elbows around in animation as he talked.

227

"Reach back and get us a beer," he said to Ziggy.

Ziggy reached behind the seat and dug around in an ice chest filled with cans of Schlitz beer.

He popped one for the driver and one for himself. His stomach had not been quite right since Nashville, but he needed camaraderie, and he found a strange and dangerous fellowship hurtling across New Jersey in a ragtag Oldsmobile with a wily drug dealer.

"Where you getting out?" the driver asked.

"I don't know," Ziggy said. "Somebody told me I could get a cheap room at the Village Plaza."

"Heh, heh, heh," smiled the driver at Ziggy. "East Village, heh? Downtown. Old drunks and cool kids. You must be one of the cool kids, heh, heh."

"As long as they got a bed, I'm good," Ziggy said.

The driver eyed him with curiosity, sizing him up.

"You could come with me, white boy?"

"What would your friends think about that?"

"I'm not worried about my friends."

"White boy like me barging in on your drug deal? Doesn't sound like a good idea."

"Heh, heh, heh, if you with me, you cool, white boy." The driver's smile was unshakeable. "Anyway," he continued, "Not going to the drug deal first. Got a lady friend first. My lady friend would get a kick out of you."

No, Ziggy decided. He didn't want to get stuck somewhere in Harlem not knowing where he was. All he'd heard about Harlem was that it was black, tough, and far from downtown. He didn't want to risk it. Did that make him a racist? Was he as bad as his parents in their Metairie suburb? Maybe, maybe not. All he knew was he did not have the energy to take a chance right now.

"No, man, just drop me in the East Village."

228

"Ha, ha, ha," laughed the driver more loudly, and then he mimicked Zig: "'Just drop me in the East Village,' he says. Man, I ain't driving all the way across Manhattan for your ass." He flipped a hand up in the air for emphasis. Ziggy studied the driver's face, weighing the mischievous against the disarming. The words were hard-hitting but delivered with apparent good humor.

"How about when we cross the George Washington Bridge I throw your ass out at the subway line. You got 20 cents, you take the A-train down to Washington Square. Now let's have another Schlitz."

Ziggy opened two more cans. If this guy was going to put down beers like this and then drive through Manhattan, Ziggy felt like he was making the right decision getting out and on his own.

It was after dark when Ziggy finally got to the Plaza. Old drunks and cool kids was a good description. The block was a squalid row of red brick structures, but it was a stone's throw from Jimi Hendrix's new studio on West Eighth Street, from NYU and Bleeker Street, with coffee shops and bars like The Bitter End, where you could still catch Bob Dylan or Joan Baez or The Velvet Underground on a lucky night. A wisp of a former dancer stood behind the Plaza reception counter, fanning herself with a flyswatter. Zig wondered about all the infinitesimal mutilated fly parts invisibly affixed to the swatter, wondered about the backwash of fly part molecules invisibly breezing across her sallow cheeks and sunken eye sockets. She showed Zig to his room: an iron frame single bed with a sink and a barred window through which one could view young backpackers weaving their way through conspiratorial drug deals and audacious streetwalkers.

"Call me, honey, if you need anything," rasped the spectral counter maid before evaporating into the hallway.

229

Zig threw his bags down. He thought he would rest for a minute, but he slept for 14 hours and woke at mid-morning. He needed to get out. To be outside. Even to sit in the squalor on the cement steps that fronted the flat red brick, to catch his breath, to soak in the squalor itself before bursting forth to new life. Someone was looking at him. A kid with wild, frizzy red hair and skin that looked fresh from a cheese grater. The kid had come up the steps without gaining Ziggy's attention, had put one hand on the doorknob to enter, and then turned and looked at Zig.

"You're new," he said. Apparently some of the hotel tenants were long-term, or at least intermittent.

"Yeah, just got here. Just passing through."

The kid sat next to Ziggy.

"Where you from?"

"New Orleans."

"Rebel, huh?" the kid chortled. Then he saw Ziggy's blank look and added: "Rebel. Southern boy. War between the states. Get it?"

Zig got it. The kid went on. "OK, Reb." He held out his hand. "Call me Frizz. Everybody else does." Ziggy couldn't tell from the delivery if the name were a marker of long-suffering indignation or a badge of honor, but he figured he'd roll with it if that's what the guy wanted. The kid definitely piqued his curiosity.

"Come on," Frizz said. "There's a thing in Washington Square Park, just a couple of blocks over."

Frizz was a weird combination of talkative and laconic. He'd blurt out in a stream about a lost scholarship to Columbia University, how the Irish took over the police force and the Italians took over the bars, how he'd gotten a guitar pick from Bob Dylan, and then he'd shut up tight for a block. Ziggy mostly listened. He liked the kid.

230

At the park, there was no discernible "thing" Ziggy could identify, but there were enough NYU students and winos, earnest pamphleteers and wannabe folksingers, for Frizz and Ziggy to share a half a joint in the grass behind one of the park benches. Now Frizz was rambling about how he'd once walked from Oklahoma City to Austin, Texas, and how he couldn't stop when he got there, just kept walking up and down Guadalupe Street, but man you better watch out for all the hippie panhandlers in this town. Then he shut up.

Zig knew it was not his calling to figure out everything Frizz said, but the last line caught him by surprise. They had passed three panhandlers along the way and Frizz had dropped a coin on each, and their manner of acknowledgment indicated that they knew Frizz well. And to hear Frizz complain about hippies, Frizz with his huarache sandals and draped purple shirt with tiny mirrors embroidered in, Frizz who had just taken in the first hippie to sit on the steps of the Plaza – it was all too strange and amusing. But Zig was enjoying the quiet patch, too. So was Frizz himself, as he pulled hard on the joint. But then Zig saw him gingerly slide the reefer down to his side, rub off the burning tip into the grass, and smash it down with his thumb. A sturdy, smartly dressed black woman was approaching, looking right at Frizz.

"You starting trouble out here?" she said.

"No, ma'am. You know me. I don't start trouble. Trouble finds me."

"Well I want to talk to you about what you gave my son, Gerald."

"What was that?"

"You know. That baseball signed by Mickey Mantle. You oughta not give away such stuff. That's going to be worth money one day. You need it more than we do."

231

"What do I need it for? Gerald loves it. I don't need anything anymore."

"Well, yeah, he sure loves it. Let me give you something for it."

"OK. You can just get the hold on my library guest card fixed."

She smiled. "Already done it." She handed him an NYU library card.

"Thanks." Now they both smiled. The woman turned, took a few steps, and turned back.

"And don't kid yourself. I can smell what you're doing out here. And I don't approve. Just because I don't report you doesn't mean I approve." And she continued on her way.

"NYU faculty," Frizz said. "She's still mad at me about the Columbia scholarship."

Ziggy didn't know how much of anything was true, but he could not escape the appeal of Frizz's company. Frizz pulled a Hershey's bar from his pocket, carefully broke it in two, and gave half to Ziggy.

"You're a good guy, Frizz," said Ziggy.

Ziggy may have uttered the words in an awkward rush of sentiment, but Frizz's thought it quite amusing. His laugh began with a wheeze and built into a coughing fit. Ziggy had a weird premonition that Frizz was dying.

"Au contraire," said Frizz. "Not good at all. Gave it up. I used to be good. Or I used to try to be good. But people aren't meant to be good. That's too high a bar for people. You try to be good, you're failing all the time, frustrated, then you get grumpy and bitter. Then you're nothing but a pain in the ass to everybody around you when all you wanted was to be good. No, I'm not good and I'm not bad. I'm done with all that. And you know what? It's liberating. You can't

232

imagine anything more liberating to the human spirit than giving up on good and bad."

Ziggy was no moral philosopher, but he had enough sense to recognize an unusual moral philosophy when he saw one. He just didn't know what to say about it.

"Go walk through the Village," Frizz said suddenly. "I got a thing to do. But, hey, later today, Central Park, in the Sheep Meadow, Simon and Garfunkel, I'm going to meet some friends around four o'clock at West 73rd, you got that?"

"Uhh, no, I don't really know my way around New York."

"OK, just do your thing and then take a subway to West 73rd. We'll be right there in the park, between the Dakota building and the lake." Frizz picked up the half-snuffed joint and shuffled off.

Zig walked through the Village not knowing what to look for and not caring. He liked the feel of it. Walking through New York. But he was doing a lot of internal work as he wandered, rebuilding, figuring out all the implications of what had just happened in New Orleans – who he was and where he was going and how the rest of his life would suddenly be built on whatever shattered fragments of that day he had brought with him. He did catch some of Bleeker Street, and walked past a place called the Stonewall Inn, which rung a newsworthy bell in his head, but he couldn't remember for what. Maybe Frizz had gotten into his head, because he could not stop walking – through the West Village and up through the Meatpacking District and Chelsea, past the new Madison Square Garden/Penn Station complex and the Garment District and into Times Square. Then he took to subway to West 73rd Street.

Ziggy walked away from the Dakota into the park, where a bicycler pointed him the way to the Sheep Meadow.

233

It was a perfectly pleasant stretch of green, with bohemian and business people gathered in bunches on the grass, dogs and Frisbees. But no sign of a concert. Was Frizz a pathological liar? No, not lying exactly. Just living life unconstrained by the facts. Ziggy smiled at the conceit.

"Hey Reb!" he heard someone shouting. There was Frizz, off in the direction of the lake, where he said he'd be. "Come on!" Frizz turned and walked toward the lake and Ziggy had to run after him, catching him just as he plopped down in a circle of three friends.

"What about the Simon and Garfunkel concert?" Ziggy probed.

"Sorry, man. I must have gotten my days mixed up."

The others in the group snorted, as if they'd seen this show before. A diverse little group, Ziggy thought: a black guy, a Latino-looking guy, and a free-spirited young woman whom Ziggy later found made a surprisingly good living selling crystals and other magical stones to tourists.

Frizz pulled out a Kool cigarette and tapped the open end against the box before lighting. The black guy immediately tore into him.

"What you doing, Frizz? First the Mexican weed, now you smoking them spade cigarettes. Don't you white people have enough of your own shit?"

"I like menthol," said Frizz shortly. "You got a problem with it, Beanbag?"

"Gimme one and I'll tell you," countered Beanbag. Frizz tossed him a Kool.

"Yeah, Beanbag," chimed in the Latino guy. "You seemed pretty happy smoking that Mexican shit too."

"Ok, ok, Pico," conceded Beanbag. "So I like the weed. Just don't give me the music."

"Oh yeah? What music is that, bro?"

"That mariachi stuff. 'Allá en el Rancho Grande.'"

Pico turned the cap on a bottle of Thunderbird and took a sip before continuing.

"You ever heard of a Mexican named Carlos Santana, tonto?" asked Pico. Then he shifted from testy to affable as he smiled and passed the Thunderbird to Ziggy. And so the conversation went as the bottle passed around, from bantering to stagey personal attacks to communal conviviality. But when they laughed together, Ziggy could see how deep the bonds had formed. This little group was uninhibited, rich in human contact, each person was all-in. The way they spoke to each other was still startling to Ziggy, but somehow the lack of rules was tied into the uninhibited, no-holds-barred human contact between these people. Ziggy could not at present sort that conundrum out.

Crystal (Ziggy assumed that she had acquired her name from her occupation) had laid her head on Beanbag and propped her feet on Pico. There was a kind of languid disregard in her posture, but she eyed Frizz seriously.

"Frizz, wasn't your appointment at the clinic today? Are you OK?"

Frizz smiled a pensive smile.

"On top of the world," he said. Then he thought of something.

"Oh, shit, I got to get back to the Village," he said. "You coming or staying, Reb?"

Ziggy and Frizz walked across the park toward the Tavern on the Green, where, as Ziggy understood it, rich people ate.

"Man, you guys play rough," Ziggy said. "I thought at first that Beanbag was going to get into it with the Mexican guy."

"You mean Pico?" Frizz laughed. "He's not even Mexican."

"But he said ..."

Frizz cut him off with laughter. "Hahaha. He's half Puerto Rican and half Irish. He was just fucking with Beanbag." Zig was amused, irritated, and curious together. He had seen for himself the rich human connection, but he still could not adjust to the roughness of the verbal play. Maybe he really was just a Reb, a laid back Southern boy. But that kind of talk, the racial jokes, the uncouth bravado – wasn't that supposed to be a Southern thing? No, everything was jumbled. Look at Lenny Bruce. The epitome of the Jewish New Yorker comedian. That was his whole schtick. Take the racist down with his own language. Poor Lenny. OD'd in Hollywood. Great, sweet, liberating anarchy in that man's mouth. No, not sweet. Rough. Ziggy wondered if Lenny could have survived the Haight-Ashbury Scene. No. Peace, love, and flowers might have been Lenny's dream but it was not his m.o. He would have rubbed everybody the wrong way. He was a disrupter. You need a disrupter first. But then you need a visionary of the new order. Someone who brings the peace and love. No, Lenny died at the right time. You can see it all over again with Ken Kesey and Timothy Leary. The disruptive Kesey, shaking all the nuts and bolts off the old order. The contemplative Leary, meditating and building a vision of the new order. Maybe, on second thought, they need to come at the same time. As twins. Twin LSD gurus. Zig had to leave that labyrinth of thought unfinished, as Frizz had veered suddenly to the steps down into the subway and was calling back at Zig.

"Gotta do my own thing now, Reb. See you later."

It was just as well. Ziggy needed his own space for whatever inner brewing was going on in his soul, in the turmoil of his life's situation. He let Frizz go and walked down the park to Columbus Circle, then hopped an A-train. At least on the A-train he could follow the same route he'd used when he first got to town. As the train rocked and

236

hummed, Ziggy felt drowsy. He wondered why people always fell asleep on buses and trains. Something about the floating movement. Maybe it was like the buoyancy of the womb. Amniotic fluid. Something about these weird steel tubes lulled people in the deepest forgotten spaces of the unconscious. He thought of his dream last week on the levee before Ragman went to Denver. Tex was probably dead already at that point, but he didn't know it yet. He thought about himself, aimlessly wandering around New York City. A day with no direction. Maybe everything was random but you just needed a day like this to see it. Randomness. The search for order in the chaos. Is that what the Scene was about? But you needed the randomness. Zig had thrown away direction today, thrown himself into randomness, and only then could he meet these new brothers and sisters, with their own joys and troubles, throwing out their own webs of connection. That's what randomness offers. Maybe that's what life is about – not about direction but about willfully losing direction.

But no, the other part was true too. Tomorrow Zig would continue his search to find Jazmine. Direction. Ziggy was once again on the precipice of sleep when he thought he heard someone say 4th Street. A ratchety announcement. He jumped up and off the train and made his way up to the surface streets. Shit. 14th Street. Oh well. Maybe he could walk to the Hudson River. The soiled map he'd found on a table at the Plaza said it was close by.

As he walked along the crumbling piers between 14th and Christopher Street, he noticed something odd. There was human life in the rubble, vivacious but clandestine at the same time. He sat to watch the sun set across the Hudson.

"You looking for a friend?" said a voice behind him.

237

Zig turned and saw a man with short groomed hair and a gym rat body.

"No, just looking around."

The gym-goer sat next to Ziggy.

"Beautiful sunset," he said.

Ziggy said nothing. He didn't mind the company, but his mental and emotional resources were running low. He couldn't think of things to say and he figured people wouldn't mind. Or they would mind and go away. No matter. Randomness. All good.

The stranger looked Ziggy up and down.

"You're not queer, are you?"

Conversations in this town never take a dull turn, thought Ziggy.

"No, I'm not queer."

"Well, you could come with me over to the pier, but ..." The gym-goer hesitated.

"But at the pier, you don't come to table if you don't want to play."

"I don't want to play."

The gym-goer gave Zig a curious look, and then burst into a short, loud laugh.

"Hahaha. You're so direct. You're not from here, are you?"

"No. New Orleans."

"Well, in your particular case," he said slyly, "I don't recommend the pier, but if you want, I'll take you to the Dubuffet exhibit tomorrow? It will be fun for you, and I'll be the envy of all the boys."

"Who is Dubuffet?"

"Hahaha. You are precious." He said it theatrically, adding an extra syllable between the 'p' and the 'r.' But when he spoke of Dubuffet, he was serious, engaged.

"It's Dubuffet's *art brut* exhibition. Raw art. He collected art from insane asylums around Europe during and after World War Two. He found all these incredible artists, totally free from any influence of art history. Just solitary souls searching the primal psyche within. It's so moving to see the terrible biographies, full of indescribable torment and despair, side-by-side with beautifully detailed original art works. Some painted, some sculpted, some worked in leather."

Ziggy was becoming fascinated. The way this guy talked, he could almost feel what it was that pulled Jazmine into the world of art. Ziggy wished Jazmine were here. Or that he were wherever she was.

"No, I gotta leave town tomorrow."

"Well you come with me later to the Zodiac or the Snake Pit."

"The Snake Pit?"

"Yeah." The guy picked up a rock and threw it hard into the river.

"Since the Stonewall riots, it's been mainly the Zodiac or the Snake Pit. Or the piers out here. But you should come with me to the Snake Pit. You're cute enough to get free drinks all night, but people won't bother you there if you don't want to be bothered. Everybody's welcome there."

Now Zig remembered where he'd heard of "Stonewall." The gay riots. The whole gay scene had come together over those riots. He thought of the cops beating those gay and lesbian kids with nightsticks.

"No, thanks. I gotta get up early and go find my friend upstate. I'm sorry."

"Sorry for what?"

"Sorry about Stonewall."

The gay guy sat for moment. Funny how a small, off-hand phrase can suddenly pull out emotion. He was actually biting back tears. Who knows what his friends had experienced that night at Stonewall, what memories were triggered?

He leaned over and kissed Ziggy on the cheek.

"I hope you find your friend," he said. Then he capered off toward the pier.

The next morning, Ziggy took the subway to Times Square first thing, and figured he could walk over to Grand Central Station and get a commuter train to Poughkeepsie dirt cheap. He could hitchhike from there up to northern Dutchess. He came up the subway steps into Times Square and stood on the corner of 42nd Street and 7th Avenue, one the most public places in the world. In a repetitive tic he had developed only recently, he reached for his shirt pocket. He felt a letter! But he had burned his induction letter! He pulled it out, shocked and staggered. No, it was not the induction letter. Not exactly. It was his draft card itself. Of course he had burned the letter but not the draft card. He hadn't worn this shirt in a couple of weeks. Long enough for him to have forgotten about the draft card. He looked at it.

Selective Service System
Registration Certificate

He thought about his inner struggle that day. Uncle Frank and his family had made some good points. There were mixed signals. But mixed signals doesn't mean there's not a right thing to do. And Zig now knew he had done the right thing. He crumpled his draft card and dropped it into the gutter. No need for bonfires this time, he thought to himself.

The small change commuter train fare was well worth it. Ziggy had a beautiful, relaxing ride up the east bank of the Hudson, with the Catskill Mountains gradually rising up in the west. From Poughkeepsie, he hitchhiked uneventfully up Highway 9, passing Marist and Vassar colleges and the Franklin D. Roosevelt estate, passing somewhere near the Millbrook commune where Timothy Leary had done his LSD experiments, and into the village of Rhinebeck. At the main intersection in Rhinebeck stood the Beekman Arms hotel with its in-house restaurant and bar, but Ziggy sought out a little coffee shop diner, Schemmy's, that looked more suitable for a backpacking hippie. Yes, Ziggy felt aligned with that countercultural thing, he could see some value in the disruptive spirit, but right now he needed to reflect, not disrupt. If only he could find a time and place of his own to reflect in.

Chapter 15

Jazmine sat on the porch, in the wooden slat armchair, finishing her mug of tea, watching the pickets of the fence blur together. She didn't really like the tea. Something, maybe the marshmallow root, was bitter. But she wanted to please the woman, the kind woman, who had prepared it for her. So she drank it in gratitude, and then rested.

An hour must have passed when the woman came back out and gently nudged Jazmine. It was time for her appointment. What appointment? Jazmine's mind reeled, ached from reeling, tried to fix itself on something. In all that phantasmagoria of joy and trauma and confusion in New Orleans, she could find no focal point.

"Jazmine, the doctor," said the woman benevolently.

241

Yes, the doctor, thought Jazmine. She could not grasp what doctor they were referring to, but it sounded right. Yes, of course, there was the doctor. She followed the woman into the house and through a rustic maze of hallways. They came out into a wood-paneled study, refreshingly lit by high windows with brown curtains pulled back. The small room was easily filled by the couch, two upholstered chairs, and a desk with a straight-back chair. The room looked familiar to Jazmine. A fortyish woman with tight lips and glasses stood and stepped around from the desk when Jazmine came in.

"How are you feeling today, Jazmine?"

"I think I'm a little better, Dr. Meyer." Yes, she recognized Dr. Meyer now. It was all coming back to her. "Definitely a little better. I guess it just takes a while for things to fall back into place."

"Yes, that was quite an event you had, Jazmine." She sat in one of the upholstered chairs and gestured for Jazmine to sit on the couch.

"You were quite broken down. Do you remember where you were when we found you?"

"Not exactly. I mean, it's coming back but not completely. We were sleeping in the car in a parking lot. A train station parking lot. I got out to go use the bathroom in the station. But something in the station. Something horrible. Then the car wasn't a car. It was a box. It was all some big mistake. I needed to get out and get away from that box. I remembered I needed to get to another station to meet someone. I needed to get to Rhinecliff. Everybody said to go to Rhinecliff Station. Somehow I got there."

"Yes, good," said Dr. Meyer. "Yes, you were in Rhinecliff. Do you remember talking to me about it?"

"Yes, now I remember. I've been here a few days. You and I talk about it every day at the same time."

242

"Good. Now we just need to unravel the story backwards until it fits, until you remember the parts you've blocked."

"It's all coming back. The tan acid. I took the tan acid and it gave me weird flashbacks. I was in Medieval Germany. Rebecca was my name. There was some kind of divine thing in my body. It appeared like a disease, but it was divinity. It was like the divinity was in my body but I couldn't feel it right. Like I was repressing something."

"Yes, good, Jazmine. We've been through this, but now you're awake, you see it yourself."

"Yes, Meister Berold knew. He wanted to help me. And Jeremiah was going to help me. But something bad happened. Something bad happened to Ragman. But that's where I lose the thread. Ragman was in a whole different time and place. New Orleans, recently."

"Do you know what we found in your pocket, Jazmine?"

"Something. I can't quite remember. I had some coins. A coin purse. I don't know."

"Do you remember what it was at the train station? The horrible thing?"

"No, no," said Jazmine, becoming agitated.

"You're close, Jazmine, we need to look at these things together, consciously, so you can control them instead of having them control you. Think, Jazmine, think. The train station. You put something in your pocket."

"Yes, I put something in my pocket." Jazmine was starting to break down again.

"Don't you want to know what it was, Jazmine? Are you ready now? Do you want to wait until tomorrow?"

"Yes, I want to know what it was. I'm ready. I can almost feel it in my hand. In my pocket. I had my hand in my pocket and was squeezing, crumpling. It was paper."

"Good, Jazmine. I think you're ready to cross the next bridge."

Dr. Meyer stood up and stepped around the desk. Everything seemed to be happening in slow motion to Jazmine. Her heart pounded. Dr. Meyer opened a drawer and took out a piece of crumpled paper. She started to come back around the desk. The slow-motion trauma was killing Jazmine. Would she never get around the desk?

Dr. Meyer sat back in her upholstered chair with the crumpled paper in her hand, resting on her lap.

"What was it, Jazmine? What was the paper you put into your pocket?"

Jazmine gasped for breath. "Ragman," she whispered, and a flood of tears came. Dr. Meyer sat next to her on the couch and put her hand on Jazmine's shoulder. She had not touched Jazmine before – perhaps there was some professional ethics thing about touching your patients – but Jazmine was grateful for the human touch.

With her other hand, Dr. Meyer dropped the paper on Jazmine's lap. It was a story from a crumpled newspaper, a small and apparently insignificant article, suitable filler for the back pages of the newspaper. The headline read: "Notorious Drug Dealer Killed in New Orleans Raid."

"I knew him," Jazmine sobbed. "He was my friend."

Dr. Meyer squeezed Jazmine's shoulder and rocked her gently. Ethics be damned, this girl needed empathy.

"Are you sure you knew him?" Dr. Meyer asked.

The question stupefied Jazmine. She was uncomprehending.

"Do you want to stop for the day, Jazmine?"

Jazmine took that as a challenge.

"No. Now is the time. I need to get this over with."

"Jazmine, think hard. Did you really know this Ragman person in New Orleans?"

Jazmine had stopped crying. Something more disturbing than tears was taking shape inside of her. She was confounded by Dr. Meyer's line of questioning.

"Are you just fucking with me?" she blurted out, not angry, but rather in sheer bewilderment.

"Jazmine, we found no evidence on you that you were even from New Orleans. All we found was the article. And the discussions we've had the past couple of days leave me unsure. We need to solve this puzzle together if we're going to get you out of here."

"What discussions?" whispered Jazmine, unable to regain her breath.

"Do you remember how your father died, Jazmine?"

Jazmine was confounded over and over again. She felt her face flush.

"I came home from school that day. There was a pile of dirty clothes on the living room sofa. I made myself a glass of chocolate milk. I walked back into the living room. The glass fell from my hand. It was not a pile of dirty clothes. It was the lifeless body of my dad. He'd had a heart attack hours ago and no one had been home. And like an idiot I was in the kitchen making a glass of chocolate milk."

"Yes, yes, you told me that. Do you remember now?"

"Yes, you asked about my family and I told you that."

"But you don't know for sure that you were in New Orleans?"

"No. I mean, yes, that's where I was living."

Jazmine stopped at the sound of her own voice saying "was living." Everything, every phrase, every memory was unsettling.

"Well, we don't know for sure yet, Jazmine. Let me tell you this story. Just a story of what might have happened.

245

And you can confirm the story or reject it or you can just listen for any clues you might use in your own recovery. Ok?"

Jazmine could not breathe. "Ok," she said almost inaudibly.

"In my story, you wander into that train station and see the newspaper article, right?"

"Right."

"And the guy who died a horrible death was called 'Ragman.'"

"Yes."

"I think that story triggered a long-forgotten obsessional neurosis. Do you know what that is?"

"Well enough. Yes."

"Somewhere, deep down, unconsciously, you felt responsible for your dad's death. Of course, that was a horrible trauma for any child to go through."

Jazmine simply nodded.

"A kernel of self-loathing was buried in your psyche and began to grow. Abjection. And what's the opposite of abjection? Divinity. Like any young girl, you wanted to grow and become a fully realized, fulfilled being. But that kernel of self-loathing was in there, and every time you felt yourself taking a step toward that beautifully fulfilled being, that kernel would slap you with guilt. 'How dare you!' it would say. 'Did you forget how you behaved when your father died? Do you want to kill your father all over again?' Does that make sense?"

Jazmine nodded in the affirmative.

"Should I go on, Jazmine?"

Jazmine wanted so strongly for Dr. Meyer to go on that she mustered the voice to say so.

"So your quite natural wish for fulfillment as you grew up was linked with the idea of a wish to kill your father. The fulfilled being you could not become you projected out as Rebecca. Rebecca, the avatar of the divine. But if you think of yourself as divine, something bad will happen to Ragman. The man who was a pile of dirty rags. 'Ragman' is the name your unconscious gave to your father, Jazmine."

Jazmine's lips were dry. Her mouth was too dry to speak. But she had to hear this. It made sense and she had to hear it. She mouthed the word water and Dr. Meyer stepped out and brought her a glass of water.

"We don't have to keep going today, Jazmine."

"No," said Jazmine, gaining some strength from the water. "We DO have to. I need to hear this in one piece."

"'Ragman' is a name for your father, Jazmine. When you saw the newspaper, your psyche saw an incredible coincidence in the name of the criminal, 'Ragman.' It brought back all of that old stuff about your father. It triggered real delusions this time. You imagined this whole life in Medieval Germany and in New Orleans. That's why you were incoherent when we found you. But you're improving rapidly, Jazmine. Can you feel that?"

"But what about all the other stuff. The Greek stuff. Wait. Did I tell you about …"

"Yes, Jazmine. You told me. Think of it this way. In the unconscious, as in dreams, often the different characters are different aspects of the self. In your visions, you were Prometheus, the divine fire-bringer, you were Eudoxia, the punisher, the Law-giver, in her divine form, as you punished yourself for causing the death of your father. You were Ioanna, the mediator. And Guda was the punisher in abject form."

Dr. Meyer could see Jazmine processing this information. She could well see Jazmine's intelligence and

247

drive to understand. So she gave Jazmine another angle to chew on.

"Think of it this way, Jazmine. It's a variant of the messianic delusion, which often counterpoints flights of omnipotence with countercurrents of masochism or self-punishing. Is it OK to talk about it like this?"

"Yes, good," said Jazmine. "This way is good. But …"

Dr. Meyer could see the wheels spinning in Jazmine's brain, so she remained silent and waited for Jaz to catch up.

"Ok," Jazmine said, "but what about Michaelskloster? It turned out to be real."

"How do you know that Jazmine?"

Jaz felt herself falling into bewilderment again.

"How do you know it turned out to be real?" Dr. Meyer gently pressed Jazmine, trying to get her to think it through.

"Because," started Jazmine slowly, "because it was in the library book."

"But is it possible – just hypothetically – couldn't you have made it all up, including the library discovery?"

Jaz pondered that silently. Yes, I suppose that is possible, she thought to herself. But it was mind-boggling. Could someone live a whole lifetime, an eternity of lifetimes, in a single day's dream?

"But … Rebecca," she fumbled. "Rebecca … her illness … how …" Jaz stopped there for lack of strength.

"Think it through, Jazmine. Rebecca's illness. What was Rebecca's illness? It was punishment for her messianic fantasy."

"But …" Jazmine was still stumbling into the story, finding her way. "But the divine thing, the messianic thing,

248

came later, after the illness. At least, she didn't know anything about the divine thing before she got ill."

"This often happens with an obsessional neurosis, Jazmine. The logic is flipped so the punishment comes first and then the transgression. We don't know why this happens but it's a common feature of the disorder. It was you all the time. You punishing yourself for your divine aspirations. Punishing yourself for the divine aspiration that would kill the rag man, your father."

It all made cruel sense to Jazmine now. But she could take no more. Not now.

That night, she lay awake thinking. It was the strangest thing. Here were two narratives. In one, she had gone through that whole beautiful scene in New Orleans, so rich in human connections to Ziggy and Ragman and Stormy and all the others. Even after it got weird, that depth of connection was the defining aspect of her being. In the other narrative, all those connections were illusory. Simply not there. But the other narrative was real. She was mentally and emotionally in shambles, that much she had to admit. Not crazy, but in shambles. And if the other narrative could restore her to reality, it would be worth it. Sure, it would be hard to give up her illusions, all that supposed human contact, the whole hippie scene they were building. But whatever had brought her to New York, she now had Dr. Meyer. For all she knew, Dr. Meyer might be her last lifeline to sanity. She sat up in bed and cracked open the window of the small bedroom to let in the chilly air. The stars flickered in the black night, beautiful and faraway and cold. "There's Venus," she said to herself. "And the moon."

The next morning scattered the stars and brought a new sun. Jazmine sat on the porch, in the wooden slat chair, with a mug of tea. This is "my spot" now, she thought.

249

Sitting on the porch here, with a mug of tea. Life seems to find its own fence posts and drill them in.

In the field between Jazmine and the apple orchard, a transaction was taking place. A young woman and man were delivering some boxes and sacks to Dr. Meyer's assistant. The delivery people were explaining something about the products to the assistant, who pulled her hair back into a ponytail as they spoke, to protect herself against the wind. The boxes appeared to be freshly grown vegetables, as the stamp on the boxes said "ORGANIC FARMS" in bold lettering that curved up and around a small unicorn logo. Jazmine felt a ruffle at the edges of her memory, but put it to rest with another sip of tea.

Another assistant joined the group with a two-wheeled dolly and the two staff members started loading the boxes. Meanwhile, the visitors who had delivered the packages turned and began walking toward Jazmine and the white picket exit to the one-lane road. Their approach astonished Jazmine. Every step staggered her still more deeply. She felt herself falling apart again as they wandered her way, ever so slowly, chatting carelessly. That tightening in her chest, the inability to breathe. Why was she feeling it all over again? The young woman she had never seen before. But the young man was familiar. Either it was a trick of her mind or the young man was Ziggy. But he did not seem to recognize her. The young couple stopped and turned back to the assistants wheeling the dolly toward the back of the house. Jazmine was in an agony of expectation. Would they never move on? They whispered something between themselves, then turned and continued in Jazmine's direction. No, the young man did not recognize her.

Chapter 16

Ziggy sat in Schemmy's diner in Rhinebeck, his pack beside the booth, drinking coffee and thinking through his next task. The villages in this part of Dutchess County – Rhinebeck, Red Hook, Tivoli – were small and closely knit. Lots of people had no doubt heard of the Red Queen's Naked Circus. These were not wallflower variety hippies. And their property, Unicorn Farm as Ragman had called it, had to have gained some attention in its own right. Ziggy would ply the locals a bit before digging through his tattered phone book looking for long shots.

He gazed out of the window distractedly, watching pedestrians pass on the sidewalk, cars on the street. Three kids stood in the street bouncing superballs against a brick building on the other side. A VW bug ratcheted by. Then a red carry-all. The kids scattered as the carry-all pulled over to park. The carry-all door opened. Zig felt a hot flow of adrenalin from the heart out to the forearms and thighs. A woman with a medium 'fro and an earth-tone dress stepped out of the carry-all. Mr. Anthony's carry-all. Ziggy knocked over his cup and saucer as he ran out. Stormy did not see him at first. Then she did. They met street center and hugged cheek-to-cheek, body-to-body, losing themselves in a poignant embrace that seemed to go on and on. Ziggy broke the silence.

"The Red Queen's Naked Circus. Unicorn Farm."

"Yeah," Stormy said. "Just four miles out. Between here and Tivoli."

"My bags," he said and went back into Schemmy's to gather his stuff.

The corkscrew-haired waitress was standing guard but broke into a smile when she saw him.

"I knew you weren't the type to cheat me. You owe me a dollar fifty."

As Ziggy fumbled with his money, he heard voices raised across the street. He looked but saw no Stormy. He paid and went back out. The voices were louder now, coming from a small bakery. He thought he heard Stormy's voice among them. He stepped through the door. Stormy stood at the counter. She had three loaves of French bread in her arms. Two guys just inside the door smirked.

"What you mean, you never seen her before?" one of them was saying. "That's Gladys Knight. Hey Gladys, where's the Pips?"

Ziggy was so close he could feel the heat of the man's breath.

"Come on, Gladys, I got some Pips waiting for you," added the bully menacingly.

Reflexively, Ziggy slipped one foot behind the man's heel and flipped him back to the floor with his elbow in his chest. The man hit the floor hard, without time to brace himself, and he felt his heart vulnerable under the ball of Ziggy's elbow. The other man held back, not knowing whom they were dealing with and not wanting to escalate with his compatriot in such peril. Stormy stepped over with her peep-toe, low-heeled shoe, put the three loaves of French bread on a table, and put the point of a shoe heel on the troublemaker's throat. She pushed Ziggy off with her hip. "Mine," she said. They could all see the heel resting on the hollow of his throat, just above the breastbone, but no one dared move, as the smallest slip or pressure would risk a fatal result. "You could learn his way." She spoke to the stranger but nodded at Ziggy. "Or my way." The calmer she seemed, the more nervous everyone else became. "You learn faster his way, with a good hard smack. But you learn better my way." Her hand reached toward the table where the loaves lay and grasped the back of a chair for balance. They could see the hollow of the man's throat move as he swallowed under the shifting pressure of the heel. "My way is to treat you the way I want to be treated." She took her heel from the man's throat, reached down and grasped his open sweatshirt with both hands, and pulled him to his feet. He stood confused, paralyzed, and she made a gesture as if to brush dirt off his chest. She picked up her loaves, nodded to Ziggy, and they turned and walked out.

On the drive out to the Farm, Ziggy was still recovering from the inner shifting that had resulted from his behavior at the bakery. He had acted without thinking. That was good, wasn't it? Don't overthink. But maybe acting without overthinking has its dark side, too. Sometimes it means aggressive pushback. Does that mean Saul was right? No, Stormy was right. Stormy showed him the way. But could Stormy have pulled it off without Zig's own pushback? Could Rag have succeeded without Saul? Did they have to go down together? Was his own action heroic or just buying into the network of violence? What are heroes, anyway? People with no insides. Ziggy knew he was still growing morally, figuring things out, that the whole horrible ordeal of last week had forced him to grow, but he would never be a hero. Heroes are just story book characters. You can only see them from the outside. As soon as you get inside somebody's head, you see inner struggles, second guesses, doubts between epiphanies. No, he, Ziggy, would never be a hero. Then he thought of the sheer physicality of Stormy picking the troublemaker up by his sweatshirt. He watched her pounding through the gears on the carry-all like a master trucker, her head bobbing and throwing occasional smiles his way.

"I didn't know you could pick up a man like that," Ziggy said.

"Have a kid, Zig. Pick'm up a thousand times when they're crying or fighting or biting your hand, when your back hurts or you got the flu. Then you'll know."

This raised an interesting question for Ziggy.

"Where is Rose Petal anyway?"

"With Julia."

"Julia?"

"Watch. We're coming right up."

She turned up a hilly gravel road into the woods. It was not what Ziggy expected. But then they hit a couple of clearings, a woodworking shop, a barn and an open patch of strawberries, green beans, and potatoes. They arrived at a farmhouse, where a few kids scrambled around the front yard and someone in the distance chopped wood. Inside, everything was clean and fresh, and Ziggy was suddenly very tired, feeling the weight of a long trip. He nearly collapsed as Stormy handed the loaves to a couple in the kitchen, chatting quietly. When Stormy turned back to Ziggy, he asked the obvious question.

"Where's Jazmine?"

"Come on," Stormy said. "Let's get you to a bed. I'll tell you about it along the way." She led him down the hall.

"Everything's OK now Zig, but it was quite a trip. The tan acid must have messed with her mind."

"Where is she?"

"She's a couple miles down the road. I lost her in Poughkeepsie."

"You what?!"

"No, calm down. We know where she is now. Julia delivers produce to this place, this facility. She heard about them finding Jazmine. She saw Jazmine on the porch."

"Well let's go get her!"

"It's not that easy, Ziggy. It's like a mental health place. Bearview Manor. They're not just going to take a

254

patient who's been freaking out and give her to the first bunch of hippies that comes along."

"But they don't know the whole story. She belongs with us. We just need to check her out."

"I know Zig. But we're not exactly family. Not legally. We can't just check her out. Not with paperwork. But the place is not a lockdown. It's not like they have her guarded. Julia thinks we can just quietly get her when we're making a produce delivery."

Ziggy like the idea. He was ready. But Stormy was right. He needed to fortify himself for a day or two. They were taking care of Jazmine in their own way. She'd be alright for now.

After a nap and a shower, Ziggy joined Stormy in the living room.

"This place has great hot water pressure. I feel recharged."

He noticed a woman across the room with her back to him, sitting at a piano. All he could see was long black hair, straight and shiny and sleek to the waist. She tinkled a few notes. Ziggy sat at a high-backed chair across the coffee table from Stormy, who sat on a couch.

"It helps," the woman said, "to have a master plumber and his family living on the commune."

The woman stood up, turned, and walked toward the couch to join Stormy. Ziggy was stunned by this woman's appearance. She was Guatemalan, with jet black hair and green eyes, medium height but she seemed taller, with elegant posture and an air of dark nobility.

"This is Julia," Stormy said.

"You must be hungry," Julia said. "But first how about some tea?"

"Y'all got coffee?"

"Sure."

As she walked out, the thought struck Ziggy. This was not just some Julia. This was THE Julia. The Julia who had been Ragman's open lover in the early days of St. Roch. She brought coffee for three and shared a bit of her story. She had been born in Madrid, where her father was a staff member in the Guatemalan ambassador's inner circle, but after the CIA-sponsored coup in '54, she returned a toddler to Guatemala, where her politically connected family was buffeted by the winds of successive military juntas. Her parents disappeared without a trace in 1960, and she escaped to New Orleans with an aunt. And here she sat, sipping coffee with Ziggy and Stormy.

"So this is it," Ziggy said. "Unicorn Farm. The commune Ragman talked about."

"Don't get your hopes up," Julia laughed. "It's not paradise. It's hard work, and kids getting sick, and cleaning out the blood and placenta after a calving."

Ziggy smiled back. He could see in Julia's face what she was trying to say indirectly, that it was all worth it. And what a face! This woman gleamed like a star, exquisite, polished, looking on the human drama from above. Ragman was all hands-on, all close-knit camaraderie, heart-to-heart, breast-to-breast. Julia was on a cosmic pedestal. Ziggy felt for a moment as if he had wandered into a Greek pantheon to witness one of the immortals.

"Oh shit," Stormy said. "I gotta go get Rose Petal from the kids' center. Y'all want to meet at the dining hall?"

"Why don't you bring her here," said Julia. "Let's stay in tonight. Eat something here. We don't want to throw Ziggy out into the deep end of his paradise before we take care of business."

After an enormous bowl of hearty vegetarian chili, Zig pranced around with Rose Petal on his shoulders, a height that she found dangerous and exhilarating. Then they

256

rolled around on the floor while Stormy and Julia sipped wine.

"Look at them," Julia said. "Two kids."

* * *

Jazmine's plight at Bearview seemed to have been dangling forever before her. She sat on the porch, watching the produce delivery couple come toward her, trying to concentrate her mind. Here were those two narratives. Total insanity on one side and complete sanity on the other, and she had to choose which was which, like picking a card from a deck. Both sides seem perfectly rational, possible. The dilemma itself was insane. Was this really how people made life-changing decisions? The couple continued toward her. Could this be "Ziggy" or was she projecting, as Dr. Meyer said she'd projected Ragman. The young man did not seem to recognize her. Then they were upon her, at the side of the porch, passing. He turned to her at the last second and whispered, "Come on, Jaz. We're getting you out of here." Was she inventing this? She felt the two narratives again. She had to decide without any positive evidence, and her whole destiny, her whole being, depended on the decision. She could go straight to Dr. Meyer now for an emergency session. This could be it, her breakthrough session. She could walk off with this guy. She would be thinking he was Ziggy, when he might be freaking out, not knowing who she was. The thought amused her. She quietly set down her mug and joined the couple in their nonchalant walk toward the Volkswagen van with the unicorn logo on the one-lane road.

Julia drove the van, and Jazmine and Ziggy sat in the second row of seats. The van torqued and gasped up and down along the road through the wooded hills. Jaz looked into Ziggy's eyes and saw everything she needed to know.

257

This kind of connection could not be fabricated. She saw tears welling up in his eyes, something she had never seen before. And she felt the certainty of that "before." Yes, this was Ziggy, whom she had known at a depth of being before and beyond Dr. Meyer's ken. It was not Dr. Meyer's fault. How could she know? But Jazmine had chosen her narrative. And she had chosen correctly.

Now Jazmine broke down quietly. The van rumbled on. She and Zig held on to each other and wordlessly let their lives begin the slow process of settling back into place.

As they entered Unicorn Farm, Jazmine immediately noticed the difference between this property and the one on which she'd spent the last few days. Bearview was more picturesque but static. Here was the smell of goats and manure, frustration at a potter's shop needed but not yet finished, people sweating in the fields, the gawking eyes of curious kids. Here there was life being lived.

They stopped at the main house, where Julia put Jazmine into the same crisply furnished guest room where Ziggy had slept. The freshness of the place served Jazmine well, and she improved rapidly over the next few days. Yes, she realized she had freaked out after the tan acid and after finding out what had happened to Ragman. She had felt lost and she had gotten lost. She had not been able to feel her own identity, at least not to feel it right. But what she needed was not to be fitted to some model of analysis. She needed something simple and human. She needed Zig and Stormy and Julia. In their presence, she was stronger already. She knew who she was.

Only once did she even feel a flicker of flashback. Dr. Meyer had shown up at the Farm with two assistants. No secrets could last in this small community, and Jazmine's whereabouts were soon enough known.

Julia met Dr. Meyer on the porch of the main house. Jazmine had seen Dr. Meyer's approach and thought it best to retreat indoors. This was not the time and place to test her newfound strength. No sense putting herself within reach, not with friends such as Julia and Stormy and Zig to count on.

Stormy and Ziggy were on a porch swing. Ziggy was learning to play the guitar, and he was picking at it when the incident took place. He set the guitar down. He and Stormy remained seated in the background, but attentive. Dr. Meyer stood at the bottom of the three steps leading up to the broad porch, flanked by her own pair of backers.

"Julia," began Dr. Meyer. "You know why I'm here."

"Yes." Julia stood straight as an arrow, her long black hair glistening in the wind, looking for all the world like an ancient Mayan princess.

"You violated my trust, Julia. You were on my property to deliver produce, not to interfere with patients. You know that."

"Yes."

"Julia, that girl needs help. I don't know what you're thinking. She is struggling to stabilize. I can give her therapy, treatment, 24-hour observation, psychiatric drugs if she needs them. What can you give her here, on a farm?"

"Love."

One of Dr. Meyer's assistants took a step forward. It did not seem a bellicose move, but Ziggy instinctively stood up from the swing. Dr. Meyer took notice of him for the first time.

"Are you with Julia in this, young man?"

"Yes ma'am."

"You know you could get into trouble?"

"Yes ma'am."

259

She studied the young man's expression. He stood as straight as Julia but much taller, with long wavy black locks hanging past his shoulders.

"Would you be willing to give me your name?"

"Ziggy."

Dr. Meyer stood thunderstruck. Ziggy. Wasn't that one of the characters in Jazmine's delusional universe? She caught her breath without giving any sign that she had lost it.

"Ziggy," Dr. Meyer said out loud. "You know a fellow named Ragman?"

"Yes ma'am."

"Then you knew Jazmine's father?"

"No ma'am. Never met him."

Dr. Meyer was staggered. Ziggy went on.

"I don't know what you're thinking, Dr. Meyer. Ragman was our friend in New Orleans. Jazmine's friend." With every sentence, Dr. Meyer weakened.

"He was an inspiration to everybody who met him. And if you're thinking he would hurt Jazmine. First, he wouldn't, because he was the best man we ever met. And second, he couldn't because he's dead."

By this time, Dr. Meyer was seated on the steps.

"Shot dead by the cops. Every visionary the same. Shot dead for loving the world too hard."

Dr. Meyer could almost feel the shot piercing her own heart. So she had been wrong about Jazmine. But still. Her point of view was still correct in the big picture. She tried to sound firm in her frailty.

"But Jazmine ... she's ... she's not well. She still needs help. Professional help."

"Good day, Dr. Meyer," said Julia.

Dr. Meyer's assistants seemed unsure of what to do next, and Dr. Meyer herself seemed too weak to stand. Julia sat next to her for a few seconds, then lifted her up. Dr. Meyer regained some of her composure.

"I'll ..." She started to speak but seemed like she did not know what to say. She blurted: "Maybe I'll be back." She immediately thought of how foolish that sounded, but decided it best not to add anything. Then off she went with her assistants.

"Do you think she'll make trouble?" asked Ziggy.

"No," said Julia. "Thanks to you."

"Thanks to me?"

"Did you see how she looked when you told her your name? She knows she was wrong about Jazmine. Her diagnosis was way off. Once she saw you, heard you back up Jazmine's so-called delusions, what could she do? No, she'd rather let sleeping dogs lie."

"She didn't look like she'd give up so easily to me."

"Don't worry, Ziggy. First, they can't keep Jazmine at Bearview against her will. And we have the body." She shook her black hair in the wind. "'Habeas corpus,' as they used to say."

"Plus, Dr. Meyer just met her so-called hallucination in flesh-and-blood." Julia smiled. "And he looked like he might be ready to get serious with her attendants."

Ziggy blushed. He couldn't remember the last time that happened, but he blushed.

"Anyway, Dr. Meyer's not evil, Ziggy. She's just wrong on this one. Maybe all of her conventional techniques work sometimes. But Jazmine doesn't fit the paradigm."

"Maybe none of us out here fits the paradigm," Ziggy said.

The event with Dr. Meyer having come to a felicitous conclusion, the work of communal life went on. Besides the main house, eleven simple rectangular cabins and currently two vacant guest cabins dotted the woods and fields, along with various sheds, workshops, and support buildings. It more than sufficed for the 42 adults and 15 kids who were permanent residents, and the Farm seemed ready to take on more if more came. Ziggy was alternately assigned to the mechanic's shop, painting crew, and then library. He liked the library best, where he could browse the books and record albums and even play the albums if no one was on site and concentrating. Jaz was set up in a guest cabin, where she could go out or rest and rebuild as needed. Stormy and Zig and Rose Petal stayed in the main house with Julia, but most always took meals in the communal dining hall.

It made sense to Zig that he and Stormy, as guests, might end up in the main house, but he wondered about Julia. Did it smack a little too much of class rank for her to be permanently stationed in the main house? Was she the de facto lifetime leader? Grand vizier of the commune? This came up one night in the dining hall. They were seated together – Jaz, Zig, Stormy, Julia, and Danny, a mild-mannered, heavily tattooed circus juggler who had been there since day one, energetically building the place by hand with Julia. When the issue of housing came up, Julia smiled that smile of hers – no one could deny that it was an aristocratic smile.

"It's true," she said, "Danny and I were de facto leaders when we were getting this place set up. That was almost three years ago. Now the leadership rotates. Zig, you've already rotated between a few crews. If you become a permanent member, get to know our long-term needs inside and out, you'll rotate onto the Leadership Committee. They coordinate the various on-going projects, make land use decisions, and send work crews off site to bring in a little money for the community. We still need money too," she added demurely.

262

"So we send out construction and paint crews, and we got some members now making beautiful pottery. The money gets pooled for the people doing all the internal work on the commune that week. But it only works with a Leadership Committee. Somebody's playing the management role all the time. But it's not hierarchical. They get the same hours logged in as the kitchen crew. And next month the same people might be on the kitchen crew themselves. Oh, but what about me. We were thinking we might have to rotate the main house, too, for the same reason, so nobody was singled out. But everybody liked where they were, and we decided that the human element was worth more than the rule. So, yeah, the rule is no hierarchy, no permanent leaders, but when it comes to housing, we all just decided to use rule # 2." Julia paused.

"Ok, you win," said Stormy. "What's rule # 2?" Julia seemed pleased with her little game.

"Rule # 2: Break any rule when it doesn't work."

"Sounds great, but could get a little dicey," said Stormy.

"No doubt," Julia smiled. "It's been hard tested a few times. We're still navigating the rapids. But we're all here for a reason and that helps us manage."

"Sounds like the kind of non-rule rule Ragman would have liked," Jaz said.

"Poor, sweet genius Ragman," mused Julia.

In the moment of collective nostalgia, Ziggy thought of how much Ragman would have liked Unicorn Farm. A real commune. Ziggy was almost embarrassed that they used to call the place at St. Roch "the commune." Or "the co-op." Ziggy had never really known what the terms exactly meant or the difference between them. Now things were getting clearer. Commune and co-op were both cooperative living arrangements for people with shared ideals, but in a co-op the members still owned their own stuff. In a commune, everyone held everything in common. Zig figured every group could find its own level along that gradient. But he and Jaz and all the kids at the Island and the Duck – they didn't know one from the other – they were just making things up as they went along. Jazmine's brother, Tom, had been right. A few underemployed hippies in a house doesn't make a commune. Unicorn Farm was a commune. Poor Ragman could only dream of a place like this.

Julia must have read Ziggy's mind because she turned those penetrating green eyes on him as she spoke.

"Ragman could have had this any time of day. He visited here. And Timothy Leary's place in Millbrook. And Wavy Gravy's Hog Farm, too. But in a way, Ragman was too good for all of this. He was always one step ahead of us. This?" She swept her hand out to indicate the full dining hall and the land beyond. "This is easy. Once you get the hang of it, no lifestyle in the world is easier. But Ragman chose the front lines. He was out there pulling people up through the weeds in the Man's own jungle. Flying without a net. Or like the guy trying to get people into the life raft when the ship's going down. You and Jazmine and Stormy, too. You were out there doing the real work of changing the world, building those life rafts with nothing to go on. Us, we're just sitting on the shore, well-fed and waiting for everybody else to come home."

There was a pause, a moment of reflection for the whole group. And in that pause, Jazmine thought she heard Rebecca's voice. "Ragman's happy," said the voice.

"Ragman's always happy," Jazmine said out loud.

The others looked at her and saw in her face joy and wonder.

Julia lifted her glass. "To Ragman," she said. And the others joined in, turning on the communal joy and wonder with a toast.

Danny grabbed a bottle of wine, which they dispatched in short order, compiling each from their own past selected tales of the Rag.

"Why did they come after him anyway?" pondered Jaz during a lull in the conversation.

"The tan acid," said Julia. "That was his downfall. The cops – not even the cops but the levers of power above them – were never going to let the tan acid or anything like it get past St. Roch. Rag's fate was sealed a long time ago. Ragman was a real hero. An idealist. A subversive in the best sense. And it killed him."

"But," started Jaz, feeling a little complicit because of her special role with the tan acid. "But how did they know?"

"Biggles," said Stormy.

"Yeah, what's the deal with Biggles?" Ziggy asked.

"Back in '67," Stormy started. Then she swirled her wine and took a sip, as Jazmine and Ziggy adjusted their seats to hear this thread of their own history.

"Biggles was branching out into heroin and coke sales around that time. He saw Ragman's army as customers. Ragman saw them as people, people reconnecting to something human beings had lost. People longing for a vision. So there was a kind of power struggle between Biggles and Ragman."

"Seems like Ragman was the obvious best choice," said Zig.

"Not obvious to everyone," said Stormy. She took another sip, seeming a little reticent, and Julia stepped in.

"The desire of addiction fights as hard inside a body as the desire for true happiness. And addiction can dress in the finest costumes. 'Take me and you'll be happy,' it says. But it's a false happiness, a selfish pleasure that grates, not the happiness that soothes. Trust me, we had our fights with this in the first days of Unicorn Farm."

Danny had opened another bottle of wine, and he and Julia seemed to have a little private toast over that remark.

"So what happened then with the power struggle between Biggles and Ragman?" inquired Jaz.

"Me," said Stormy pensively.

"When Rag took me and Rose Petal in – she was a tiny thing – that did it for Biggles. Biggles knew he'd lost. Nobody in the Co-op could *not* feel protective of Rose. Biggles just had to recoil and get away."

"So Rag won the power struggle," pressed Jaz.

"Or Rose won it for him," continued Stormy. "But not forever. I don't know what happened after Biggles left, but he was seething, vengeful. At some point, I imagine the cops got a hold of him – or the levers of power as Julia says – and they used him to get at Rag, through that lanky kid y'all seen at the lake, through Beachbum."

"So Rag won first and then Biggles won after all," said Jaz, trying to piece things together in a way that made sense on the logical plane of things.

"I don't know if Biggles won in the end," said Stormy. "Biggles was a pawn. Whose spirit will survive? Who gave us something to live by, to carry on?" she continued, as if trying to figure out how to ask it right.

"That's the moral way to look at it," said Julia.

"What other way is there?" asked Zig, whose curiosity was piqued even as his heart was torn. Danny was busy keeping all glasses full.

"In the ancient Mayan calendar," said Julia, "time moves forward and backward. Why? Because cosmic time

266

moves forward and backward. Did you know that the equinoxes move backwards against the constellations at a rate of 1 degree every 72 years?"

No, no one in the group had known that, but they were all ears.

"In the forward dimension of time, Biggles betrayed Ragman and Ragman died. In the backward dimension of time, Biggles' betrayal, and all it represents, comes first and Ragman rises from the ashes of that betrayal." Julia paused, thinking it through herself.

"So the good guy wins after all," smiled Jaz.

"Maybe," said Julia. "But this Mayan thing isn't a moral way of looking at it. No good guys and bad guys. It's more like a religious way. Not so much who's right and who's wrong but more about the fundamental miracle of creation, of how creation works. Take Jesus. The whole point is that he doesn't just give meaning to those lives that come after him, but sends meaning back, in the other direction, rolling new life into all those who lived and died before him."

"That's a cool way of looking at it," said Zig. "But I still see it together. The moral way and what you're calling the religious way. Together. When I look at Ragman's life, his actual life, I have to see them together."

"Good for you," said Julia mysteriously. She downed the rest of her wine. "What is a life anyway, one life? There is no one life. Just a tangled mess of lives."

"I know what you mean," Jaz said.

Chapter 17

The next morning, Stormy shifted her duties. She had worked until then in construction, repairing a shed and then finishing the pottery workshop. Her rapid acclimation to the journeyman's tools had been the talk of the commune, but the next day she moved to the Kiddy Cabin, an overgrown playhouse and a large grassy area surrounded by a foot-high stone wall that had all the markings of a pony ring. Rose Petal had adjusted quickly to her situation as well, but then she had an accident with the Kiddy Cabin's resident hamster. She was perhaps more upset than expected, and Stormy thought it best to spend the days with her for a while, which meant Kiddy Cabin duty.

Ziggy and Jaz had taken the day off to go into Rhinebeck in the carry-all to get cleaning supplies for one of the work crews. Ziggy was on the lookout for the bakery boys, but everyone on this day seemed to go out of their way to be nice. Ziggy and Jazmine treated themselves to the luxury of a beer at Foster's Coach House Tavern, where the owner, upon discovering that his visitors were from the faraway south, threw in a clam chowder on the house.

Still later, after their chores were done and the sun had set, Ziggy and Jazmine sat behind Jazmine's cabin, which abutted the woods. There was no bench in the back so they had spread a blanket out, just to peer into the darkness descending on the woods and listen to the crickets.

"Listen to all that tiny life," Jaz said. "I wonder what they're feeling."

"I know," Zig said. "Tuning into their little universe right there in the woods." He and Jaz took a moment to tune their own senses to that little universe themselves. Zig saw

Jaz with her eyes closed, smiling, steadying her breathing to a deep and slow pace.

"How about you, Jaz? How do you feel?"

"Don't laugh, Zig."

"Why would I laugh?"

"Because I've been so sick and run down."

"Why would I laugh at that?"

"It's not that. It's just that – after all that – I feel better than I've ever felt before."

Ziggy thrilled to the sound of those words. Jazmine was doing well. Wonderful, in fact. The world was wonderful.

"How about you, Zig?"

He could feel her breath.

"How you doing? I know it hasn't been easy for you either."

"I feel good. Great. I can't even remember when it was bad. Was it yesterday or a million years ago?"

"You're becoming our philosopher-king, you know, Zig," Jazmine poked.

"Smart, sexy, and ready for revolution," he teased back.

"It's getting chilly. I'm going get a sleeping bag," Jaz said.

Ziggy lay back on the blanket, engaging with imagination as well as his senses the sounds and smells of invisible life in the woods a few steps away.

Jaz came back, shaking out the sleeping bag, and nudged Ziggy over with her foot.

"You're not wearing shoes, Jaz?"

"No, just my wool socks. I want to feel free."

She spread the sleeping bag over Ziggy, over the whole blanket, and crawled under.

Ziggy could feel her breath again. Her body next to his. He almost kissed her but held back. He had kissed her before – theirs was an affectionate friendship – but he knew that if he kissed her now it would be different. It would be more than a kiss of friendship. No, he loved her too much to change the terms on her now.

"What are you thinking, Zig?"

"I don't know. All that tan acid stuff. Wasn't that weird, Jaz? The regressions? What was all that about?"

"I don't know. I just know it's not a one-to-one correspondence like Dr. Meyer wanted it to be."

"But what did it all mean?"

"I don't know, Zig. I don't care either. I think that was one of my problems, one of the knots tying me up inside. I wanted it to mean something. But it doesn't matter. I was there. I felt it. Rebecca felt me. So what does it matter what it means?"

Zig didn't get it.

"Remember that day with the saints cards, Zig. And the Oat Willie stickers? Running around with Tex and Rag and the Hare Krishna kids? Remember how we felt that day?"

"Yeah, what a nice, sunshiny day that was."

"Well what did that day mean?"

Zig didn't answer.

"The sunset over the Catskills tonight, Zig. The smell of magnolias back home. What do they mean?"

"I'm not sure I understand the question," Zig finally said.

"My point exactly," said Jazmine. She turned toward him and cuddled up, with an arm on his chest and her head on his shoulder. Then it clicked for Ziggy. He shared her moment of recognition.

"The whole big universe out there," she continued musing. "We think it's out there but it's in here. It's an inward universe, and it doesn't mean anything, but we're all in it together. I'm learning through Rebecca. She's learning through me. And it's not too late for her. Time doesn't work that way. We're all writing and rewriting each other's stories all the time. We can write it how we like. It just takes a little vision."

They looked at the stars and pondered, each in their own way, but together.

"Walpurgisnacht," Jazmine murmured.

"What?"

"Walpurgisnacht. The night when witches meet in the mountains in Medieval Germany. I looked it up. We just missed it. It would have been last week, or maybe the week before."

"Weird," Ziggy said. "But when I look at the sky, I can feel it."

"Sure you can. Up there are the same stars they looked on in Medieval Germany."

Jazmine took out her braid and let her hair fall across Ziggy's shoulder and the edge of his chest.

"Did I do the right thing, Ziggy? Leaving college? Quitting the Marketing program all of a sudden like that?"

"Yeah. You were right and I was wrong. I was pushing you to stay in toward the end, because I thought … well, I don't know what I thought. It's just you were always so driven to do this thing. And then with the tan acid … I don't know, I didn't want you to quit something just because of the tan acid."

Jazmine smiled.

"Well, I called Dean Hecht anyway, and he said I can take my exams from here at Bard College. So at least I'll finish the semester."

271

"You're great, Jazmine."

"I know," she giggled, and hoisted herself up so her face was looking down at Ziggy's. Ziggy could feel it coming. The thing he was avoiding. He couldn't remember why he was avoiding it.

"Walpurgisnacht," she said again.

"Witches in the mountains," Ziggy said with a smile.

"Witches right here," she whispered.

Jazmine's face came down closer to his, hesitated, and then her lips gently touched his. He could still feel the scar against the softness of her lower lip.

Now she was kissing him in earnest, and he kissed back. The flow of genuine affection was uninhibited. Ziggy felt it as a tingle inside, a fantastic euphoric quiver. There was no trace of that conflicted feeling, no shame. He fumbled with her bra, and Jaz reached back and unfastened it. They embraced, laughed, rolled around under the sleeping bag, the earth below and the stars trundling above. Ziggy slowly explored the landscape of her body, attending to every curve and nuance. Layers and layers of scent and taste: heavy musk and wild mint, olive and sea salt, the graze of her fingertips on his stomach, the exquisite feathery tip of her tongue, the creamy softness of her breasts and the sudden darkness of the nipples. He moved down, feeling, tasting his way down, layers and layers of landscape, the curve below the belly, the pubic tuft, and the swollen pink and purple-tinged folds below. He moved up, sinking his fingers into the opulence of her black hair, gazing at her in wonder, the Egyptian-Frankish mystery in her deep violet eyes and charcoal lashes, the ivory skin, Jazmine, whom he knew so intimately, the true Jazmine, in cosmic and physical splendor, with all the petals of her body open and hungry and free. This was one of love's secrets, the freedom, the absence of all possessiveness. Zig now knew that this was

272

his hesitation, his fear, his conflict. He feared possessiveness. But now, with Jazmine in his arms, his love knew no possessiveness. It was exhilarating, liberating. This too was the secret to the song.

> We were so close, there was no room
> We bled inside each other's wounds

It wasn't the Viet Nam War or even Woodstock, but something underneath both, an internal reference point. That capacity for self-effacement combined with empathy, the capacity to bleed inside each other's wounds. And chase the internal dark away, heal the disease. He and Jazmine had reached that point. This wasn't just about sex. Well, sex was part of it. Beautiful, delicious, tantalizing sexual bodies. But it was about much more. He and Jazmine had reached that point of intimacy where they could bleed inside each other's wounds. Right now, wrapped in their own tangle of body and souls, he could feel it. And he knew she could feel it. They had reached the point at which time stood still.

Jazmine pressed her palms against Ziggy's skin, from the smooth triceps around to the tightened abs and back up to the shoulders. Then along the sides of the backbone, all smooth skin and muscle. His shaved whiskers scratched her belly and the fullness of her breasts. Her hands moved along his back, down to the flex-tightened bulk of his buttocks. She felt his desire growing, stretching, gorging up against her. She felt the warmth and firmness of her own thighs against him. Then his black locks hung over her face. She pressed her forehead hard into his chin. This was Ziggy, blood and bone and sinew, Ziggy who had always eased her, calmed her, Ziggy who had loved her without thinking, without expectation. She was overwhelmed with emotion. She felt him probing her body, gently at first, then with

273

power. She clenched her arms to his back, in desperation and love, grasping the flesh, squeezing himself, herself, toward some primeval animal release.

Afterward, as Jazmine lay resting her head against Ziggy's chest, she understood what Ragman was saying about sexual liberation at the Tree of Life. The sexual body, the physicality of sex, was beautiful when it's an expression of full human connection and degrading when it's an abstraction from human connection. That's what he was trying to say when he talked about commodified sexuality. Ragman had taught her something. She smiled. She, Ragman, Rebecca, even Dr. Meyer, everybody helping each other along, making mistakes, learning on the fly. And Ziggy. Ziggy liberated her and all the world. Ziggy opened her back up. She had been closed for so long. It was back to her Mom's fucked up boyfriend, Ken. Just the suggestion of sexual desire from Ken, his hand grazing her. She suddenly remembered what Ken had said on that day that he had laid his hand on her butt, Ken with his hot breath: "Work it, girl. Tell me when, and we'll work it together." Simple, non-committal, but devastating to her. The devil is most evil when he's most subtle. It had not even been that long after she'd started her period. "What work?" she had stuttered back, short of breath, helpless in her confusion. But she knew what he meant. She knew it was something sexual. So that was her introduction to sexual desire. Maybe it wasn't even sexual desire. Maybe it was just power. After all, he never actually tried anything after that. Ken never followed up on anything he said. For once that was a godsend. But anyway, it registered in her young mind as sexual desire. That could sure as hell explain why she implicitly acted as if sex were dirty and love were pure, why they had to be separated. Maybe she had learned something from Dr. Meyer after all. That explained something of Rebecca too.

274

Her fear of Meister Berold, of his hot breath. Rebecca in some vague way was remembering Ken.

But the sex and love thing, how they had to be closed off from one another, it took Ziggy to open her again. Not Ziggy himself exactly, but being with Ziggy. That had opened her up again, had shown her what was so simple for some and so difficult for others, that sex and love go together. Only Ziggy, the one person she could trust most, the one she could open up to completely without emotional risk, if not for Ziggy she might have lived out her life building walls upon walls. She leaned over and kissed his neck, then his mouth. He responded, not with passion but with gentleness.

"What you thinking, Jaz?"

"Nothing. Just how fucked up my whole life would have been without you."

Ziggy smiled and lightly caressed down the length of her tricep. Without pride or false humility, he knew what she meant. Nothing needed to be said. That's what he found so great, so enlightening about Jazmine. They could integrate souls completely – this night had proven it – and still be totally individuals, thinking their own thoughts, finding their own way. It was a paradox, really. Only by staying true to themselves, by not giving themselves up, could they integrate their souls completely, to that vanishing point where time disappears. And only by the communion of souls could the individual be complete. This was as true for Ziggy as it was for Jazmine. And for Ziggy, it was the possessiveness thing. It was only by giving up any false instinct to possess that you could feel real love, the transcendental kind of love. But it's only when you feel that love that you can shed any last trace of possessiveness. He thought of all those loves ruined by lies. And how without possessiveness, all those lies could have been avoided. Why couldn't people just see that? He felt compassion pooling and flowing outward.

"What are you thinking, Zig?"

"My own hangups." He hiked his head up on one elbow. "I think what I feared most about this moment …"

"You knew this moment was coming?" she cut in.

"Not before it happened, but looking back, I guess so. But I thought it would change us. I thought love would be possessive, and then we'd need commitments, and things would get all tied in knots."

"We have love, Zig. We don't need commitment."

She suddenly seemed so wise, so certain. Ziggy was still wrapping his head around the idea.

"Look up there, Zig."

"Venus. And the moon."

"No deeper. Further back. The constellations. The timeless cosmos. Our love is forever etched on that screen. What is commitment, Zig? It's a relationship in time. Commitments last 10, 20, sometimes 40 years. We're beyond that."

She pulled him back down and kissed him, and they fell pleasantly back into each other's arms.

"We have eternity, Zig. We don't need the timebound thing. We're like archetypes up there in the sky."

"You make it sound like art."

"It is art, Zig. It's the basis of all art. And it's right here with us. In us. We're experiencing it here and now. We are the archetypes. Cupid and Psyche, Apollo and Daphne, they're all shadows cast by us, by what we're feeling at this moment."

Ziggy's attention alternated between Jazmine and the stars.

"Something divine has chosen us, Zig. I was resisting. All that effort to find meaning. It was actually

276

resistance. I'm resisting less now. But you and I, Zig, we're carrying some torch, something that's also etched in those timeless archetypes up there."

A low-flung cloud whisked between them and the stars, and when it passed the lights of the sky seemed even more crisp.

"We have a torch to carry, Zig. Rag's torch, Rebecca's. We have to do it deliberately or the light will go out."

Ziggy thought for a moment that Jazmine was the light. He saw it in her eyes, in the radiance of her body.

Zig kissed her. "You're beautiful," he said. "Beautiful and dazzling and it doesn't mean a thing."

They smiled, laid back, and became thoughtful again.

"I get what you said about timelessness, Jaz. I feel it too. But I'm thinking, people can feel what we feel and still make that commitment in time, can't they?"

"What are you thinking about? Montreal?"

"I'm still going, you know."

"I know." She ran her finger along his cheek.

"Yeah, Zig, people can feel what we feel and still make that commitment in time. Rule # 2, remember?"

Ziggy remembered.

"So maybe us too someday, Zig. We can have it if we want it. But we don't need it, and that makes all the difference. We'll be choosing it from a position of total freedom every day." She was surprised at the depth of her own rolling realization.

"We love each other more than we need each other. Now I know what that means."

Chapter 18

The next morning, Jaz and Ziggy were in a fog of ecstasy and the commune was in a chaos of expectation. It was mock-circus day, as the Red Queen's Naked Circus had broken out its instruments in preparation for a hippie gathering of the tribes across the river in the village of Woodstock. The village was some fifty miles from the famous Woodstock Festival, but it was the village that was the sometime home of Bob Dylan and Robbie Robertson and The Band, and you never knew who would show up on Tinker Street to join in a song. Anyway, there would be tourists with money, and the Naked Circus hoped to bring home a small windfall for infrastructure projects.

The patch of Unicorn Farm that tapered down to the creek was abuzz. Two young women in headbands tuned up an accordion, a mime busily painted himself in gold, a stilt walker pranced in colorful shredded rags, and half the commune seemed to be donning themselves in the costume garb of fantastic creatures. The other half were down in the creek, some naked, some topless in cutoffs, taking a cool dip. The kids were either naked in the creek or shrieking with delight as the costumed creatures prodded and tickled. To Jazmine, it looked like a scene from Hieronymus Bosch's *Garden of Earthly Delights*. To Ziggy, it looked like the future of humankind.

Night fell to the rhythmic primal sound of a drum circle calling kids and all back from the creek to the pony ring by the Kiddy Cabin. Jaz had Ziggy's arm tucked into hers as a campfire crackled and embers flew.

"Like that night at St. Roch," said Zig. "Remember that night a few weeks ago with Hoss and Pepper and Rag and the stars?"

"Yeah, I remember," Jaz sighed.

"But with more kids' voices," added Ziggy. "I like the kids' voices."

"Me too."

They both smiled, pensive but happy.

"You know I've seen this circus before," said Jaz.

"Yeah?"

"Yeah, at the lake in New Orleans. Before I met you. But this time they look like the gypsies in Rebecca's village."

"I know, it's weird, isn't it, Jaz. First you think there's all these separate people working out their own lives in their own time and space, and then ..." He stopped.

"And then what?"

"And then I don't know."

"The strand-entwining cable of all flesh," said Jaz.

"What?"

"That's what Joyce called it."

"Who's she?"

"It's 'he,' silly." She poked him in the abs.

"Well he better not mess with me." Zig poked back.

"Let's go to the cabin," whispered Jazmine. And the two left the merriment of the drum circle and campfire to drink of deeper pleasures.

The next morning brought an unusual knock on Jazmine's cabin door. She lifted Ziggy's arm off of her belly and crept to the door. A phone call in the main house. It was Pepper.

"Hey, Jaz, what you doing?"

"Where the hell are you, Pepper?"

"At my redneck brother's place in north Louisiana. He's got a couple of acres and a trailer behind the house just outside of Monroe. He says y'all can come."

"That's so nice. He doesn't sound like a redneck to me."

"Oh, don't worry, he's a redneck alright. But when he says something, he means it. And he says y'all are welcome."

"Even Stormy?"

"I oughta not even answer a bitch question like that. Of course Stormy."

"It's nice to know your brother hasn't washed your mouth out with soap."

"He's my brother, not my personal fucking manager."

After the conversation wound about for several minutes – who was doing what, old times, new dreams – Pepper came back to the point.

"So y'all coming or not?"

"We'll think about it. We're good up here, Pepper. You should come here."

"Maybe I will one day. Stay in touch. Love you sweetie." And then she was gone.

Jazmine floated back across the grass and crawled back into bed with Ziggy. He stirred and put his arm around her.

"Who was that?

"Pepper."

"No shit? How did she find us?"

"Through Claire and Cool Breeze. She's putting together an address book. Hoss and Gina are on a pot farm in Humboldt County, California. Oh, and Pepper said we can go stay with her redneck brother in north Louisiana."

"No, I'm still going to Montreal. This draft-dodging thing isn't going to go away. At least not yet. Meanwhile, I've got a feeling there's a bistro somewhere up there needs a pizza maker."

280

Jaz straddled on top of him.

"You stay right here for now," she said provocatively.

That day was a day off for most of the commune, but the Kiddy Cabin was open for kids to be dropped as adults caught up on their own household needs and avocations. Jazmine and Ziggy took in the mid-morning sun on the pony ring wall as Stormy managed a handful of toddlers with the help of an older boy. Jazmine slipped her fingers into Ziggy's, enjoying the feeling of them interlacing. She reached her other hand over and ran it along Ziggy's wrist. Such delicate wrists for such a strong man. She remembered noticing those delicate wrists at the nighttime gathering at St. Roch a few weeks ago, the gathering that seemed so long ago, the one Ziggy had reflected on at the drum circle last night. She lifted his wrist and kissed it, without disentangling their hands. Holding his hand was not merely a physical act, but a trigger, an indicator, an objective marker of all sorts of transcendental knots and connections forming at the emotional and intellectual and spiritual layers of being. It wasn't something she was thinking, really. It was something she felt deep inside herself.

An older girl had now joined the kids, and Stormy took a moment to join Jazmine and Ziggy. She was beaming.

"They even have a separate library play space for the kids," she called out as she approached. Of course, Ziggy knew this. He had been the commune's de facto librarian for the past week. But he had never seen Stormy like this. She was like a kid herself, laughing, playing, radiating a devil-be-damned innocence. She sat on the pony ring next to Jaz. In this atmosphere – an open green space with older kids mixed with younger – the kids could practically take care of themselves.

281

The three sat silent for a moment, watching the kids running around in the sun.

"You gonna be in Kiddy Cabin for a while?" asked Jaz.

"As long as it takes," Stormy said carelessly. "I liked the tool belt but I like this too. I like everything."

"I've never seen you so happy," Ziggy said to Stormy.

"Maybe never been so happy. This place is good for me, Zig. Really good. And look at Rose Petal."

Zig watched Rose Petal. Two kids around her age had just arrived, and she was weighing out the excitement against the trepidation at their presence. She had found some object on the ground, probably worthless to adults but of infinite novelty in world of children. She held it out to the newcomers, who surveyed it with awe.

Ziggy picked up some of their awe himself. Stormy had taught him something about dealing with racism back in Rhinebeck, but here was a new dimension. "Become like little children," he ruminated to himself. They might be curious about hair textures, they might fight, but they wouldn't even know how to form a judgment based on race. He looked at Jazmine, at those soft lips he had kissed the night before. He watched her as she watched the children playing. Jaz had that non-judgmental thing down. She had that little child wisdom in her bones. Purity of heart. And Stormy. Ziggy suddenly realized that these were the role models for the Age of Aquarius. They were alive and here. Jazmine. Stormy. And Ragman, too, in his way. And Rose Petal.

"Rose never been so happy either," Stormy continued. "She feels like a little princess in a land of princes and princesses. She loves the attention of other kids."

282

"I know," Ziggy said. "Look at her with those two. It's like she found a rock of solid gold."

A moment passed.

"A secret bigger than gold," Jazmine said distantly.

"What?" Ziggy wasn't sure he'd caught her words exactly.

"Nothing. I was just thinking of something I heard a long time ago."

Ziggy was too relaxed to push further, and went back to the sweet observation of the kids. As he watched Rose showing her hand-held curiosity to the other children, concentrating as if concentration would persuade them of the magnitude of wonder in store for them, he noticed something odd. One of her eyes scrunched up as she cogitated on the subject, and she seemed to chew the inside of her cheek. It reminded Ziggy of something. Of someone. No, it couldn't be. He let drop the first inkling of his thoughts.

"Hey, was Ragman in Haight-Ashbury in early '67?"

Stormy looked at him closely, keenly, looked through him. Their eyes connected and a Mona Lisa smile curled at the corner of her lips. Then she changed the subject.

"Danny and I made a deal, Zig," Stormy said.

Ziggy still held Jazmine's hand, fingers lacing fingers, and he noticed now that Stormy held her other hand. It was exhilarating. In a way, he supposed, they were all in love. He knew they were all feeling the same thing, though they might access it or express it differently.

"He's going to teach me pottery and I'm going to teach him akua ma and mask making. He's really got me thinking of digging back into my West African roots. I can really do it here, no clutter in the air, wide open to do what I want."

"So you're going to become a permanent member?"

"Permanent's a big word. But I'm all-in for now. I got a long-term cabin."

"A cabin just for you and Rose Petal?"

"Not just." She hesitated. Ziggy saw a blush spread across Jazmine's cheeks.

"I'm staying too, Zig. Stormy and I took the cabin together. And Rose, of course."

She paused.

"Julia wants me to do the marketing for everything – the organics, the pottery. I already sketched some logos and we talked to a print shop in Rhinebeck. There are a couple of hippies with retail shop in Kingston. And their friends in New York." She beamed. "So I'll be marketing for the movement, not for the Man."

After a moment, she added: "You could stay too, Zig."

Ziggy felt a wrench of love and longing.

"No. I got to keep going to Montreal. I'm already packed. As perfect as this place is for y'all, it won't last for me. I'd be trapped. At least right now I got to keep going."

"I know."

She leaned over and kissed him.

"It's good that you go. The world out there needs people like you."

"Me?" Zig stammered. "I'm just a regular guy."

"That's why," Jaz said. "To you, you're just a regular guy. But you make people feel good. You make them feel connected on the inside."

"People keep saying that," Ziggy mused. Or maybe it was the song, he said to himself – *we bled inside each other's wounds* – but no, it was true, people kept telling him that.

"Every novel needs a keynote," Jaz teased. But then she became more serious with her own mixed metaphor.

284

"I mean it, Zig. It doesn't have to be the loudest note or the longest note. It might even be near-invisible. But it has to be there, holding the melody together for the other notes. It's something people feel."

"If by keynote, you mean a leader, I don't know. I'm not going out there to lead anything. Yeah, I'm with everybody in the Scene, but I wouldn't know how to be a leader. I don't understand politics."

"That's why," Jaz said. "It's not about politics. You tried to save Beachbum, you tried to save Rag, you did save me. Nobody told you to do this. Rag didn't tell you to do any of this. Your parents weren't telling you to do any of this. The government sure as hell wasn't telling you to do any of this. You're doing your own thing. And your own thing is to connect to people without thinking about them this way or that. You just connect on the inside. Everybody you meet feels it. It's like a weird kind of strength. A strength that comes from gentleness."

"My strength comes from you," Zig said. "All from you."

"Wherever it comes from, Zig, people feel it. You don't quite get it because you're too 'there' to get it. But trust me, people feel it."

"I trust you," he said with a smile. He noticed Stormy still holding her other hand.

"And I trust you and Stormy together. Y'all have a good place."

"You can always come back when you want, Zig."

"And you can always come meet me on the road."

She simply nodded. She knew.

They sat, the three of them, holding hands and watching the children play, and thought about their lives and destinies and all the things you never know. All the things you don't need to know, thought Jazmine. Was the tan acid

285

the next thousand-year chance at humanity's breakthrough, about which Berold spoke? Scuttled, like Rebecca's moment of transcendence was scuttled. The tan acid and the flower child revolution. Maybe it wouldn't change the whole world this time. "Who knows, the world might wake up and burst into a beautiful flower." Kerouac had said that. Not this time. Maybe next cycle. But if the chance is gone, or postponed for a thousand years, then what did it all mean? Then she remembered her own epiphany. It's not the meaning that matters. With every epiphany, you get two unsolved mysteries. It's the mysteries that keep you pushing forward. Or back in for another go-round. She had meant what she said to Ziggy that night behind her cabin, about the search for meaning, how meaning can sometimes be a distraction from living. Why did she feel so good about it, about everything? Maybe it's not about changing the world. It's about something inside. Something that she and Ziggy had. All the things you don't need to know. She felt pure, with the purity she had seen in Rebecca. She thought of Rebecca. And then she thought she heard Rebecca's voice, telling her something obvious. But what?

"Don't you see, Jazmine? It was never about my purity – that was just an idea, a doorway, a tonic to open you up – don't you see?"

And all in an instant Jazmine saw, a second epiphany. With Zig, behind the cabin, she had reclaimed her body from Ken. She had regained her purity. Now she knew what Ziggy had seen in her all along. She blushed at the thought but it was true. She thought of how people, all of us, let ourselves get distracted from our purity, she thought of the goat girl from Cuzco. She thought about Ragman. Yes, she felt good, but still she wondered, why could she not have saved Ragman. She pictured Julia speaking, that night at the communal dining hall, saying something about how meaning

286

moves in both directions. Then it was Rebecca speaking again.

"Yes, Jazmine, the meaning of Ragman's life moves in both directions, into the so-called past and the so-called future. Ragman chose that box so Jeremiah could live with me. The story is rewritten."

Yes, thought Jazmine, it was Ragman's face in the box.

"The man in the box," Rebecca said. "He always walks away at the end of the magic show. Things are connected in ways you don't understand, ways outside of time. You know this. You've been thinking this all along."

Jaz smiled. "Yes, I've been thinking this all along."

"Thinking what all along?" Jaz opened her eyes and saw Ziggy beaming down at her. It was so nice, the connection so deep, that she could say everything or nothing at all.

"You," she said.

That night was all bittersweet joy in Jazmine's cabin. It was her last night with Ziggy, at least for a while. Who knows what the future holds? And what does it matter? We co-exist with all of our pasts and all of our possible futures right now. They folded into each other's arms and unfolded their souls, as if they had lived a thousand years in the past three days. And perhaps they had.

* * *

 Gary Gautier was born in New Orleans, has hitchhiked through 35 states and 8 countries, run two marathons, and once, due to a series of misadventures, spent six months as the chef at a French restaurant. He holds a Ph.D. and has taught writing and literature at flagship state universities. His publications include children's and scholarly books, novels, poetry, articles in peer-reviewed journals, and book reviews.

Selected books by Gary Gautier:

Spaghetti and Peas
This beautifully illustrated hard-bound picture book brings a zany, heartwarming adventure to life for 3-8 year olds.

Mr. Robert's Bones
Three kids searching for silver in an abandoned house awaken memories of racism and betrayal, and join with some quirky old-timers to save the neighborhood from its own past. This family-friendly novel suits ages 14 to adult.

Year of the Butterfly
In this chapbook of poems, two figures meet, cross landscapes and oceans together, and part in a lyrical journey that is archetypal in scope but intimate and nuanced in human connection.

Contact Gary or check out his current events and musings:

Web: www.garygautier.com
Email: drggautier@gmail.com
Blog: www.shakemyheadhollow.com

Made in the USA
San Bernardino, CA
28 April 2020